Lilac CREEK

Lilac CREEK

ABIGAIL MORGAN

First published by Abigail Morgan 2026

Edited by Kellianne Gammill
Cover design and typesetting by Brooke Jacques

First Edition 2026

This book is dedicated to the mountains between Logan and Garden City, where I spent hours coming up with stories in my head (including this one) and reading my favorite books.

19 Years Ago

Prologue

Wade

The wooden stairs creak behind me, racing my heart as I try to quiet my breath. I crouch just a little bit lower as the sound of footsteps gets closer to the dark broom closet I'm hiding in. Her footsteps are slow and calculated, as though she's trying to be quiet.

But Haze has never been good at that.

The smell of fresh grass and lake air wafts into the rickety old building through open windows. As long as I can remember, this two-story shop floating on the end of a dock has been my favorite place in the world.

"I know you're in here, Wade, you'd better not jump out and scare me again," a sing-song voice rings out, a little closer than I would have guessed.

My own mouth betrays me, letting out the quietest of chuckles. I slap my hand over my lips, but it's too late. Light pours into the closet as the door whips open. My eyes adjust to the brightness, and there she stands.

My best friend. Hazel Mae Connor.

Her family just moved to Juniper Ridge a few months ago, back when I was nine years old. I'm nine and a half now. Hazel is only six, so my dad says I have to watch out for her. But I don't think she needs it.

She rides horses at her family's new dude ranch, fishes in the river with me, and can even swim all the way out to the big rock in the lake. Hazel is fearless. She's good at everything she tries. Especially hide and seek.

"Gotcha!" She yells, a wide grin spreading across her face. Her coffee brown curls hang wild around her face. Sometimes I think Hazel is the prettiest girl I know, but I'll never tell her that.

I scoff. "I'm just taking it easy on you because you're little."

Hazel rolls her eyes, kicking absentmindedly at the floorboards with her purple tennis shoes. "You are not, Wade. Don't be a liar. I'm just better at finding you." She reaches an arm out to me, pulling me up. "I bet I know this place better than you, and it's not even mine."

She's probably right. On the day we met, Hazel talked to me like we had already been friends our whole lives. We spent all summer exploring the tackle shop, the marina that surrounds it, and Connor Ranch. I've never been very adventurous, but for some reason, she keeps pulling me along. Now, when she's not around, it feels weird. Too quiet.

"That's because when you're not here, I just help my dad with inventory and stuff downstairs," I retort. My older brother Wyatt and I have worked at my dad's tackle shop on Bear Lake for as long as I can remember. We get the first pick of all of the new fishing lures and poles.

"Okay, fine," she says, a spark of challenge in her light blue eyes. "Bet you can't find me this next round."

Hazel reaches out her hand to me, and we shake on it. "You're on."

She grabs my shoulders, turning me around to face the Woodsy the Owl poster hanging from a nail on the wall. I cover my eyes with my hands and start counting down from twenty. Her footsteps shuffle away, heading away from the stairs next to me. The office above the tackle shop has a bathroom, a closet, and a storage room surrounding the larger space where my dad's big wooden desk sits. My brother and I come up here in the wintertime to sit by the fireplace when it gets below zero outside.

I'm almost positive Hazel is heading towards the storage room in the back. There isn't much in it, since we have all of our file cabinets and store supplies in the one downstairs. But there's a secret door in the storage room I didn't think anyone else knew about. It's a sort of laundry chute that we have never used.

"I'm coming to find you," I announce. Instead of going right to her, I wander around the room a bit, checking different places I know she's not hiding in. Under the desk, in the small shower we use to wash lake water off of life jackets, in the cupboards on the wall. Only when I'm sure it's been longer than it took Haze to look for me do I open the door to the storage room.

Sun shines into the room in long rays through the dusty air and fogged window panes. It's just like I remember it, a few old cardboard boxes and some extra chairs. Dust covers the floor, small footprints leading towards the wall to my right—the chute.

"Maybe I'll check behind these boxes," I say just loud enough for Hazel to hear. A muffled giggle comes from within the wall, putting a smile on my face.

I walk over to the boxes, pushing the top one aside just enough –

"Wade!" A small voice yells from the wall behind me.

I sigh, turning towards the chute. "Haze, you're not supposed to give away where you are."

A frustrated grunt shakes the chute door as she pulls it up. She's crouched with her knees to her chest, dust and cobwebs stuck in her dark hair. "No, come here. I found something."

She holds up a piece of rich tan leather, eyes wide. I rush over to her and help her out of the chute. She tumbles out, clutching the leather thing close to her chest.

"What is it?" I ask.

"I'm not sure. It was stuffed back behind the rope in that little cupboard."

I shake my head, "That's an old laundry chute. You should be careful in there; it moves down to the first floor if you pull the rope."

"Cool!" Her face lights up, eyes darting back towards the chute as if she'll go try it out right now.

"What is it?" I repeat, hoping to turn her attention away from anything that will get me in trouble with my dad.

Hazel holds the leather out to me. It's soft, worn in. I open the strap on the front.

"It's a diary," she whispers.

I nod, flipping through the pages. It looks like an old journal. It's heavy. I get the feeling this is something important.

The only page with any writing on it at all is the very first one. Scrawled in messy cursive are the lyrics to the chorus of "Check Yes or No" by George Strait.

Hazel's squeal of excitement almost bursts my eardrums. "What is it, what is it?" She jumps up and down at my side.

"It's the song my mom always plays, Check Yes or No," I tell her.

"Oh. That's it?" Her face falls.

"We should put it back," I say, warily. My hand absentmindedly rests on the back of my neck. "It might belong to one of my parents, and we aren't supposed to play in here."

Hazel's face falls immediately. "No way, we can't put it back. It's so pretty, we should keep it and write something in it."

"What would you even write in it?"

She considers this. "I don't know, maybe we could make a map to buried treasure. Or, we could write a story about the ranch."

I shift back and forth on my feet. Disappointing Hazel is not fun. But neither is getting in trouble with dad. "Let's just keep it in the chute, and when we know what we want to do with it, we can come back and get it."

"Okay, I guess so," Hazel shrugs.

The chute is dark and dusty, just like the rest of the storage room. I carefully set the leather journal back into the space behind the rope where Hazel found it, and I swear for just one second, I can hear waves crashing against the shore even through the walls of the tackle shop.

“Come on, Haze,” I say, wrapping my arm around her shoulder. She’s almost as tall as me already, but Dad says one day I’m going to shoot up like a weed. “Let’s see if Wyatt will take us to get shakes.”

She bounces up and down, unable to contain her happiness like always. “I want raspberry!”

We race down the stairs side by side. “You didn’t win, you know,” Hazel says as we jump down the last few steps.

“Didn’t win what?”

“Hide and seek. You didn’t find me. I would have won if I hadn’t found that journal,” she says.

I chuckle. “You’re right, you would have won. That was the best hiding spot.”

She holds her chin high, a smile threatening to break through. “I know, I told you I’m the best at hide and seek.”

One day, she’ll be better than me at every game we play, I already know it. Hazel is one of the smartest kids I know, and she’s three whole years younger than my friends and me. But I don’t mind if she beats me at everything. I don’t care who wins or loses, as long as I’m with my best friend.

Present Day

Wildflowers and Wild Horses

Hazel

"Wade, where do you want all of the waterlogged boxes?" Water drips in a steady rhythm from the sagging box in my hands. I slosh it around a little, feeling for extra weight. Yep, this one is definitely full.

"Over by the window is fine." My best friend's voice comes from around the other side of the file cabinet between us.

"Sir, yes, sir." Water splashes under my sandals, still leftover from the flood. Out of all of the things I thought I'd be doing today, clearing out Wade's dad's office at Black Bear Rentals was not on the list. Stepping foot into this room wouldn't even make the top 100. As far as I know, he hasn't even been in this room since James Monroe passed away five years ago.

At some point, it was silently decided between the Monroe brothers to leave the office as James had left it. I know Wyatt has been in here a couple of times to grab important forms or belongings, but it has always been too painful for Wade to venture through the wooden door.

Until now, that is.

Mother Nature herself forced us both in here with a flood. Not so surprising, since the building is literally on the edge of a dock surrounded by lake water. But devastating all the same.

Wade awoke to a few inches of water covering the entire first floor of the rental shop. By the time I arrived, it was mostly drained, and Wade was standing in front of the office door as if it were the entrance to a tomb filled with skeletons.

The box hits the damp wood planks with a squish instead of a thud. I open the lid cautiously, then step back to assess the damage. It's filled with mostly files, which are probably lost.

"This one's a goner," I toss over my shoulder.

Wade lets out a long sigh. "I figured most of them would be. He never had time to buy bins. I should have bought bins."

"You can't blame yourself for the flood, Wade. We'll save what we can, I promise." My chest squeezes. There's nothing worse than seeing Wade sad. "If it'll make you feel better, we can drive to the city tomorrow and buy as many bins as your little heart desires."

"Yeah, you'd probably love that, you weirdo," he scoffs. "Organization freak."

"I might be a slut for organization, but at least I use my powers for good," I say.

"How would you use them for evil?" He laughs.

I tap a finger on my chin. "Hmm. Probably reorganize everything you own into so many bins over and over again until you couldn't find anything, eventually leading to psychosis."

Wade shakes his head, setting down the damp book he's been holding.

I shrug. "You ask a silly question, you're gonna get a silly answer."

"I just don't know what to do with all of this... stuff," Wade says after a while. "It's not like it's useful to the shop, but I feel like I'm letting him down if I throw it away. Is that crazy?"

"Of course not. You don't have to throw it all away right now. We can pick out everything that's actually important, like his writings, and throw away things he probably filed away once and never looked at again," I offer. "If it helps, we can separate everything into piles and decide later. When you're ready."

He offers me a bleak smile, pulling a new book out of a ruined box. "Yeah, I guess that's fine."

I bend down and reach into the box, pulling out files. They're each labeled a different month, full of waterlogged invoices and fishing guide logs. At the very least, I can grab my hair dryer from the ranch, and we can try to salvage these. I'll just get them all out of here and onto the sunny dock in the meantime.

My fingers brush across something more solid in the box. Nestled in between the files is some sort of book. I fish it out of the box expecting it to be dripping wet like the rest of the contents, but it's not.

It's completely dry.

I whip the cover open, flipping through the pages as quickly as I can. They're all dry. Not even a little bit damp. Closing it again, I search the cover for a title. It's a brown leather journal, with a thin strap and loop to hold the cover closed. Nothing is written on the front, just worn, cracked leather and white saddle stitching.

Carefully this time, I open the journal to the first page. The lyrics to "Check Yes or No" by George Strait stare back at me in messy cursive.

"Wade!" I jump up, rushing over to the file cabinet.

"Wha–" A loud thud interrupts him. "Jesus, Haze, you scared me." He rubs the back of his head that hit the bottom of the hanging cabinet.

"Oh, sorry," I start.

He waves me closer, "It's fine, what is it?" Wade's bright blue eyes meet mine. One of his hands remains in his sandy blonde hair, still messy from sleeping on it. I almost forgot that all he's wearing are some sweatpants. He hadn't bothered to get ready yet in the panic of the flood.

I clear my throat. "Right! Sorry. Look what I found in that box."

I wave the journal high enough for him to see over the piles of boxes in between us. He squints, eyes trailing over the journal in my hands. "What is that?"

"Remember that first summer we met? When we played hide and seek upstairs and I found the laundry chute or whatever that thing is?" I say.

"Yes." He steps around the wall of boxes until he's at my side. "You could have fallen an entire floor and gotten hurt."

"Yeah, yeah, anyway," I dismiss. "That journal I found in there? It was in that box!"

"What?"

"The journal. The one we found. It was in the bo–"

"I heard you," he sighs. "Let me see it." He reaches out to grab it, but I snatch it away right before his fingers brush the leather.

"No. You have to be nice to me first." I hold my chin up as high as I can. Which probably looks a little silly to him from seven inches above my head, but the effect is the same.

His head tilts a bit, expression softening. "I'm sorry for being snappy. It's been a day. Thank you for all of your help."

I smile, handing the journal to his waiting hand. "I forgive you for being annoying. Try not to let it happen again."

"Back at you, weirdo."

"Hey!" I exclaim. Wade lifts the journal all the way to the ceiling as I jump to grab it.

"No take-backs," he teases.

I fold my arms and take a step back. In all of the excitement, I ended up an inch away from his bare chest. "Just open it."

He smiles, peeling back the cover. His brows furrow as he reads the scratchy cursive. A couple of loose waves of hair fall into his face. He brushes them away, pursing his lips together.

"Well?" I urge, rocking back and forth.

He meets my gaze, handing the journal back to me. "Yeah, looks like the same one. Wonder why it was in a box."

I close my eyes and sigh as dramatically as I can. "Did you notice anything weird about this journal that came from the *soaking wet* cardboard box I found in a puddle of *water*?"

Understanding lights up his face. "It's dry!"

"Yep. Bone dry."

Wade hums, looking past me. "Maybe it wasn't all the way on the bottom, and the leather protected the sides or something."

"Yeah, maybe." I run my fingers down the first page. The paper is thick and textured. I remember wanting to take this home when I first found it. It practically begs to be written in.

Absent-mindedly, I turn the page, and to my surprise, it's not blank. I suck in a gasp of air at more messy cursive decorating the second page.

"Look at this!" I yell to Wade. I feel his elbow brush my sweatshirt as he steps closer to read it over my shoulder.

It's more lyrics. This time, an entire song. In the same scratchy cursive as before.

"Love Story," he says. His voice just close enough to my ear to send goosebumps down my arms.

"What?"

"That's the song. It's a Taylor Swift song," he clarifies.

"Oh. Right." I turn the page again. "There's more."

We read through the third page of lyrics. This time, it's "Something Like That" by Tim McGraw. The cursive has greatly improved, as if the writer took more time on this song. The fourth page is "Strawberry Wine" by Deanna Carter. It's not until we get to the fifth page of the journal that there isn't anything left to read.

"Freaky," I mutter. Wade hums in agreement. "Do you think..." I trail off, turning back around. He looks down at his shoes.

"I'm not sure. I never saw him with it, but I don't see how it could be anybody else's. It was in the chute, now it's in a box in his office."

"Yeah." We stand in silence for a few moments, surrounded by ruined memories.

"Hey." I reach out and grab his arm. He meets my gaze, eyes swirling like a storm cloud. "Do you want to take a break later and go on a ride? I've got to get Sage and Thistle out anyway; they've been cooped up."

He stares at me a little longer, and I think he may not have heard me until he finally nods.

"Yeah, a break sounds good," he says. "Let's put that journal up at the front desk. I don't want it getting ruined back here."

We make our way around the maze of boxes and chairs and out into the hallway that leads to the store. It's not a huge building by any means. Small rooms separated by a tiny hallway with a steep staircase in the middle.

Wade places the journal carefully into a drawer in the shop. The sun is shining through the windows, waves reflecting bright, sparkling light onto the rows of life jackets, paddles, and wakeboards. Black Bear Rentals hasn't been this quiet in the summer since Wade and Wyatt first opened the shop a year after their dad's death.

I've probably spent just as much time here as I have on my family's dude ranch ten minutes away. It feels like home.

Wade and I aren't very good at being alone. Especially since he lost his dad. His brother was already married at that point, living in a house on the other side of the mountains. Wade was left with a whole lot of responsibility running the shop and helping out at his mom's cafe while she grieved.

But he was grieving too.

So I helped. A lot.

I used all of my business knowledge from managing the dude ranch to help him and Wyatt start a new business. I volunteered at Heidi's, taking whatever shifts they couldn't fill, and I spent all of my free time with Wade. Sometimes we didn't even talk at all.

With time came a little less of the heaviness, and the dark storm clouds parted a bit. But even now, I worry about him sometimes. I can't help it.

"You don't have to stay and clean up all this stuff, you know," Wade says. "Wyatt will be here tonight. I'm sure you have plenty to do at the ranch."

"There is literally nowhere else I need to be right now more than here. Stop trying to chase me away," I laugh.

"I would never."

Chapter 2

August

By the time we finish up enough in the office to feel okay about leaving, it's about two hours before sunset. Perfect timing to get up to the ranch, get tacked up, and see the sunset from the peak. My favorite time of day in the mountains.

We spent the rest of the day sorting papers, positioning gigantic fans, and singing along to extremely loud music. It's a good thing Wade closed up shop.

"Would it kill you to fill this thing up all the way just once?" He says from the passenger seat of my Bronco, reading an honest-to-goodness print newspaper. He pushes his glasses up his nose.

I smile, adjusting my sun visor. "Yes, it would. Just like the sight of you reading that, when the internet exists," I tease, starting down the winding road that heads up into the mountains. "Seriously, Wade, you look like an old, grumpy grandpa checking your stocks. And you know a full tank of gas freaks me out."

That earns a chuckle from him.

I reach towards the radio and click it on. Taylor Swift's "August" starts playing loudly, flowing out the open windows and into the pine-scented air.

Wade scoffs. "You have the nerve to call me old as you drive a 70's rustbucket while listening to an actual CD?"

"Hey, it's not my fault this thing doesn't have Bluetooth. It barely has a working radio."

"My point exactly." He turns the newspaper over in his hands.

I glance over at his green t-shirt with a little beaver yelling "Dam it!" on it, and think about how happy I am to have days like this. Driving up a winding mountain road with my best friend on our way to ride horses on the mountaintops.

"Where are we headed today?" Wade says as we tack up in the barn.

"I was thinking up to the peak. It's so clear we'll probably be able to see pretty far over the valley," I call back from next to my small, tan Palomino horse, Sage.

The setting sun spills through gaps in the trees as a cool mountain breeze blows in the scent of sagebrush. I close my eyes for a second and listen to the soft trot of my horse, the pine trees swaying slowly in the breeze, and birds chirping in the evening sun. I love this place. I never imagined actually leaving it.

Until college, that is. I fell in love with history, and unfortunately, there aren't any jobs for an archivist or historical technical writer in Juniper Ridge, Idaho.

Even the closest large towns had nothing that would fit my interests. Since graduation, I'd virtually interviewed all over the country, and only actually landed one offer: in Tucson, Arizona, at the Arizona History Museum.

It's an archivist position, and it's honestly a dream job for a history graduate. I haven't told him yet about the offer or the possibility I'll move away.

My whole life, everyone has always expected great things from me. I remember my dad saying to me more than a few times, *You are bigger than Juniper Ridge, Hazel. You're going to see the world and do great things out there.* I loved to read about far-off lands, even throughout college when I started traveling more with friends.

And, I love to travel. But, I'm never as happy as I am on these mountains above where I grew up with my very best friend. Sometimes, I wonder if something is wrong with me for not quite wanting more for myself as much as my parents do.

"You're quiet today," Wade says from his saddle as we start the trek up the mountain.

"Just enjoying this beautiful August day." I tilt my head up towards the sun.

"Usually, the sound of you enjoying a beautiful day is slightly louder than this." The corners of his mouth turn up in a smirk.

"Gimmie a break, Wade. I'm just trying to be more like you."

Wade chuckles and rides up next to me with a smile on his face. We trot over to a shady tree and tie up the horses for a quick rest while we take in the view of the valley below.

"So, how are the ranch guests this week? I thought I saw someone in a nice-looking suit trying to find cell service earlier this week." Wade's legs stretch out in front of him as we sit on a rock.

"Oh yes, I believe that would be Mr. Thompson, who took no less than *seven* calls on our last ride. It's so funny to me that people come all the way up here to get away, and then simply refuse to let go of their regular lives for a couple of days," I laugh. "If we didn't have wifi at the cabins, I think we might be out of business."

"People love the dude ranch, Haze. And they love your parents. And you. You love it so much, it rubs off on people. The wifi is just a plus. You're not a Starbucks," Wade laughs, nudging my shoulder with his arm.

"Maybe not, but we could really use one. If not for the guests, then just for me. I could go for a slice of coffee cake right about now."

Wade turns onto his side, facing me. My heart flutters for a split second under his full attention. He's great at that, the whole undivided-attention thing. My brain is heading in a hundred different directions at all times, on the other hand.

"Race you down the mountain." His voice is so low I almost don't hear him.

I laugh, "Fine, winner pays for dessert at Heidi's."

"You're on."

"You're like a human tornado." Wade laughs as I throw my jean jacket over the beanbag chair in my room, kicking my boots off in the direction of my closet.

My room is technically the primary suite on the second floor of the ranch house. My parents have always preferred the first floor, turning one of the bigger office spaces into a bedroom when we first moved in.

I thought it was so cool that my room was so big with sweeping floor-to-ceiling windows and an attached bathroom as a kid. It's probably why Wade and my other best friend, Katie, always came to the ranch for sleepovers when we were little. It felt like a whole separate apartment when I was a kid.

"I'll organize everything tomorrow," I reply, knowing there's about a fifty/fifty chance of that actually happening. I'm very neat and organized on a computer and in the barn, less so in my room.

"Good, because I'm starving. I could probably eat three burgers right now."

"So dramatic." I roll my eyes, turning towards my closet to grab a change of clothes. "Don't forget you're paying, slowpoke."

Wade chuckles. "You'll never let me forget. By the way, your mom just texted me and asked if I could please change the porch light while I'm here." He pushes off the wall.

"That is so typical," I laugh. "She must have seen you on the barn security cameras. You so do not have to change the porch light."

"Of course I'm changing the porch light. Being Elyse Connors's favorite is something I take great pride in." A smug grin paints his face.

"You're only her favorite because she hasn't had to sit through years of your constant dad jokes that somehow get worse with practice," I point out. "She also hasn't seen drunk Wade try to hit on pretty girls with those same jokes. It's highly embarrassing. I've considered voiding my friendship contract with you on several occasions."

"Oh, there's a contract now, is there?"

"Sorry, did that slip out?" I put on my best shocked face. "Of course, there isn't a contract, and those monthly deposits I get from your mom aren't paying me off to deal with you every day. I just work for her on the side." Wade's grin grows bigger as he punches my arm on our way out into the hall.

"You're such a little sh-" He's interrupted by the intercom beeping and my mom's voice crackling through the house.

"Hazel, honey, I'm having a little trouble in the barn. Would you mind helping me out if you're home?"

I walk up to the intercom box in the hallway and press the talk button. "Heading there now, Mom. Wade is coming too." We start down the stairs, grabbing our hats from the hangers on the wall.

"Oh, how wonderful, has he changed the porch light by chance?" she asks on the intercom, a little out of breath. I look over at Wade and roll my eyes as he laughs, putting his hat on and folding his glasses into his shirt pocket.

"Guess I'd better get on that the second we get back," he murmurs as we step out the front door.

I'm not sure what I expect to see when Wade and I walk into the barn, but it's not my mom on her hands and knees by the door to the pasture, covered in mud, muttering curse words with a screwdriver in her hand.

The doors are closed, and the horses are all out in the field grazing for the evening. Mom stands and swipes a stray piece of brown hair out of her face with her wrist upon seeing us, letting out an exasperated sigh.

"Oh, Waylon, thank goodness you're here. I can't get the door to open. I think it's stuck, and I need to get these horses inside for the night," she says, hugging Wade and handing him the screwdriver. "Hi, hon. You look adorable today."

"Thanks, Mom." She squeezes me into a hug, crushing my ribs.

"How was your ride this morning?" She asks.

"It was good. Not too hot yet. We went up to the peak and back, it was super clear today. We could see all of the lake and into Utah."

"Sounds like it'll be perfect for this week's dude ranchers. They're very excited about the views. All the way from Kentucky! Can you believe that, Waylon? We've had so many far-travelers this year." Her eyes light up with excitement.

"I can't think of a single person in the world who wouldn't want to visit Idaho's best dude ranch, Mrs. Connor." He flashes a charming smile her way. I take the chance to flip him off out of my mom's view.

"You're such a sweetheart," she gushes. "We are so lucky to have you around here so often." Mom gives me a pointed look, "Very often, indeed," she adds, quietly enough for just me to hear.

"Wade doesn't have a life, Mom, that's why he's always bumming around the ranch," I say loudly. Wade turns back towards us, a hand over his heart, feigning offense.

"I resent that," he scoffs.

"You two bicker like an old married couple, I swear," she scoffs, turning to walk out of the barn. "I see the barn is in capable hands. I'm headed in to call your father. He should be just about back to his hotel room after today's auction. I'm sure he'll want to give you the snow globe he got for you this time, the second he gets home. I swear, I don't know how he finds one of those damn things every trip, even in the summer."

After we wave goodbye to my mom, I plop down cross-legged on the dirt floor in the middle of the barn.

When we were little, Wade and I used to spend so much time here brushing horses, mucking out stalls, and running through the barn playing hide and seek. My dad has kept up on it well throughout the years, making sure it still looks as new as it did when we built it all those years ago.

I trace my hand along the red paint of the wood-plank wall, remembering all of the times I've re-painted the barn with Wade, splotches covering our clothes and arms.

We'd spend hours in the rafters pretending we were pirates or international spies. Then, later on, talking about our days, our classmates, our big dreams.

One of our many hangout spots at Connor Ranch. Growing up here gave me the coolest childhood. We'd spend days out in the woods, always finding a new corner of the large property we hadn't explored yet. I'm lucky I got to grow up wild like that, and even luckier to have Wade by my side.

"Done," he says once the door clicks back into its track. "You ready?" He grabs my hand and pulls me to my feet.

"I'm always ready for free dessert."

Group Chat

No Scrubs

Katie: HOLY SHIT

Katie: I have a book recommendation for you.

Hazel: Did you finish it?

Katie: Yes. I am unwell.

Katie: Five stars. No notes. One of the best books I've read this year.

Katie: The guy is so sexy. Broody and dark. Perfection.

Hazel: Oh, but I usually like a golden retriever guy.

Katie: I know, but you'll like this one. I promise. He's hot as fuck.

Hazel: So I should read it?

Katie: YES. Please.

Katie: The sex was so good.

Hazel: I'm in.

Katie: Literally the perfect amount. Miles is going to be getting some suggestions for sure.

Wade: Why am I here?

Chapter 3

Butterflies

"It's cool seeing all of his notes and research like this." Wade turns to another warped page in an old notebook. "I always saw him taking notes and sitting for hours at his desktop, but actually seeing all of the work he put into guiding is something else."

"He really loved Black Bear Guiding." I take another sip of water before picking up the next file. A news article from 2003 on fishing regulation changes.

"Maybe we can keep some of the research in the office and add on a guiding service to the rental shop. It might be a fun side project for Wyatt to run. Or maybe, we can bring in a new guide that wants to set up a shop in the area," he says.

I laugh. "One thing at a time, there, hotshot. We still have about a million and two boxes to get through in that office before we can even start to clean. Are you thinking you want to keep it as an extra office for the shop?"

Wade tilts his head just slightly to the side like he usually does when he's mulling something over, pushing his glasses up.

I love it when he wears his glasses. "Yeah, it'd be nice to have a separate office space from the apartment upstairs. Maybe I'll actually feel like I'm going to work every day instead of always being on the clock upstairs," he nods.

I remember the day he moved into the apartment on top of Black Bear Rentals. It was about a month after his dad's passing. We hauled in the concerningly few boxes of his things from his mom's house. I remember teasing him about being able to fit all of his belongings into a suitcase.

"I don't need a lot, Hazel," he had told me. "Plus, when the FBI finally comes for me for catching a fish without a license when I was twelve, I can make an easy getaway to Canada."

He has gained a few things since then, more fishing rods, a few framed photos, and paintings. But he's still the same Wade he always has been. I'm glad for that.

I tuck my fuzzy sock-covered feet back into the fluffy blue blanket on his couch. Wade immediately clocks it and gives me a pointed look.

"I don't understand how you could possibly be cold in the middle of the summer."

I punch him lightly in the bicep. "It's nighttime. Normal people get cold at night. Also, we are literally on top of the lake, it's always colder here."

"Whatever you say." He rolls his eyes, turning another page.

"Hey," I say. "Did you leave that journal with the songs in it downstairs?"

"Yeah, why?"

"No reason, I just wanted to look at it again. There's nothing else like it in any of his things," I say.

He quirks a brow. "And?"

I sigh. "*And* don't you think it's a little unlike him?"

"I guess so," he mumbles.

"Okay, so let's bring it up here. See if we can figure out if it's his handwriting or not." I stand up from the couch, knocking the blanket onto the cold, wood floors. Wade reluctantly follows me down the staircase, turning on every light as we head into the shop.

It's not often we spend time in the shop at night, besides coming and going. I've always thought it was a little bit spooky at night. The waves lapping against the dock outside of the windows, blue moonlight pouring in, and casting shadows all over the walls.

It's a full moon tonight, bright in the room before Wade reaches across my shoulders to turn on the little lamp on the front desk. A warm glow illuminates the shop.

I stand on the other side of the desk from him, resting my elbows on the cool wood counter. Wade reaches for a key under the countertop, feeling around for a bit until it's in his hand and he's opening the drawer below. He sets the worn leather journal on the counter between us before meeting my gaze.

"Here you go. Happy?" He gives me a pointed look.

I smile, grabbing the journal. "Very."

Despite being alone in a cold, damp building for hours, the journal is warm in my hands. I slip the leather strap out from the loop, keeping the cover closed.

Wade watches in silence as I run my fingers along the lyrics to the first song. Then the second. When I get to the third, he chuckles softly.

"What?" I ask.

"Nothing," he smiles. "You're just cute when you focus." He reaches over and flicks my nose.

I roll my eyes, turning to the next page. The first blank one.

Only, it's not blank anymore. Perfect cursive letters decorate the textured paper, dark and new. My heart races in my throat as I read furiously through the words until I recognize the song. It's the lyrics to Kacey Musgraves's "Butterflies."

"Wade, look!" I snap my gaze up only to see him staring wide-eyed at the journal. He whips the journal around to face him as he reads the words. For a heartbeat, we stare at each other. I'm the first to snap out of it.

"Did you write in this?" I whisper.

"Of course not, did you?" He steps back, running a hand through his hair.

"Why would I ask you that if I had written it?"

"I don't know, Haze. Are you one hundred percent certain this was blank earlier?" He paces behind the desk.

I grab the journal again, reading the words that definitely were not there when I found it. How could this happen? It was locked away. Maybe one of the shop employees got hold of it today. That has to be it.

"I'm certain. Who was working today? Did they have a key to the drawer?"

Wade's face lights up. He closes the distance between us, grabbing my shoulders.

"That has to be it. Brody and Emily were working today, one of them had to have written in it."

"Why would they write song lyrics in a journal and leave it in the desk?" I ask.

He takes a step back, analyzing the desk drawer as if it's going to jump out and tell him exactly what happened. A single sand-colored lock of hair falls onto his forehead. He's quick to push it away again.

Brody and Emily are two of the three college students who work at Black Bear Rentals in the summer. On weekends, Wade usually has two of them working to help with the rush of customers spending time out on the lake. I've always thought Brody and Emily, in particular, would make a cute couple. They always seem to be chatting or looking at each other when they think no one is watching.

I'm a hopeless romantic at heart.

I look down at the lyrics written on the page. They're so similar to the ones on previous pages. It looks like the exact same handwriting, more practiced over time.

"Wade, look at this." I flip through the pages. "The handwriting is the same. It starts off a little scratchy with the first couple of songs, but it's the exact same style. See the loops on the 'g's?' They match."

"Do you think–" He stops himself.

"What?" I say eagerly.

He sighs, running a hand through his mussed hair. "Do you think one of the employees has been writing in this? And putting it back in the office?"

I look down at the pages, the careful strokes of cursive, deep black against the parchment. "If one of the employees is writing this, my money is on Emily."

He nods, gaze far off in thought. He takes his glasses off, resting them on the counter. "Why song lyrics though? Is working the desk that boring?"

I flip through the pages again, reading them in order. "It reads almost like a story," I point out.

Wade walks around the counter until his arm rests lightly against my shoulder, his warmth enveloping me in the chill of the night air.

"See?" I point to the first song. "It starts with light-hearted young love with 'Check Yes or No,' which we knew was in there before, then 'Love Story.' Then it develops into deeper love with the last couple of songs."

"Only you would read this like a love story," Wade chuckles.

"Maybe that's exactly how it's meant to be read. I see the way Emily looks at Brody, it doesn't take a genius to notice she has a crush on him." I close the book, turning to face him.

"Anyone could see that," he says.

"Exactly. So maybe she saw the journal one day with a song written in it, and decided to continue it." The corners of his mouth curve into a small smile as I crane my neck to look up at him. The familiar scent of him wraps around me like a comfortable blanket. Linens, his ocean-scented cleaning spray, and something else.

"What do you suggest we do about it?" His gaze dips just slightly from my eyes to my lips, and I feel my cheeks start to heat. It's too late at night, and too much has gone on today. We shouldn't be standing this close, alone in the dark shop.

I take a step back, cold air filling the space between us and killing the buzz of energy that was there a minute ago. Confusion fills his features for a second before he clears his throat.

"I think we should launch an investigation," I practically shout. Wade startles, jumping back an inch or two.

"Sorry," I continue in a normal tone. "I think we should launch an investigation. If Brody or Emily is writing love songs in the journal at work, it's got to be about the other. We can keep an eye on the journal tomorrow and see if anything changes."

Wade nods slowly, looking out the window. "Alright, we'll keep an eye on the situation while we clear out the office. For now, let's put the journal back where it was in the drawer."

I walk over to the desk, placing the old journal carefully where it was, on top of countless sticky notes, pens, and broken fishing lures.

I'm not sure how either of them would have gotten into James's locked office or upstairs to find it in the laundry chute. It doesn't totally make sense. But the writing matches up so perfectly. There's no way anyone could replicate it that well in one day.

As much as I should probably just let it go, the journal feels personal to me. Wade and I found it as kids. It had one of our favorite songs in it. We hid it in a secret location that only we knew about. It feels like mine.

And I want to get to the bottom of it.

Chapter 4

Linger

On Monday morning, I wake up around five to a text from Wade. I groan, reaching over to my side table where I threw my phone last night. The battery icon glows an angry red.

Wade: Today works for me too, see you then.

Another rolls in as I'm still reading the first. It's a photo of him, hair sticking every which way, eyes barely opened, shirtless, and holding a bright purple stuffed pony. His navy eyes twinkle as he tries not to smile.

I can't help it. A grin breaks out on my face.

Wade and I have had a running joke of leaving the stuffed horse where the other can find it since I was ten years old, and left it at his house in the first place. I've found Harriet in the middle of a stable, between the branches of a tree, on the fireplace mantle downstairs, hidden in plain sight. I suspect she'll pop up somewhere new in the next couple of days for me to find again.

Wade: Guess who was hiding under my sink?

Hazel: Harriet! How did she get in there?

Wade: Very funny. One of these times, Harriet isn't going to come back.

Hazel: Waylon Monroe, it's not nice to threaten your best friend.

Wade: I'm threatening this ball of fluff.

I save Wade's selfie to my camera roll because it's just too funny not to, and push my comforter off. I give myself ten seconds to lie in the comfort of my bed before rolling off and into the bathroom to get ready for the day.

Wade and Wyatt got a good start on cleaning up after the flood this past weekend. They dried out the floorboards, set everything back in the shop where it was before, and brought all of the waterlogged boxes of James Monroe's files up to Wade's apartment.

As it stands, the only things left in the office downstairs are the old wooden desk, chair, and the shelves on the wall. The fluffy grey rug Wade and I used to sit on as kids had to be tossed. The standing lamp in the corner, too, but it probably stopped working long before the flood.

It's eerily empty.

And Wade's already tiny living room is even more cramped. We've got to finish going through all of the files still, placing them into separate piles and getting rid of the ones too damaged to read. Hopefully, soon, he'll have his apartment back to normal.

Pulling on a soft, blue sweatshirt, I grab my cowgirl hat and head downstairs. The ranch house my parents built when we moved to Idaho is a sight to behold.

A black metal railing curves down the spiral staircase and into the open living area. I remember my dad asking my mom why they were building a spiral staircase. She replied, "Why not?" and that was that.

The kitchen sprawls out across the house, wide enough for an island and the reclaimed wood kitchen table. Sunlight creates a sort of glow in the warm wood tones of the cabinets. Just past the kitchen is my favorite room in the house.

The den.

I'm not sure why we've always called it that, since it's the only living room in the house, but that's what it feels like. A rock fireplace fills the center of the wall, and everything else in the room was built around that. Floor-to-ceiling windows span across the perpendicular wall, the rising sun spilling across the room.

I spy movement on the deck just outside the windows. As soon as I step outside, breathing in the cool mountain air, I instantly feel more awake.

"Morning, hon." My mom smiles as I sit across from her at the small iron table. I look out past the deck railing at the rolling hills and jagged peaks of the mountain range surrounding us. Red, yellow, and purple wildflowers paint the lush hillside like splotches of watercolors.

"Hey, Mom."

"Want some coffee?" She hands me a steaming mug, and I immediately take a long sip.

"Thanks," I say.

She nods, looking back out at the mountains. "Another beautiful day. Your father just left for the stables."

"I should be going down there right about now, too," I say. "We're splitting up this morning between the two groups." This week is a busy week at Connor Ranch. Three corporate retreats and a family vacation at our little dude ranch. If we hadn't added those three extra cabins last year, we wouldn't be able to accommodate them all.

Working in a vacation town means we have a really busy season and a slow season that's so slow it's almost non-existent. The next few weeks will be our busiest of the year before summer tapers off, and we start thinking about winter renovations.

I manage most of the dude ranch by now on my own, with my parents dialing back their workload to guiding horse rides and big picture planning. Of course, we have a team of cabin cleaners and a couple of extra ranch hands, but the lion's share of the work lands on me.

I don't mind it.

In fact, I love it. Running this place and implementing systems is my favorite thing in the world. There's nothing I love more than a new idea and a fresh spreadsheet. Well, maybe a happy guest at the end of their stay. That's pretty cool, too.

"Have you heard back from Arizona?" Mom asks before taking another sip of her coffee.

And there it is.

Dread mixed with hope. Happy and sad. Because as much as I love this place, I might have to leave it.

"Not since their offer letter," I say. "I still have a few more weeks, their current archivist is finishing out the summer."

She tucks her golden brown hair behind her ear, nodding thoughtfully. "How are you feeling about it?"

I sigh, "I don't know, Mom. I'm conflicted." I pick at a loose thread in my sweatshirt. "It's a really good position, it's just so... far. I'd be leaving you in the lurch at the ranch. We'd have to bring someone in to manage the dude ranch. And what if I get the job and end up hating it?"

"What if you love it?" She asks. "Don't make your decision based on the ranch, sweetie, that's your father and my dream. I love that you love it here, but I want you to go out and find your own dream. This could be it."

"Yeah," I whisper.

"Not that I want you to leave, of course, I'd keep you here all your life if I could. But you're meant for great things, Hazel Mae. I know it," she says.

I nod, slowly, not taking my eyes off the mountain valley I've called home for most of my life. It's hard to imagine leaving, even though I always planned to. I'm not sure anywhere else could live up to this place.

Placing my cowgirl hat on top of my braided hair, I stand from my chair and give Mom a quick hug.

"I'm heading down to the barn. I'll see you after trail rides," I say.

We say our goodbyes, and I head back into the house to find where I kicked my boots off last night. Probably somewhere on the porch. It was late when I got back from Black Bear Rentals.

I spend the rest of the day moving through the motions of trail rides and talking to dude ranch guests, but the job sits in the back of my mind, eating away at my attention.

It's a good thing I'm going to Wade's. I could use a distraction.

Twelve hours later, I'm freshly showered after a long day on horseback and walking down the floating dock to Black Bear Rentals.

Wade isn't in the shop when I arrive, just Brody working behind the counter. I wave hello as I make my way to the back.

"Hey, Hazel. Wade just ran out, but he should be back any minute," Brody says.

"Thanks," I nod. I start to head back to the back room, but an idea stops me in my tracks. I pivot right back towards the front desk. "Hey, Brody, is Emily working today?"

Brody looks up from whatever rental form he's filling out. "Yeah, she's in the marina putting away the jet skis. Do you need her for something?"

"No, just curious." I rock back and forth on my feet. "I have a friend I was thinking of setting her up with on a date, but I'll ask her about it later."

That gets his attention immediately. Brody stiffens, eyes wide. "Oh, really?" His voice shakes a bit.

I can't help but smile. Suspicion confirmed. "Yeah, she is still single, right?"

"I– I think so," he says, unmoving.

"Great," I smile. A bell rings on the front door, and in tumbles Wade with a couple of brown paper bags filled with what smells like garlic fries. My favorite.

His eyes land on me right away. "Oh, hey, you're here. I got us food." He turns his attention to the front desk. "Hey, Brody, anyone come in while I was gone?"

Brody stares out the window in a daze. Wade looks over to me, brow furrowed. I shrug.

"Brody, are you okay, man?" Wade says a little louder.

Brody snaps out of his trance, smoothing out his navy board shorts, the official uniform of Black Bear Rentals. "Yeah, yeah, sorry. It wasn't busy at all."

"Okay, cool," Wade says slowly, walking towards the back of the shop.

I follow him up the narrow staircase and into his apartment, rounding the corner and running right into a stack of boxes taller than I am.

"Sorry," Wade grimaces. "I had to move a couple of stacks so I could get into my bathroom."

I laugh, "We've gotta get to sorting so you can have your life back."

"I still have my life, it's just a little more cramped than usual." He sets the paper bags onto the tiny kitchen table and gestures for me to sit. "Do I want to know what you said to Brody down there that haunted him so badly he couldn't speak?"

I pop a fry into my mouth with a smile. "I just mentioned Emily."

"And?" he asks, taking a bite of his burger.

"And... I might have mentioned that I want to set her up on a date with a friend."

"You're evil." He laughs, leaning back in his chair. He stretches his arms behind him, pressing his shirt tight against his chest. My eyes fall for a split second before I realize what I'm doing.

Nope. This is Wade.

"I had to see his reaction!" I exclaim. "As it turns out, I was right. I'd bet you anything that he wrote those songs in the journal. I've never seen someone so obviously in love."

Wade rolls his eyes. "Maybe it's just a coincidence. Or, maybe he doesn't want to say anything to her. I don't know if we should push it, Haze."

"I would never," I wink.

"You're such a meddler," he laughs, stealing a sip of my drink. "What's your master plan?"

I hadn't really thought it through yet. I was so focused on figuring out if it was true or not, I didn't really think much past that. I tell him as much, and he thinks for a minute, chewing on a fry.

"Maybe we should just ask him if he wrote in the journal," he says finally.

"Wade," I sigh. "Where's your sense of adventure? We can't just ask him."

A laugh rumbles in his chest as he shakes his head. "We both know you're the adventurous one, Haze. Not me."

I'm not sure why that disappoints me so much. I know that about him. It's one of my favorite things about him.

He's so steady. Sure.

I tap my index finger on my chin with a hum. "Maybe we should set them up. Didn't you say Brody is picking up a new jet ski for the shop from Salt Lake City? We could send them down to Utah *together*."

Wade sends me a sideways look, burger in hand. "I have Brody scheduled to go with Colton."

"So unschedule Colton and slot in Emily."

He considers this. After another bite, he shrugs. "I guess we could try it. See if anything else comes up in the journal afterwards."

"*Wade.* This isn't about the journal anymore. This is about true love!" I exclaim, my arms flailing through the air. In my excitement, I accidentally smack him on the shoulder.

Wade chuckles, rubbing his palm across the spot I hit. "Okay, okay, fine. But don't be disappointed if nothing comes of it."

For the first time in weeks, I'm actually excited about something. Just excited. It doesn't come with extra worries or a nagging voice in the back of my mind. There's nothing to plan for. No one will get hurt based on the decision I make. *I* won't be hurt.

This is exactly what I need. Something to do with Wade, just like the old days, to get my mind off of everything with the Arizona job. Sure, I'll have to spend a good amount of time getting the ranch ready for someone else to manage it. I'll need to get everything set up in Arizona for myself. But when I'm with Wade, I don't have to think about any of that.

We can have one last magical summer in Juniper Ridge. Running around town like we used to do, not a care in the world. Maybe we'll even have time for a few days out on the lake, lying in the sun and swimming in the clear water.

A memory tugs at me, lying on the boat deck next to Wade. Sun shining down on us, drying us off. My wet hair hangs off the edge of the boat, our knees touching. Wade's navy blue eyes looking over at me.

"Something will come of it. You'll see. I'm always right about these things." I shift out of my seat, standing to throw away the paper wrappers and brown paper bags. Nothing is better than dinner from a lakeside burger joint. "Thanks for the food."

"No problem," Wade mumbles, mouth full.

Chapter 5

Just Out Of Reach

Friday night comes along quicker than usual, and I can't tell if it's because we're busier than we've ever been at Connor Ranch or if time just goes faster when you're avoiding your email.

My foot taps against the oak flooring of my built-in office in the big barn. I've checked my phone so many times in the past hour that I should just leave it on at this point.

Finally, after probably the thousandth tap on the little glass screen, my best friend's familiar face pops up in a little bubble. It's my favorite photo of him. Mid-laugh, wet hair, the bright turquoise lake shining in the sun behind him.

I took the photo right before his dad's death. Wade and I had spent an entire day on the lake, fishing in the morning and swimming in the afternoon. It's one of my favorite memories with him.

We didn't go out on the lake for at least a year after that day.

Wade: All closed up for the day, wanna grab shakes?

I smack my knee into the desk, springing up to my feet. I shoot back a quick *on my way* and grab my keys. That'll probably bruise tomorrow.

It takes almost no time to get to Black Bear Rentals. The short canyon drive between Connor Ranch and Juniper Ridge is unusually fast. Only three other cars wind down the hill to the lake with me. I pull into the marina, showing my season pass to the attendant.

Waves rock the dock as I make my way to his door. A small storm rolled in and out today, churning up the water. The marina is eerily quiet as a result; all of the boats are docked early. I like it out here when it's quiet.

Wade rounds the corner from the staircase just as I walk in the door in a blur of head-to-toe navy blue. The corners of his lips turn upward into a small smile when he catches my gaze.

"You ready?"

I nod. "Yep. How was the shop today with Brody and Emily gone?"

"Fine," he says, looking down at the notepad on the front desk. He crosses something off, then shoves it into a drawer. "It wasn't too busy today with the rain."

"When are they back?" I make my way around the desk and open the top drawer.

"Tomorrow afternoon."

I lean down, searching for the little leather notebook. Something brushes my arm.

"I already pulled it out for you. I knew you'd be too curious," Wade says, nudging the notebook toward me.

I grin, taking the book out of his hand. "The whole point of all of this was to check on the notebook," I point out. My fingers catch on the loop, opening the book to the first page. I flip through page after page, but there's nothing new. Just blank, open possibilities after the last entry. My stomach sinks. I'm not sure whether I'm disappointed or not.

I know I should want it to be Brody and Emily writing in the journal, but it almost seems too easy. I guess I'm kind of hoping for one last summer adventure. Now, it might be over before it really even started.

Wade shrugs, reaching for my hand. "We'll check it again in a bit. Come on, let's get in line before the crowd shows up."

I snap the book shut, setting it back into the drawer. He takes my hand, tugging me to the front door.

It turns out, all of the crowds from the empty lake are in town today, doing exactly what we had planned. Every single shake shack has a line out the door, winding down the sidewalk.

We pick our favorite one and settle into the back of the line. It doesn't take long for a few families to jump in behind us.

"How can this town even hold this many people?" Wade mumbles. "This has to be a fire code violation."

"Call the marshall," I tease. He looks down at his phone for a second like he might do just that. "Just enjoy the view, Wade."

I love this time of day in the mountains. The sun has just set, turning the sky a mix of purple, pink, and blue. It's just dark enough that all of the neon signs and strings of lights are on and sparkling. The lake matches the cotton candy color of the sky, and everything looks like a painting. It's magical.

He nods towards a group of teenage boys yelling *bro* as loudly as they can. "Yeah, great view– oof." He grunts as my elbow connects with his ribs.

"Don't be such a Negative Nelly. I was talking about the sky."

He rubs his ribs in mock pain. "Sheesh Haze, violence isn't the answer."

"No, it's the question," I tease. "And the answer is yes."

He shoots me a pointed look. "Ha-ha."

The line disappears in front of us one by one until it's our turn to order. We go with our usuals, raspberry for me and chocolate for him. One of the small bistro tables opens up out in the grass, so I run over to grab it.

"I can't believe you actually got a table," he says, sitting down next to me with our shakes.

"I can't believe it didn't take thirty minutes to get shakes." I take the long, red spoon out of the oversized shake cup and take a bite. "Especially with these crowds."

His thigh pushes against mine as he leans over with some extra napkins to place under my already dripping paper cup. His sleeve snags against the white paint peeling off the wooden table, so worn it's mostly brown at this point.

Ever since we were kids, we have always sat on the same side of the table. Habit, I suppose, when our parents would take up the opposite side.

As we got older, it was always Katie on the other side. Katie has always been more like a sister to me than a best friend. She's the sunshine to my rainy day.

Over a year ago, she went on a work trip to Jackson Hole, Wyoming, and decided to stay. It's been a hard year adjusting to life without her in Juniper Ridge, but I'm so happy she found her home.

I can't imagine any other place feeling like home to me as much as Juniper Ridge, Idaho, with its turquoise water and purple wildflowers. It's slow summer nights and cozy mountain winters. Connor Ranch, coffee at Heidi's, and Wade.

Nights like tonight, where the sound of the waves lapping on the shore mixes with the low murmur of people exploring the town. Where everyone seems to wear a contented smile, relaxed and far away from the everyday worries of life, where they come from.

When the sky puts on a show every night with pink cotton candy clouds, deep blue hues that change as the sun sets behind the tall peaks, and a blanket of stars so bright it doesn't feel real.

"I love the lake this time of year," Wade says, reading my mind. His eyes seem to glow just a bit in the soft light as his gaze traces across the tops of the mountain range.

I nod, "Me too, it's the best. I wish it lasted longer."

"Nah," he waves me off, taking a bite of his shake. "Then we wouldn't appreciate it. Plus, I like the snow too. For a few days."

"Yeah, I heard you're really into skiing," I tease.

If there's anything Wade isn't, it's a skier. When we were teenagers, I brought him along with my family and me to the local ski resort. He spent eighty percent of the time putting his skis back on when they popped off, and twenty percent of the time almost missing the chair lift. At one point, he rolled down the hill for so long after a fall that the snow actually accumulated on his coat. A gaggle of little kids called him 'snowman' all day.

He chuckles, and I catch a twinkle in his eye.

"How do you know I haven't been practicing every day in secret so I can show you up one of these days?" He says.

"When would you even have time for that?"

"You'd be surprised at what I have time for, Haze," he says. "I could be playing the long game."

I roll my eyes. "I'll believe it when I see it, snowman."

By the time we finish our shakes and start walking back to Black Bear Rentals, the sky is dark. Streetlights make little golden bubbles of light in our small town, a blanket of stars twinkling brightly above.

There are definitely some perks to living out in the mountains.

The shop is so dark when we stumble through the door that I can't even see the front register. Wade's deep laugh fills the small floating dockhouse.

"Are you headed back to the ranch?" He asks. "You can stay if you want. I replaced the blanket you stole from my couch last month."

"Wade!" I exclaim. "I was going to bring that back to you, you didn't have to get another one." I had taken it home with me on a rare chilly summer morning on a night I probably shouldn't have stayed over, since I was due back at Connor Ranch at four the next morning.

I can't even remember why, but if I had to guess, we probably got sucked into some movie marathon. Wade and I tend to pick a movie theme and stick with it for a long time. Last year, it was only Christmas movies. For six months. It didn't matter if they were cheesy or heartfelt, it's all we watched. After that, it was anything with Stanley Tucci.

He waves his hand with a shrug. "It was getting old anyway. Scratchy. The point is, I got a new one, so it doesn't matter."

"Sure, I'll stay over. I don't have anything to do tomorrow until later." He smiles in the low light, and for some reason, I have to look away. "I'm bringing that journal upstairs, though. I want to flip through it and make sure we aren't missing anything."

"Have at it." He starts up the steep staircase to his apartment above.

The journal is in the same place we left it when we locked up earlier. I grab it out of the drawer, the leather cool against my skin. When I round the corner at the top of the staircase, the journal is already open to the first song, and Wade is already sitting in his usual spot on the couch.

I throw myself onto the other end of the couch, sinking into the soft cushions as I flip through each song.

The couch dips as Wade scoots closer to look over my shoulder at the journal. His thigh presses into mine, and I lean into the familiar touch. The scent of pine and dust mixes in the air, settling around us.

Maybe there's a pattern in the lyrics. A code. Some letters are capitalized, or a hidden meaning in each one.

I've already noticed that each one isn't necessarily the entire song. Rather, a verse and a chorus, or sometimes a bit longer. Two verses. In one case, just a chorus. There doesn't seem to be any rhyme or reason why the songs are written that way, or why the songs are in the journal at all.

The handwriting gets slightly darker and a bit cleaner with each song. The style looks familiar, but I can't place it. Especially with how much it varies between songs.

When I get to 'Butterflies,' I pay closer attention to the page. It's not quite as worn as the first pages of the book, and the ink is darker. Newer. Whoever is writing in this is either using a different pen for each page or the ink is fading impossibly fast. I bite the corner of my lip, concentrating on each word of the song.

But, there's nothing. No pattern. No explanation.

A shadow catches my eye as I fiddle with the page. Turning the page to the next empty page, my stomach drops.

It's not empty anymore.

Chapter 6

When Did You Get Hot

"Ready?"

Sunlight glints off the ripples of Lilac Creek, making me squint in the late morning heat. I grab my sunglasses off my head, untangle my hair from them, and put them on before my eyes start to water.

"Ready," I call back to Wade. We woke up later than usual today and decided to head up to the creek on our way up to Connor Ranch. Probably because we were up all night talking about the new song in the journal.

The lyrics to "Just Out Of Reach" by Willie Nelson and Patsy Cline were written in that same dark, neat writing as the last song. Almost the entire song this time.

Another song appears without explanation.

Wade and I had locked up before we left. Brody and Emily were currently driving back from Utah at this moment, nowhere near the rental shop last night. We were right back to the drawing board again.

We threw out a few ideas of possible culprits last night, but they all led to dead ends. No one else has a key for the shop besides Wyatt, who lives far enough that he wouldn't have had time to get to the shop and out in time.

Eventually, we both passed out on the couch mid-conversation and woke up around ten this morning. Suppressing a yawn, I take another sip of coffee, trudging down to the banks of Lilac Creek.

The creek is nicknamed after of the mountain peak it rushes down. In the spring and summer, fields of lilac colored wildflowers blanket the grass so heavily that from a distance the entire mountain looks purple.

I take my sandals off, setting them safely on the riverbank, and wade into the water. It's cold. Biting cold. But after a few minutes, I'm already used to the mountain run-off. Wade stands downstream a bit, casting his flyrod into a lazy patch of slackwater on the opposite bank. His dad's old flyrod.

That fishing pole was the very first thing he ever moved into the small apartment he lives in now. It was there the first night he moved in, leaning against the far wall like it was a piece of decor, not a constant reminder of his father.

He wouldn't let me put it away, so we moved his things into the apartment around it. Two chairs sat in the middle of the floor facing the window overlooking the lake. I'd stayed over late that night to make sure he was settled. We played poker on the floor, ate takeout from Heidi's cafe, and listened to old music on a tiny speaker I brought with me for the move.

It became a tradition.

For months, we'd listen to Patsy Cline's "I Fall to Pieces" sitting on the floor. I'm not sure why we picked that song, probably because it was one of his dad's only records that wasn't so scratched you couldn't hear anything.

It was one of those seasons that solidified our bond. We were always close, but after going through that, it was different.

Something new. A rock hiding under the sand, revealed by the brush of a wave.

The creek water rushes around my ankles as I walk towards Wade, moving slowly. His line floats across the summer breeze as he casts, settling softly onto the top of the water. This late in the season, the river is cold and clear.

"Anything?" I ask when I finally reach him. We stand a few feet apart in the water, at the curve of a creekbend. The scrub oak blankets the bank behind us, shielding us from the rest of the mountains.

He shakes his head, turning towards me. A soft smile plays on his lips once his gaze meets mine. "Not yet," he murmurs.

I hum. "Well, I guess that's why they call it fishing–"

"Not catching. Yeah, yeah, yeah. Nice one, gramps," he interrupts. The sun reflects off the water, casting waves of light across his face, lightening his hair.

"I'm sorry, do you not like my dad jokes?" I bring a hand to my chest.

He rolls his eyes. "I think I'm the only one who tolerates them, Haze."

"That's not true, Katie does. Sometimes."

"No, she doesn't."

"Fine," I concede. "She doesn't, but sometimes she pretends to, and that's worth something."

"Have you heard from her lately?" He asks. "She hasn't been active in the group chat lately." He flicks his wrist again a few times, casting the line back out across the creek. A single tuft of floppy blonde hair lands on his forehead.

"As a matter of fact, I have. She's coming to visit in a couple of weeks," I reply. I was so excited when our friend told me she was coming to work on her vacation rentals in the area. I squealed into the phone and almost broke her speaker.

"For work?" He asks, gaze locked on the fly he cast out, floating on the water.

"Yep," I nod. "She'll be at the ranch at least one of the nights, I'm sure she'll want you to come hang out."

"Is she bringing Miles?"

Wade met Katie's boyfriend, Miles Autry, the last time she was here. They got along well enough and even went fishing together for an afternoon. It's still crazy after all the years she spent single to see Katie's constant dreamy expression whenever she's around Miles.

"Not this time," I shrug. "He has some sort of big to-do at the ranch to end the season, branding something or other. I don't know, I work with horses, not cows."

Wade nods, taking a step upstream towards me. "I take it she's not staying long, then?"

"Nope, just a couple of days. I'm sure she'll be back in the fall," I say.

Wade casts again, his forearms flexing with each movement. He's gotten tan this summer, like he does every year, and the white button-up t-shirt he's wearing accentuates it. At some point today, he rolled up the sleeves to his elbows. Veins line the inside of his forearms, settling when he releases his grip on the line pinched between his fingers.

Cold water droplets hit my face, startling me out of my head.

"Hey!" I exclaim, bringing my sleeves up to my cheeks to wipe away the creek water. "What was that for?"

"Stop staring at my reel like that, it's creeping me out. You're making me all self-conscious about my casting," he laughs, drying the hand he used to splash me on his shorts.

My cheeks instantly flame. Had I been staring that long? I shouldn't have been staring at all. It's *Wade* for god's sake. I don't stare at Wade.

Ever.

"It's a cool reel. Blue. Mine is silver," I sputter out. I look over my opposite shoulder, turning away so he can't see my face. How embarrassing.

He laughs, reeling up his line. "Alright, let's head out. I'm starved."

I spring to action, climbing up the bank as fast as I can.

"Me too," I call over my shoulder. "I'd better get back to the ranch anyway; they probably need me for something."

The rush of the water drowns out his reply. Sticks crunch beneath my feet as I make my way up the hill, dodging sagebrush bushes along the way.

My stomach is in knots. I've never allowed any of this to surface between us. What's wrong with me? This is the worst possible time to be... noticing things about Wade.

I'm probably leaving. Moving a thousand miles away at the end of the summer. And here I am, making it even harder on myself than it needs to be.

The thing is, it's really hard shutting Wade out of any part of my life. He's the one I ramble to, every thought that comes to my mind. I've never kept anything important from him.

It's eating at me.

He's just now back to himself, the happy version of Wade I knew growing up. His dad's death wrecked him. I can't just tell him I'm leaving for good.

I reach the car, leaning against the passenger door. The heat seeps through my shirt, warming my skin. Wade still stands on the banks of the creek in his waders, breaking down his fishing pole into three smaller sections for the ride back.

His cheeks have turned just slightly pink from the morning sun. I'm sure mine are too. I take a deep breath, the mountain air soothing my mind. I don't need to think about any of that right now. Today, I just need to have a good day with my best friend.

Chapter 7

I Can See You

The couch sinks as I plop down onto one of the soft leather cushions.

Light flows in through all of the windows in the great room, brightening my mood. The mountains stand in stark contrast to the clear, blue sky behind, never changing.

I take a swig from my water bottle as Wade sits down next to me, holding a plate with a warmed-up burrito. My mom greeted us at the front door in a mad rush of ordering more horse tack over the phone, but she still made time to let Wade know there was food in the fridge.

I've never seen Waylon Monroe turn down free food.

My back goes rigid as he sits next to me. I still have no idea what that was earlier. I'm not used to looking at Wade like... that. He's my best friend. We grew up together. We were just spending a lot of time together lately, that's all.

Or maybe it's because it has been so long since I was with anyone. Dating hasn't been that appealing to me after Shawn. And that ended almost a year ago.

It's not like I've missed it much. Dating brings another headache I don't have time for into my already busy life. Running the ranch is much more than a full-time job, and I'd rather spend my limited free time with Wade or Katie when she's in town.

Most of my previous dates have been either annoyed or intimidated by how much I work. How much I care about the ranch, and the time I put into making it the best it can be. That just doesn't work for me.

Shawn didn't start that way, but he got there eventually. They always do.

My phone buzzes against the couch cushion from inside my pocket, startling me. I reach for it, keeping the screen angled away from Wade.

It's an Arizona number.

I press three times, trying to send the call to voicemail, then stuff my phone into the couch cushions like it's on fire.

"Who was that?" Wade raises a brow. I guess it's too much to hope he didn't notice me acting so weird.

"No one," I reply. *What a stupid answer. Damn it.* "Just a spam call," I stutter.

He purses his lips, mulling over my answer, then turns back to the plate in his lap. I let out a small sigh of relief. He may be suspicious, but at least he isn't pushing it.

For now.

I've got to tell him sometime. I know I do.

What if he never wants to talk to me again? Or worse, what if I go down there and it's not what I wanted? What if it's all for nothing and I'm stuck somewhere I don't even like?

I take another deep breath, inhaling the mountain air that always seems to calm me down. I can't freak out in front of Wade. Especially when he doesn't even know what's going on.

"Did you think of anyone else who could be writing in the journal?" I ask, changing my train of thought. We'd checked it again this morning, and there were no new songs written on the pages.

He sits back into the couch pillows, leaning a little closer to where I'm sitting. "I did think of someone it may be, actually. They have a key to the shop, they're around at weird hours, and have access to the front desk–"

"Are you kidding me, Wade?" I interrupt, throwing my hands in the air. "Why wouldn't you tell me about this? It literally *has* to be whoever that is. We have no other options."

"Because I don't think it was him. He has no motive, and he's not exactly the most romantic guy. There's no way it's him," he says.

"*Who?*"

"Earl," he deadpans. "The bait guy."

A laugh bubbles out of me. Then another. "Earl the bait guy? Now I *know* you're fucking with me."

He rolls his eyes. "I tried to tell you it's unlikely."

"I mean, he is single," I manage to get out through giggles. "But I seriously doubt that Earl the bait guy is writing songs into a random journal during deliveries."

"Maybe he's bringing someone with him? I don't know." He drags his palms down his face on a sigh. "He's the only other person with a key besides Wyatt, and Wyatt hasn't been to the shop in months."

"Yeah, maybe," I concede. "We could always get your security camera up and running again and see if there's anything off."

Wade's security camera hasn't worked in years. He left it up as a deterrent, but we don't even have police in Juniper Ridge.

"I don't know what I was thinking; it's a stupid idea. We can just drop it," Wade says. Red creeps up his neck, staining his ears.

"It's not stupid," I say quickly.

He rolls his eyes. "Seriously, Haze. It's fine."

"This is an investigation, Wade." I pound my fist onto the coffee table. "We have to completely clear every single suspect, and that includes Earl. Even if he's not the most likely. We should check it out. Get the cameras back up or else."

His eyes light up as he chuckles, shaking his head. A small sigh of relief escapes my lips. "Fine, Dictator Connor, I'll get right on it."

"Good."

We spend the next hour or so talking about nothing. Making jokes, making plans to go out on the lake, and discussing dude ranch guests. By the time the front door closes behind Wade, all of my anxiety from earlier has melted away.

It's not like a new job one state away is a death sentence. I'll be back visiting my parents and Wade all the time. We've been best friends for over a decade, and we aren't going to lose all of that over a little bit of distance.

I shake my head and walk back to the couch, fishing my phone out of the cushions. Before I can think too much about it, I press call on the Arizona number highlighted in red.

It rings twice before a cheery voice saying hello fills the speaker by my ear.

"Hi," I stumble to reply. "My name is Hazel Mae Connor, and I just missed a call from this number."

"Oh! Hazel Mae! Yes, it looks like Dana wanted to speak with you," the woman exclaims. "I'll patch you through."

"Thank you." I absentmindedly twirl a lock of long, wavy hair in my fingers until another, slightly huskier voice answers the phone.

"This is Dana."

"Hi Dana," I say, suddenly nervous. "This is Hazel. I just missed a call from you?"

"Yes, Miss Connor, thank you for getting back to us. As I'm sure you know, I was calling again to see if you have decided on our offer yet." Dana's stern voice does nothing to calm my nerves. "I'm afraid we'll need an answer by the end of September so we can prepare for you to join us."

I nod even though she can't see me. "I completely understand. Thank you for being patient with me during this process. It's been busy at my family's ranch lately, so I've been a bit tied up, but the museum is a priority for me. I will have an answer by the end of September for sure."

A pause.

"Miss Connor, my team and I were wondering if you'd like to join us at the museum to get to know the work and your future colleagues a little better, as well as take a tour of the facility. Is that something you'd be interested in?" She says, voice completely devoid of any emotion.

They want me to come to Arizona for some sort of... trial run? Right now?

"Yes, I'd be interested in that," I hear myself say. What am I saying? I can't just run away to Arizona for a couple of days. A week? "When would this take place?"

"Well," she sighs. "Ideally, as soon as you can."

My heart drops. "Thank you so much for the offer. I'll check my current schedule and get back to you if that's alright."

We say our polite goodbyes, and I lower the phone from my ear. Staring out the window, I replay the call in my head. I've been dragging my feet on this offer for far too long, and I know it. It makes sense they'd want me to come down there and see it for myself.

It'd probably be good for me, even. I'll get to see what it's like. Who knows, maybe it won't be as bad as I think it'll be. Maybe I'll even like it.

When my heart slows back down to a normal pace, I head to the mudroom and pull on my boots. My hands are still shaking when I open the sliding door to the horse barn.

I wanted this.

Right?

Chapter 8

Getting Good

The familiar sight of Katie MacPherson's auburn barrel curls bouncing in the sunlight fills my vision, lighting everything up in a bright orange-red. She mutters something to herself about grout as she scrubs large tiles within an inch of their life.

Between all of the stress of closing up the summer dude ranch books and moving into winter, trying to make a decision on my future career, and sorting through the rental shop office with Wade, my brain is just about at capacity.

So, I volunteered to chat with Katie as she checks in on this condo between rentals. It's a much-needed break from the ranch spreadsheets and the perfect excuse to finally catch up with her while she's in town. Which, much to my dismay, is only three days this time.

I miss her so much.

"Are you sure you don't need another property manager, Kate?" I ask, taking a bite of the apple I brought with me.

"It's just crazy right now, not forever. It'll slow down sooner rather than later, and then I'd be stuck with a property manager with no work to do. I can handle it for now. Sometimes I just wish guests would make my life a little bit easier, and not drop spaghetti sauce on my white tile and leave it there for more than twenty-four hours," she says with an eye roll, switching cleaning products again on her scrub brush.

"I hear ya," I sigh. "A couple of weeks ago, we had an entire set of plates in a cabin go mysteriously missing. It took three days to find them stashed by the garbage cans, broken into pieces. I just don't get why people can't notify us when these things happen, so I don't have to find out about them from the next guest."

"C'est la vie," Katie shrugs, grabbing a washcloth to rinse the tile. It's starting to look white again, instead of the bright orange it was when I arrived at the scene. "So how's Wade doing these days? I haven't seen him yet on this trip. Is everything okay with the shop?"

"Wade is Wade," I say with a wave of my hand, "He's always the same. I haven't seen Wyatt around the shop much lately. I think Wade has taken over most of the hours this summer."

Katie nods, her forehead scrunching together in the middle. "I've actually got to get a hold of him tomorrow, I have a guest that needs a couple of wakeboard rentals. Think he has anything left?"

"I think I saw a few left when I was over last night."

"Last night, huh? What were you doing over there?" She waggles her brows, a smile spreading across her face.

"I've uh... been helping him with cleaning out his dad's old office in the rental shop. It was past midnight when we got done yesterday, and I didn't want to drive up the canyon to the ranch, so I stayed over on his couch. Probably why I'm so tired today. That thing needs to be replaced," I say with a yawn.

Katie hums, carefully taking off her rubber gloves.

We do a final walkthrough of the condo and make sure everything is in order for the next guests. The cleaners have already been through to do all of the light cleaning, and the place looks like a luxury lake house right out of a movie.

We walk out to the parking lot, arms linked together, running through our calendars to find a time to get together before the end of the season.

"Look at us, two hard-working women running freaking awesome businesses for vacationers. Who would have thought?" Katie muses.

"Definitely not me. It's almost too good to be true," I wink. "Speaking of, I want to run something by you. I'm thinking of breaking the Arizona news to Wade this weekend, and I was wondering if you had any of that special order wine you love so much to help soften the blow. If I don't chicken out again, that is."

"You still haven't told him you're thinking about moving away?" Her emerald eyes widen. "Hazel, he's going to think you've been hiding it from him, telling him this late in the game!"

Guilt twists in my chest. I meant to tell him, I really did. I just... couldn't.

"I know, I just haven't found the right time. It's been so hard to clean out his dad's office. I don't want him to feel like I'm abandoning him. And it's been hard enough for me to think about leaving the ranch and all of my friends and family," I sigh. "Plus, I don't even know if I'm going to take the job. What if I hate it?"

"If you hate it, then you quit and move on to something else, it's not the end of the world. Wade loves you, he's not going to make you feel guilty for leaving if that's what you really want." She squeezes my shoulder. "*Is* it what you really want, though?"

"What do you mean?" I say. Her gaze turns softer. I look towards the ground. I hate it when she looks at me like that, it feels like she can see right into my soul.

"Because every time we talk about it, you spend the majority of the time telling me how much you'll miss Connor Ranch and Juniper Ridge. I'd hate to think you'd leave and not be happy where you're going." Katie says.

"I don't even know anymore. I feel like I'm driving myself crazy overthinking every possible scenario of leaving, not leaving, running into the mountains to live as a wolf," I let out a dry laugh, "I think I'm just not going to think about it for at least a day and see where that gets me."

"A day?" She challenges with a pointed look. "How about a week? You need a break. You're doing way too much for everyone else. The ranch, Wade's shop, this job stuff. Go ride some horses without guests, convince Wade to get out of the apartment and onto a boat, read a book, whatever will get your mind off of this for a good while, then come back to it with a clear head. Sound good?"

I nod.

"Promise me you'll give it a break for a week?" she insists.

"Yes, okay, I promise. One week of fun," I concede.

"Good. This is gonna be good for you, Hazel, I can feel it," she pulls me in for a goodbye hug.

One week.

I can handle one week of distraction, right? Of course I can. It *would* be nice to get Wade out of the shop and do something a little bit lighter. It's been kind of heavy lately, going through all of his dad's old things. He'd probably have a good time on the lake.

Maybe, if we're lucky, it'll be just like old times. No lingering sadness, no stress creeping in at the edges of every laugh. None of... any of the weirdness in the air.

It'll be great. Fun, even.

I put my sunglasses on, crank up the radio in my Bronco, and head into the purple-hazed mountains towards Connor Ranch.

"Come on," I mutter to the car in front of me. The road from the ranch to Juniper Ridge is usually pretty clear in the morning, but today I've been stuck behind a car going about ten under the speed limit since they pulled out of the small campground about halfway up the road.

Now it seems as though they're waiting for a written invitation to turn out onto the main road to town. Granted, the main road is pretty busy too, cars whooshing by one after another down the narrow, winding path between hills.

That's the downside of living on a mountain bench, I suppose. The roads always contain some sort of hazard, from ice and snow in the winter to tourist traffic galore in the warm months. The car finally turns out onto the main road, thankfully heading in the opposite direction, and I'm on my way to Black Bear Rentals again.

Wade and I planned to go through the office again later this afternoon, but I'm antsy to get out of the house this morning after a cancelled trail ride. My plan is to see if he's free, and if not, I'll head down to the lake and read a book on the white sand beach. It's a win-win situation for me.

Though I'm hoping he's free and wants to tackle more of the office organizing. We've been on a roll lately, and I can see the finish line. Everything is dried out and mostly sorted through.

I pull my Bronco into the marina, parking in my usual shady spot. The lake is calm and bright today, turquoise shining in the sun. A small family swims in the clear water on the other side of the marina lot, splashing in the shallow water.

Hopping onto the hot pavement, I make my way to the dock I've spent most of my life walking down towards Black Bear Rentals. Emily stands on the back dock behind the building, helping a hesitant couple onto one of the rental jet skis.

Great, I think. *If he has help today, maybe he'll be able to take some time to organize with me.*

I push the door open, hearing the familiar chime of bells announce my arrival, but the shop is completely empty. No customers, no one standing at the front desk. I round the corner, heading up to Wade's apartment. Maybe he hasn't come down yet.

His door is propped open just a crack. "Hello?" I say, softly knocking on the door. "Wade?"

There's no answer.

I pop my head into his apartment, but no one is there either. Silent and empty. I close the door, walking back to the stairs, when I hear a small thud from the first floor.

"Wade?" I call again, rushing down the stairs. Another thud comes from behind the office door. "Are you in there?" I lean onto the office door, listening for an answer.

"Haze?" Wade's voice cracks. I turn the knob, slowly opening the door and peeking inside.

"Hey, are you okay in there?" I say. Light spills into the dark room from the opening, landing on Wade's tall frame sitting on the floor in the middle of the room. He's turned away from me, looking over one of the boxes that didn't get quite as damaged.

The room is still a mess. Boxes everywhere, books flipped open to dry out all the way, three garbage bags stuffed full in the corner. His glasses lay discarded on the floor behind him.

I pad over to Wade, squatting down next to him. An old photo album lies open on his lap.

"Sorry, I didn't hear you come in." His voice is unsteady and raw. I turn him to face me, a hand on his cheek. A tear escapes his eye, landing on my palm.

"What's wrong?" I whisper. "Are you okay?"

He breathes a dry, sad laugh. "I'm fine, I just came across this," he holds the photo album up. "My mom made it for him when I was little. It's all of their memories from when they were first married, then when Wyatt and I were little. I just couldn't pull myself away. I'm sorry, I should have waited for you, I'd probably be in better shape."

"No, Wade," I say. "Don't apologize. "I'm glad I came by so you're not alone."

He shakes his head, meeting my gaze. "I don't know why it's still so hard. I just– I don't remember a lot of this, and it's frustrating. Why don't I remember anything? He's gone, and I can barely picture his face anymore."

"Wade," I frown. I wrap my arms around his neck, pulling him into a hug. He immediately pulls me in so I'm sitting in his lap on the floor, his head resting on my shoulder. The photo album slides to the floor.

Wade holds onto me as if I'm his only lifeline, saving him from drowning in this grief that never goes away. His arms wrap around my middle, squeezing me until all I can feel is his desperation. For contact, for comfort, for love.

"Breathe," I remind him. He takes a deep, uneven breath, relaxing a little bit more.

"Hazel–" he cuts off.

"I know."

I let him hold me on the floor of his dad's office for a while. It could have been a couple of minutes or half an hour. When he relaxes his grip a little, I pull away, wiping the tears from his cheeks. He tries a watery smile.

"Can you show me the photos? I'd like to see them." I whisper. He nods as I slide onto the floor next to him. I press my thigh against his, not ready to be too far apart just yet.

He brings the photo album to rest on both of our knees, flipping back to the beginning.

"This is right after they opened the tackle shop," Wade points to a photo of James and Heidi Monroe standing on the marina dock.

"It hasn't changed all that much, has it?" The sign is different, the boats in their slips are older, but it's the same building we're in now. Heidi smiles at us from under a baseball cap. James stands behind her, circling his arms around her waist.

"Nope, it's pretty much the same," he agrees, turning the page. We look through photos of the tackle shop in its glory days, James fishing with strangers who were clients of his guiding business, Heidi's very first creations for her brand new restaurant, just a few miles away from the marina.

We're laughing by the time we get to Wade's grand entrance to the photo album. James holds an infant Wade off the edge of the dock, dipping his toes in the water as toddler Wyatt watches with a very concerned look.

"You're not even crying," I giggle.

"That's where it all started, I guess," he laughs. "I have to send this to Wyatt, he'll love it." Wade takes out his phone, snapping a photo to text to his brother.

"You can tell even from baby photos that you guys were a handful," I say. The next photo is of Wade, probably around a year old, leaning off the dock to point at a school of black carp in the water as Wyatt feeds them cereal.

"I was a handful," Wade says. "Wyatt was much calmer. Oldest kid stuff, I guess. He looked out for me."

"You should take this over to him next time you visit. I bet Lainey would love to see it, too."

He smiles, closing the photo album. We looked through the entire thing, laughing and pointing out our favorite photos. James might not be here anymore, but looking through these snapshots of his life, it kind of feels like he is.

"Yeah, I'll do that." Wade stands, helping me up. I shake out my legs, which have definitely fallen asleep sitting on the wooden plank floor. "Thanks, Haze, I'm really glad you came by. I probably would have locked myself in here all day under a storm cloud."

I pull him in for another hug, wrapping my arms around his chest. His shirt is soft against my cheek. "Next time you need me, please text me. You don't have to do any of this alone."

He sighs against my head, squeezing me a little tighter once before letting go.

"I will, I promise," he whispers, pushing a stray curl behind my ear.

I nod, taking his hand and leading him out into the midday sun. "Come on, let's go for a swim."

Chapter 9

I Can Love You Better

WADE IS ALREADY WAITING outside when I pull up to Black Bear Rentals for the third time this week, leaning up against a pole on the shop's porch. His sandy blonde hair is hidden under a navy blue ball cap, his hands tucked into the pouch pocket of a gray hoodie.

I'm five minutes late, and I know I'm going to hear about it. I don't care. As long as he's back to himself, he can get on me all he'd like.

A frown crosses his face as I wave. He looks at his watch pointedly, shaking his head. I beep the horn twice in response, unable to help the smile creeping onto my lips.

"You know, if you leave your house about five minutes earlier, you'll arrive at your destination five minutes earlier, making you on time for once. Just some math for you," he jokes as he slides into the passenger seat of the Bronco.

His arm flexes on the armrest. I snap my gaze back to the dashboard.

"You know, if you're slightly less of an ass to people each day, they will think slightly better of you over time," I counter.

That earns a laugh from him as we make the short drive down the street to Cisco's. It's just far enough not to want to make the trek on foot. Cisco's is a small rectangle building made of old storage containers. Pretty plain from the outside, besides their neon sign with a Cisco fish on it.

Inside, it's a hodge-podge of metal garage signs, neon beer signs, stickers on the wall, posters from local businesses, and photos of local fishermen with their biggest catches. Dim industrial-style hanging lights above the long bar.

Ever since I was old enough to drink, Wade and I have loved to come down to Cisco's and play pool or darts on weekends. In the winter, sometimes we have the place to ourselves. Katie, being the most competitive out of our friends, always wins.

He told me he waited until I turned twenty-one to order a drink at Cisco's so we could do it together. I'm still not sure if it's true or not, but I don't really care. It's a nice thought either way.

Wade and Katie brought me to Cisco's the night of my birthday all those years ago. I had just been broken up with by Shawn for the second time (it turned out to be four by the end of it), and I wasn't feeling up to going out. They dragged me to the bar, insisting that no matter what, I needed to celebrate my twenty-first so I wouldn't look back and regret anything.

My birthday is in the middle of July, so it was still pretty busy in Juniper Ridge. We had trouble finding a room. We ended up squishing together at the bar between two groups of college guys.

We ordered our drinks, eventually line danced with the crowd, and it was the most fun I had ever had. I couldn't remember Shawn's name by the end of the night.

In between dances, I made my way down the narrow hall in the back to the bathroom, but stopped abruptly when I noticed, through the haze of a lemon drop martini, one beer and two shots, none other than Wade Monroe with some blonde girl, *kissing.*

I hadn't even considered that any of us would be kissing anyone that night. It was supposed to be a friends' night out. Before they saw me, I turned around and high-tailed it back to Katie at the bar. I remember thinking about how grateful I was to be on the verge of being drunk when I saw that.

I don't know if I could handle the awkwardness of seeing my best friend making out with a stranger in the back of the dark bar sober.

Now, the twang of a guitar coming from the speakers engulfs my ears as we make our way inside. It's still fairly light outside, but the neon signs still glow with a familiar warmth.

Wade's telling me about a particularly bad-mannered rental shop customer as we slide into two burgundy leather barstools in the middle of the dark oak bar.

When the bartender brings us the beers Wade ordered for us, I sneak a quick look around. Over in the corner booth with a pitcher of beer is a group of five local guys I recognize from high school. As a chorus of laughter rings out, at what I'm sure is a highly inappropriate 'joke,' I notice the dark hair on the end that I'm sure I've touched.

Then, I notice the charming smile I've kissed dozens of times, the hands that have touched every inch of my body, the mouth that told me I wasn't good enough with casual cruelty. Shawn glances over at me, and his smile fades as recognition sparks in his eyes.

My eyes widen, and I whip back around to face the bar.

"Haze, everything alright?" Wade's eyes search mine.

I clasp my hands together to stop the shaking and take a deep breath. *Why is he here? He had to pick the same night as me to go to Cisco's?*

"Remember how I told you it's been months since I've seen Shawn?" I whisper.

"Yes..." he starts, looking increasingly concerned by the second.

"Well, now it hasn't."

As if on cue, a throat clears behind us, and both of us turn to look straight at Shawn as he walks up to our seats.

"Hey, Hazel Mae, it's so good to see you. You look great," he says with a forced smile.

"Yeah, you too," I muster out, feeling like such a cliche. Wade stiffens next to me and grips my arm a little too tightly. I pull out of his grip when Shawn goes in for an awkward hug.

"Waylon, you're looking great too, man. Been hitting the gym lately?" Shawn says to Wade.

"Nope, just out on the lake a lot, summer boating and all that," Wade says. His lips press into a thin line, and something cold passes across his features.

"Cool, cool," Shawn replies absently. "So listen, Hazel, I was thinking we could catch up sometime. I was just thinking of texting you, but I don't want to bug you during the busy season. Now that you're here tonight, it's like the universe is sending me a message," he chuckles, "Let's grab coffee sometime."

I nod curtly. I hate that he calls me Hazel. It feels like a violation, like he has special access to using a shortened version of my name. He shouldn't be allowed that.

"Great, I'll text you tomorrow," Shawn says with another smile oozing with charm and confidence, "I've missed you. A lot." He brings his hand to my shoulder, giving me a light squeeze before walking back to his group of buddies, now on their way out of the bar.

Wade's eyes linger on my shoulder after Shawn leaves. I place a hand on his thigh under the bar, bringing his gaze back to mine.

"Hey, I'm fine, I just didn't expect to see him. It's been a while," I say softly.

"He cheated on you, Haze," he snaps. "I just don't like guys like that, and I don't like that he can just pretend to be your friend after how he treated you."

"It's okay, Wade, seriously. I have no interest in meeting him for coffee ever. Really, it's fine. I was just surprised, that's all." My thumb makes small circles on the top of his jeans.

His gaze dips to my lips. I feel myself lean a little bit closer, or maybe he does. Pulled in like the tide. Waves crashing low in my core. A glass crashed to the floor in the background. As quickly as this whole thing started, it ends.

Wade shifts awkwardly on the barstool, twirling the straw in his drink. His fingers flex around the glass, knuckles turning white.

"Let's go play some pool," I offer as a distraction. He grunts reluctantly, and I pull him over to an open table. We don't talk much during the game, but by the end, he's smiling again at least.

On our drive back to the shop, he's fidgety. His eyes dart over to me and back more than a few times. His thumbs tap a quick staccato beat on the steering wheel. Not wanting to push him, I leave him to his thoughts and open my texts with Katie.

Hazel: You will never believe who I just saw at Cisco's.

Katie: Um, rude, you went to Cisco's without me? Not fair.

Hazel: Wade asked me to go with him. We ran into Shawn.

Katie: No way!

Katie: I hope you told that jerkface to kindly fuck off.

Hazel: I was too shocked to remember to insult him. Damn it.

Hazel: He asked me out for coffee and said he missed me. A lot. It was so awkward. It really upset Wade that he was being all friendly with me.

Katie: I'm sure it did.

Hazel: What's that supposed to mean?

Her typing bubble pops up and disappears again and again. I let out a frustrated sigh and stuff my phone back into my bag. I just want things to go back to how they were. Before Katie moved away, before the job offer. The good old days when there wasn't this tension between Wade and me. Just kids, having fun at the lake.

The shoreline passes in a blur outside my window. Moonlight reflects off the surface of the lake, lighting up the night around us. The alcohol buzzes around in my head, making it feel heavy on my shoulders.

I push my hair over one shoulder and absentmindedly pick split ends off the bottom of the strands. It's a habit I picked up from my mother years ago. The longer my hair gets, the more I do it. It's down to my waist now.

"Hey, should I cut my hair?" I blurt out.

"What?" Wade says drowsily.

"My hair. Should I cut it?"

"Um... no? Why?" He looks over at me inquisitively from the driver's seat. His blue eyes sparkle in the starlight. He always looks so good.

I giggle, pulling my legs into my chest. "It's getting so long. I'm not sure if I should cut it again or not. I've never had short hair, maybe I'd look good with it."

He nods. "I'm sure you would, but you wouldn't look like Hazel. I like your long hair." His eyes are smiling at me when

I catch his gaze, sending another flutter through my stomach. I'm too tired and tipsy to fight it.

"Okay," I hum. "I won't cut it then."

"Okay," he smiles, turning his gaze back to the road in front of us.

Wade turns my Bronco into the parking lot of the rental shop. I planned to drive back up to the ranch tonight, but I won't risk it after having two drinks at the bar. I wait in my seat for Wade to come around to get my door, hands under my thighs.

Our eyes catch through the window as he grips the handle. For a split second, he lingers there. A shaky breath whooshes out past my lips.

Normally, I'd be freaking out. But the mix of the alcohol, the night air, and... Wade does something to me. I want to be reckless. I'm *never* reckless.

The passenger door creaks open, and his eyes never leave mine. He reaches for my hand to help me out of my seat.

"Wade..." I whisper.

He swallows once, his throat bobbing up and down. My eyes fall to it against my will, and I instantly regret it.

How have I never noticed this before? Noticed him? How is it possible to be around someone every day and know almost everything about them, all of their quirks, all of their habits? Then one day, slowly, start to see them in a different light completely?

How could I not see the deep navy blue of his eyes? How could I miss the fleeting way his emotions pass across his face?

How could I not feel this urge to be near him every waking second, to know him better?

I feel myself lean closer to him. His hands instinctively land on the seat below me, caging me in. Our breaths mingle, blood rushes behind my ears.

"Haze," he whispers. My name sounds softer on his lips. My gaze falls to his mouth. We're so close now that I could just reach a little further, just a hair, and–

"We shouldn't. Not like this."

My heart stops. It's like a bucket of ice water being poured on me. My buzz instantly disappears.

"Right. Sorry. I think I'm a little, I don't know, drunk or something. I don't know what's happening–" I ramble.

"Hazel–" he starts.

I wave, cutting him off. He backs up a few steps, chilly night air rushing in between us."It's fine. Are you fine? I'm fine. Well, not like *fine* fine, but you know–"

"Hazel, please–"

"No, you're right, let's just go in. I'm so tired, I think I'm just going crazy," I rush out.

He sighs, hands on his hips. About seven different emotions pass across his features, none of which I have the energy or wits about me to decipher at the moment.

"Fine," he says, looking down at his shoes. "C'mon." He grabs my hand again, pulling me out of the car. I stumble a little on the ground in my heeled cowgirl boots.

The panic I expect to bubble up through me just... doesn't. I should be freaking out right now. I should feel guilty and scared. I should want to erase it all.

But, I don't. My heart tugs towards him, a string pulling taut between us.

What's wrong with me? I'm *so* not like this. I'm not the girl who almost kisses her best friend. I'm the girl who does everything by the book, who people can depend on. The girl who has it all together.

Except, am I even that anymore? Am I that to Wade? I still haven't even told him about the possibility that I might be moving an entire state away. So far, he'll have to take an airplane to get to me. So much for dependability.

I'll tell him this week. I have to. I can't have this keep eating at me.

That must be why I'm acting like a crazy person. I feel guilty, so I'm trying to get closer to him in other ways or something. I'm sure there's a logical explanation to it all.

Sure, it's a little embarrassing that he had to be the one to stop us tonight, but he was leaning in, too. At least I have the excuse of being buzzed and being under a ton of stress.

What's his excuse?

Chapter 10

Jealous

My head is still pounding as I walk through the aisles of the local feed and tack store, Lake Supply, the next morning. Or maybe I should say late morning. It was already almost ten o'clock when I got out of bed this morning. Pretty late for someone who is usually up at dawn with the horses.

Luckily, today is a check-out day. Guests have left, and the cleaning crews are arriving to turn down the cabins for the next set.

Rows and rows of horse reins pass by as I make my way back to the wire brushes. A new wire brush is next on my list after one of the guests left one out a few weeks ago, and by the time I found it, it had rusted.

I absentmindedly reach out and run my finger along the sharp metal teeth. My mind is still racing from yesterday. Clearly, whatever this is between Wade and me isn't going to pass on its own. I keep replaying that moment in my head. Leaning in, a fog clouding my every thought. And then, of course, his whispering my name.

Saying we shouldn't do this.

It feels a lot worse this morning. I want to crawl out of my skin thinking about it. I can't believe I did that. Try to kiss Wade? Am I going crazy?

The oddest part might be that I'm pretty sure he leaned in, too. It's hard to recall through the haze of it all, but I'm at least eighty percent certain he did. Which means... did he want to kiss me, too?

No. There's no way.

He probably didn't even mean to. Or, he was trying to make me feel better or something. That's very much like Wade, to pretend something so I don't feel alone.

It's very much *not* like Wade to lean in so closely with that spark of... something in his eyes. Confusion? Amusement? I can see it so clearly in my mind, but I can't make out what he was thinking at that moment.

As much as it sucked to get rejected by my very best friend, I'm relieved. He's right, we shouldn't ruin what we have. Plus, out of anyone in the world I could have gotten rejected by, Wade was probably the best choice. He'll judge me the least.

Unfortunately, I'll probably judge myself enough for both of us.

My mind replays the moment again as it has been on a loop all morning. Wade opening my door, the air changing, crackling with something new, leaning towards him, Wade taking a step closer–

"That's it!" I whisper-shout, scaring myself. I look over my shoulder, but no one is around to hear me talk to myself in the middle of a store.

For some reason, it took that many replays in my head to remember that important detail. Wade took a step towards me.

A deep, boisterous laugh jolts me out of my head. I push up onto my toes to see over the rack in front of me. Three rows ahead, a tall man with white hair leans over the checkout counter, talking with Mary, the owner of Lake Supply. Her face lights up into a wide grin as he leans in closer, whispering something in her ear.

My hand flies to my lips to cover a gasp. Earl and Mary? Are they together?

I whip out my phone and open my texts with Wade.

Hazel: At Lake Supply. Earl is here, flirting with Mary! Thoughts?

I chew on my nail while I wait for Wade to see my text. Should I have probably started a conversation with him differently, especially with how we left things? Probably.

Three little dots pop up on the left side of the screen. My heart skips a beat. He's typing.

Wade: My thoughts are mostly that you're a big old meddler and a little bit creepy.

A laugh escapes me. I type back, smiling down at my phone.

Hazel: I'm not creepy or meddling, just passing along some information.

Wade: I stand by my previous text.

Hazel: Wade! The journal!

Hazel: If Earl is writing about Mary, this could be it.

Wade: I think you were right before. I seriously doubt my bait guy is writing love songs in a journal at my shop during deliveries.

Hazel: But did you think he'd be flirting with Mary during deliveries? Because I didn't.

Wade: I suppose not.

Shoving my phone into the back pocket of my jeans, I grab a wire brush and head up towards the checkout counter.

"Hi Earl," I blurt out.

He jumps back from the counter, turning around towards me. "Howdy, Hazel. I'll get out of your way here."

"Oh no," I smile. "I'm not in any rush. Doing some morning deliveries?"

He nods. "Just came from the Monroe boys' place, actually." He turns and looks at Mary. They exchange a look that has me shifting on my feet.

"Let me ring that up for you, Hazel Mae," Mary says. The soft cadence of her voice spreads through the air like a warm blanket.

I hand over the wire brush, and Mary bags it up. Earl doesn't leave, though. He stands to the side, gaze locked on the fish-themed nail clippers lined up on the counter.

Mary hands me the bag and my receipt with a warm smile.

"Thanks!" I say, walking towards the door, but her attention is already back on Earl and his puffy brown corduroy coat.

I kill the ignition as I pull up to Black Bear Rentals that afternoon. The sun is beating down on Juniper Ridge today, another late-season heat wave that has families covering the beaches and boaters clearing out of the marina.

Wade is at the register when I tumble into the shop, sweat already beading on my forehead. A sigh of relief escapes as the air conditioner hits my face.

"Why is it so hot today?" I complain.

Wade's eyes slowly turn up at me. His sandy hair covers his forehead, just a little grown out. "It's summer," he states.

I roll my eyes. "Yeah, I figured that one out all by myself."

He huffs a laugh, turning a page in the book he's reading. There's no one else in the shop today, but from the looks of it, he's had a busy day so far. Most of the life jacket racks stand empty on the wall. On the back side of the register, the key rack is almost empty, the only keys left belonging to a couple of older jet skis and the fishing boat.

"Just you today, huh?" I ask.

He nods, his gaze back down on the book. "Brody's out with a couple of customers getting a boat launched."

"I heard Earl stopped by."

"He did."

I wait for him to elaborate. He doesn't. "And?"

He sighs, closing the book and standing up straight. "I was here the whole time; he didn't come to the register once." My excitement drops off completely. "But, I did check the journal before he got here."

"You did?"

Another nod. "See for yourself," he says. Wade steps back from the counter, motioning for me to open the drawer.

I don't waste any time grabbing the journal out and flipping through the pages. Just after the Willie Nelson song, on the next blank page, is another song. I skim over the familiar lyrics until I can hear them in my head.

"Seriously?" I shake my head in disbelief. Wade chuckles. "The Jonas Brothers?"

"Well," he says. "Just one of them, I think."

The lyrics of Nick Jonas's *Jealous* stare back at me from the page.

"We go from Willie Nelson to Nick Jonas? Who is writing in this thing?" I say incredulously. I flip through all of the pages, verifying that all of the songs are the exact same and the page after the new song is blank. As always, it is.

"Not Earl, it seems," Wade says. His voice startles me. He must have taken a few steps up to look at the song over my shoulder, because when he speaks, his breath skirts across my ear.

"There's absolutely no way Earl knows the lyrics to this song," I laugh.

"Even if he did, he wouldn't have been able to. He hasn't been in since the last song was written, and I was here the entire time he was today. It has to be someone else," Wade says.

I nod, running my fingers across the words on the page. Just like last time, the writing style is the same. Unlike the first few songs in the book. The ink looks newer, too.

"It has to be someone," I say, twirling a piece of my hair through my fingers. Our hips brush against each other as I turn to face Wade. He takes a step back, his eyes falling to my hand holding my hair. I stop, not meaning to, and he looks away.

"I'm too exhausted and hungry to even come up with anything else, Haze," he mutters. He slumps back onto the wall behind him, running his hands through his hair.

The loose t-shirt he's wearing lifts just a bit, and I look away before I can even look. "Heidi's?" I blurt out.

"What?" he says groggily.

"Let's go to Heidi's. I could use a burger today." *And probably a bucket of ice water to go with it.*

He nods, pushing off the wall. "Yeah, let's do it. Can you cover down here while I head upstairs for a second? We can leave as soon as Brody is back."

"Yep."

I collapse onto the register as soon as he's up the stairs all the way. Why does it feel like nothing can go right anymore? I can't stop whatever is wrong with me when Wade is around. Nothing about the journal makes sense. It's unbearably hot for the end of August, and no matter what I do, I absolutely cannot bring myself to tell Wade that I might be moving away.

My head falls into my hands, and I let out a frustrated groan. Everything feels like it's slipping through my fingers, and I can't even enjoy what might be my last summer with my best friend.

Group Chat

Hazel + Katie

Katie: Guess what Miles said today?

Hazel: Oh god, what?

Katie: I braided my hair today, and he said it looked 'just like Claro's.'

Hazel: His horse?!

Katie: Yep.

Hazel: Why are men?

Katie: Speaking of men, how is yours?

Hazel: I don't know who you're referring to.

Katie: Yes, you do.

Hazel: Fine.

Hazel: He's still Wade. I don't know, I'm trying to be normal.

Katie: Fuck normal. Make it weird.

Hazel: Thanks for the suggestion! I'll take it under consideration.

Chapter 11

Wild As You

No tables at Heidi's are the same. The entire cafe was decorated one table at a time with antique chairs of all styles in every color. The baby blue walls house dozens of photos and paintings of the lake and surrounding mountains. Comfortable, warm light emanates from the various antique lamps placed on each table, each one different than the last.

The air always holds the scent of freshly baked croissants. I'm not sure how, but I have a suspicion that Heidi does it on purpose. One day, I expect to find a secret stash of them somewhere.

It's a little chaotic. An assault on the senses.

It's perfect.

At night, I prefer to sit inside near the fireplace. Even in the summer when it's not lit, it still feels cozy, tucked in a corner with a cowhide rug beneath it. But on a sunny day like today, I can't help but sit in the sun room.

Wade and I walk towards the very back of the converted house, towards the wall made of windows. We sit at the table right in the middle, under the skylight. Succulents and vines hang from the wood beams running under the domed roof. All the colors of the rainbow glint off the light catchers hanging in each corner, each one a collection of shiny prisms.

The menu is so worn, it's difficult to make out what some of the smaller words are, but it doesn't matter. I know exactly what I want.

"Hazel Mae, how wonderful to see your beautiful face," Heidi beams as she kneels next to our table. "To what do I owe this pleasure?"

"We are in desperate need of a couple of burgers," I laugh. Heidi's mix of blonde and grey hair shines in the sunlight, her eyes crinkled at the sides.

"Hi, Mom," Wade says from across the table. Heidi places a hand on his forearm, squeezing once before letting go.

"Hi baby, it's good to see you too," she smiles.

"Hah!" I exclaim. "I'm the favorite."

"Well, of course you're the favorite, dear," Heidi says. "You've never once spilled an entire gallon of red paint on my white carpet."

Wade scoffs. "You can't count that, I was three."

"The clock started when you came into this world, I'm afraid," Heidi shrugs. I catch my breath from laughing and take a sip of my water. "What are you two kids up to today? Nothing but trouble, I hope."

"I just stopped in town to run a few errands for the ranch," I explain. "Then we have some plans to organize the office at Black Bear again. After burgers, of course."

Heidi stands, stuffing the blank notepad back into her apron. "Sounds like you have quite the day ahead of you. We'll get these started for you."

"Thanks," we both say as Heidi walks back towards the kitchen.

"It's not fair that she likes you more. I bet she gives you extra fries, too," Wade rolls his eyes.

"Have you tried being more like me?" I take a sip of cold water.

Wade smiles, his warm gaze piercing into somewhere deep in my chest. His eyes are soft, and the amused curve of his lips makes me smile right back.

So familiar. Like home.

"I could never be like you, Haze. You're one of a kind," he winks.

I smile. "So are you."

He shakes his head. "No, you have a spark that I don't have. It's okay, I don't mind being your sidekick."

"It's nice to have a sidekick." I study him, and he studies me back for a moment. His eyes are so *blue.* Swirling navy, lighter in the middle. They glow a little in the sunlight, framed by light lashes. It's late enough in the summer that his freckles are more pronounced, darkened by days in the sun.

"I think your face is my favorite face," I giggle.

He lets out something between a laugh and a shaky breath. Unstable. "What?"

I shrug, looking down at the little black bear on his shirt. "You have a nice face. Very warm. Inviting. My compliments to Heidi."

Wade chuckles. “That barely makes any sense.”

“It doesn’t have to make sense to you, it makes sense to me.”

He shakes his head, pulling his phone out of his pocket. His brows furrow as he reads the screen, then pockets it again.

“Everything okay?” I ask hesitantly.

He nods. “Yeah, sorry, just Sabrina.”

My heart drops. “Oh? I didn’t realize you two were still...” I trail off, the words unable to come out of my mouth.

“We’re not.” He says. “Not really.”

“What does that mean?”

He sighs. “We aren’t back together or anything, she just mentioned she’s in town, so we were gonna grab a coffee or a drink.”

My chest tightens. I take another big gulp of water, twisting my hair between my fingers. “Oh. Those are two different vibes.”

“Go ahead,” he motions.

“What?”

“Just tell me your thoughts, Hazel. I know you have them.” His demeanor shifts, and I know him well enough to know he’s in defense mode. Not the time to push it.

I push it anyway. “I just don’t like her, Wade. It’s not a secret, you know that.”

He runs a hand through his hair as I feel heat creeping up my neck.

“That was a long time ago,” he says slowly.

“Doesn’t feel like it.”

"Well, it *was*." He leans in, voice lowering. "She's changed. We're older now. Plus, I already told you, we aren't back together or anything."

"She up and left with no word, Wade!" I say a little too loudly, my arms up in the air. I look around, making sure no one is watching, before lowering my voice. "Two weeks after your dad died! Excuse me if I'm not the biggest fan." Flashbacks pass in my mind, Wade at his lowest. Having to pick him up off the couch the day she left and force him to eat. He was already broken. When his girlfriend of two years disappeared, he had nothing left.

"Yeah, well, I'm not the biggest fan of Shawn, and I had to watch that dick try and get you back the other day," he snaps. His eyes harden, boring holes deep into me.

"That's not fair." My voice comes out shaky where I meant it to be firm.

"You're not being fair either." He says.

This is uncharted territory for us. I squirm in my seat. We hardly ever fight, and when we do, usually one of us bends pretty quickly. We generally see eye to eye.

I search for any ideas, anything at all to turn this around.

"You're right, I'm sorry, it's not my place." I get the courage to meet his gaze and find it softer, more vulnerable.

He sighs, shifting forward, leaning his arms on the table. "I get you have an opinion, Haze, that's fine. It's just that I hold your opinions highly, and I'd really appreciate it if you'd try to maybe give this one a blank slate."

He's so earnest, so hopeful, that I can't help but nod. "Okay." I take a deep breath, casting Sabrina from my mind.

"Here are those burgers, y'all," a soft voice interrupts my train of thought. Jane, one of Heidi's servers, sets our plates in front of us.

"Thanks, Jane, they smell amazing," I say as Wade takes a bite, never one to wait to start shoveling food into his mouth.

"Let me know if there's anything else you need," she smiles.

"I've got some shakes courtesy of your mom, Wade," Marcus rounds the corner with two strawberry shakes in hand.

"Wow, straight from the chef," I laugh. Wade mumbles something that sounds like 'thanks' with a mouth full of fries.

"You know, Heidi, there's no telling her 'no,'" Marcus laughs, handing us the shakes. "Hey, Janey."

"Hi," Jane tucks a strand of dark, coiled hair behind her ear. They stare at each other for a beat too long before Marcus clears his throat.

"I'd better get back to the kitchen, then," he stammers.

"Oh yeah, me too," Jane nods. "Enjoy your meal."

"What was that about?" I whisper to Wade after they both disappear around the corner.

"What," he says before finishing off the last bite of his burger.

"Jesus Christ, Wade, it's not a race," I say.

He shrugs, popping another fry into his mouth. I haven't even started my food yet, and he's almost done with his. Typical. I'm not sure where it comes from, but both Wade and his brother Wyatt eat like they've been starved for days. I push my fries toward Wade as an offering, but he shakes his head and pushes them back.

"I *mean*," I start again. "There's clearly something going on there."

He considers my words. "Marcus and Jane?"

I nod, taking a sip of my shake. "Yeah, did you see how flustered he got when he said hi to her? They literally work together all day. And she wasn't much better off."

"If you say something about that journal–" Wade rolls his eyes.

I shake my head. "No, not even that. Although if we could figure out how they'd have access to it, maybe. I was just observing."

He laughs, leaning back in his chair. His arms are crossed, the sleeves of his t-shirt pushing against his biceps. "You're always observing."

"It's your favorite thing about me," I tease.

"I like a lot of things about you," he says, taking a sip of his milkshake. I freeze. "You know, now that you mention it, Jane was in the shop the other day."

"Why?"

"Brought in lunch for the crew. Sometimes we do that, and when we do, it's always Heidi's, obviously."

"Obviously," I repeat. "So you're saying it could actually be her?"

He scrunches his nose in thought. "It's possible. I don't know, I've never actually kept track."

My heart races. This could be it. Jane clearly has a thing for Marcus, and if she's been to the shop, maybe she's the one writing in the journal. I'm not sure how she'd actually get enough time to write in it, but maybe she gets bored when she's waiting for Wade to grab payment or something.

Either way, this is a new start.

"What day is it?" I ask, a smile creeping onto my face. My hands jitter with excitement.

"Friday, why?" Wade's head cocks slightly to the side as he tries to read me.

"It's trivia night."

Chapter 12

Something to Talk About

"WHAT DO YOU THINK our team name should be?"

"You're unbelievable." Wade shakes his head, grabbing our drinks from the bar.

"I was thinking 'The Bear Lake Monsters,' but is that too obvious?" I ignore him. We make our way back to the little high table we secured about fifteen minutes ago at Cisco's Trivia Night. I can't remember when Wade and I last came to trivia night, but it's been a while. Probably a year at least.

"Yes, but I can't think of anything better, so go for it." Wade slides onto his barstool, setting our drinks on the table. I pick up the whiteboard and start to doodle a sea monster with our team name for the night. "I was talking about you inviting Marcus and Jane on a double date at trivia night."

"No one here is on a date, Wade. I simply invited them to trivia night with us because I'd like to get to know them better. Are you suggesting that *we* are on a date?" I give him a pointed look before continuing my drawing.

"No, that's not what I'm saying," he says quickly. "You know what I mean. You're trying to set them up."

I laugh, clipping the finished whiteboard displaying our team name onto the holder in the middle of our table. Wade is already holding the answer whiteboard, so I hand him the marker to go with it.

"I don't know what you mean, Wade. I'm not doing anything. We haven't been to trivia night in a while, and I thought it'd be fun. Obviously, we can't be a team of two, so I figured it'd be a great chance for all of us to get to know each other," I explain, looking towards the front door. No sign of them yet.

"Right," Wade narrows his eyes at me.

I shrug. "And, if they happen to get together after this super platonic trivia night, then so be it."

"Hah!" Wade exclaims, pointing at me. "I knew it!"

I roll my eyes, looking down at the appetizer menu. "Are you going to be this hyper all night?"

"I'm not–" Wade's eyes widen as he sputters. "You know what, never mind."

"Great. Oh, there they are!" I wave to Jane as she walks in the door, Marcus not far behind her. "They arrived together, that's interesting."

"Meddler," Wade mumbles.

Jane and Marcus make their way to our table. Jane changed into a gorgeous emerald mini-dress that complements her dark skin tone. Her eyes light up in a grin when she waves back at me. Marcus follows behind, looking like he's about to ride a really tall roller coaster.

"Hi guys, glad you could make it!" I pull Jane in for a quick hug. Marcus pulls her chair out for her to sit down. I barely hear her muttered thank-you.

"I'm always down for a Cisco's Trivia Night," Jane smiles.

"Oh, same," I say, picking up my drink. "I'd be here every week if I had a team."

"Hazel is freakishly good at trivia," Wade explains. "Don't let her tell you any different. I'm a mere accessory for her at these things."

I nudge his arm. "Hey, don't hype me up. I might not live up to it."

The lights dim, bringing our attention to the small stage set up on the dance floor. Ryan, the only trivia night host Juniper Ridge has ever had, sits behind a laptop, microphone in hand.

"Welcome to Cisco's Trivia Night!" He announces. Ryan was a sports announcer somewhere back east when he was younger, so he's always way over the top for trivia nights. I love it. "If you haven't already, decide on a team name and display it on your table so I know who to give points to. We'll do five rounds of five questions, with increasing difficulty. Does everyone know how to play?" He looks around the room. A few people whoop with their enthusiasm, most everyone nods.

Marcus leans towards me, dipping his head. "What are the rules?" He whispers.

"Nothing too complicated," I assure him. I drop my voice as Ryan brings in the familiar trivia night music track. "Just let us know if you're pretty sure you know the answer, and we'll confer. No phones out. And, try to whisper so the other teams can't hear what we're talking about."

"Got it," he says, leaning back up in his chair. Jane looks between us, her brow furrowed slightly. I smile at her, but she just nods politely, turning her attention back to Ryan, who is telling us about tonight's categories.

Oh no. Does she think I'm into *Marcus?*

That is literally the exact opposite of what I want. I was supposed to be bringing them together tonight. I replay the night in my mind, starting with me frantically running back to the kitchen to invite them out with Wade and me. Sure, I asked Marcus first and invited her when she walked in, but that's just because he was there.

When I look at it from her perspective, it *does* seem like I invited her to be polite after I'd already asked Marcus to come. But she had to know I was already coming with Wade, right?

Shit, shit, shit.

I let out an exasperated sigh, taking a big swig of my drink. Wade looks over, raising a brow.

"What's up?" he leans in and mumbles. His warm breath skirts the shell of my ear.

"Just please go with everything I do tonight. Please," I whisper.

"What?"

"Please." I turn to face him. His eyes widen and search mine.

"Okay, but you have to tell me what's going on," he whispers. It's then that I realize how close we are. Our noses almost touch.

"Tell you later. Just trust me," I hiss.

He swallows. "Okay." Questions race behind his eyes, but there's no time.

I scoot my chair closer to Wade's, grabbing his hand in mine as tight as I can. He stiffens at first, and I almost pull away, but a moment later, he's leaning into me. His shoulder brushes up against mine, comfortable and warm.

"First question from the geography category," Ryan's voice booms around us. "What is the largest country in the world?"

"Russia!" I whisper in Wade's ear just as he scribbles down the same answer.

Jane and Marcus turn towards us, looking down at the board. Jane's eyes linger a little longer on Wade, and I's hands, locked together on the table. The smallest hint of a smile forms on her lips.

"Are they always this easy?" Marcus asks, voice low. The entire bar is a chorus of whispers over the background music.

I shake my head. "No, they just start this way. Trust me, you'll be stumped in no time."

Jane laughs as Marcus shakes his head, turning back to face the stage.

"See," I whisper to Wade. "It's working."

"What is?" His deep voice in my ear vibrates through me at our proximity.

"I think Jane thought I was flirting with Marcus," I explain.

My shoulder shakes when Wade chuckles next to me. We shifted at some point so that he's slightly behind me. I lean back into his chest.

"You probably were, you flirt with everyone," he says. It's disappointing to hear the smile in his voice but not be able to see it.

"That is so not true," I laugh. "I don't flirt with *you*."

Wade opens his mouth to reply, but he's interrupted by Ryan's loud voice surrounding us on the speakers.

"Alright, Juniper Ridge, hold those answers up. Right, right, right..." He points at our sign, counting up everyone's points. "Oh, come on, Canada? That was an easy one!" He says to a table to our left.

"How much do you want to bet those guys pull a Katie-style comeback and win the whole thing?" Wade whispers so closely that his lips brush my ear. Two years ago, Katie got every single question wrong in the first round, only to pull through in the more difficult rounds and win the game for our team.

"That's impossible, seeing as we are the obvious winners," I counter.

"Okay, everyone, erase your answers and get ready for the next question," Ryan says.

Wade grabs the ratty old washcloth and wipes the answer board clean. That washcloth has seen more trivia nights here than I could ever hope to. He lets go of my hand, and my stomach bottoms out until he reaches it around me, pulling me in.

This is perfect. This is comfortable. It's not the first time he's had his arm around me at Cisco's, and it certainly won't be the last. My nerves wash away like waves on the shore.

Jane and Marcus seem to relax more and more throughout the night. During a particularly ridiculous question that no one had the answer to, they accidentally knocked their heads together laughing so hard.

Which, of course, made us all laugh even harder.

By the time the last question rolls around, there's a permanent smile on my face. I've had a ton of fun tonight. Small town trivia night with friends beats going to a club any day. I didn't realize how much I've missed doing things like this since Katie moved away.

As much as I love staying in by myself or with Wade most nights, it's good to get out. Katie was always the one instigating nights out. Without her, I've become a shut-in. Working all of the time or helping out at Black Bear Rentals.

Tonight has been a refreshing change.

"It's that time of the night," Ryan calls out. A chorus of boos fills the air. "I know, I know. But I do have a life outside of announcing trivia for you people, so let's get to it. The final question."

"If we get this one right, we win," Wade whispers.

I turn to him, eyes wide. "Are you serious?" I haven't been keeping track of our points at all.

He nods, a glint in the bright blue of his eyes.

"You guys," I whisper-yell across the table. Jane and Marcus lean in. "Wade says if we get this one right, we win."

Marcus's eyes go wide. They exchange a look. When Jane turns back towards me, there's a firm determination in her gaze.

"We've got this," she whispers. The four of us fist-bump, then turn our attention back to Ryan.

"Alright, here's the question. Everyone ready?" He asks. A few people cheer. "What was the first music video shown on MTV?"

A confused murmur spreads through the bar. I look over at Wade, who shrugs.

"That's right, the very first music video shown on MTV. What was it?" Ryan repeats. Everyone looks around at each other. No one is going to get this one right.

Damn it.

We gather as far as we can lean towards the center of the table.

"Any ideas?" I whisper.

"No, I've got nothing," Jane replies.

"Same," whispers Wade.

I nod. "I have no idea. I've watched MTV plenty, but it was years ago, and I have no clue what the first video would have been."

"I think I have a guess, but I'm not one hundred percent certain," Marcus says warily.

Jane perks up, nudging his shoulder. "Your guess is better than the nothing the rest of us have come up with. What is it?"

Marcus looks around the room, down at his feet, then up at Wade. "Okay. I guess we can try it. I think it's 'Video Killed The Radio Star.'"

"Seriously? That'd be really ironic," I laugh.

"I think that's why I remember it from somewhere. I love that song, and I remember thinking it's funny that it was the first MTV video. But I can't be certain," Marcus explains. He fidgets with his hands on the table. Jane reaches over and covers his hands with one of hers.

"Let's go with it," she says, looking at him.

Wade uncaps the dry-erase marker. We all watch intently as he writes down the song title, then uses his arms to block our board from the other teams.

"I have a good feeling about it," Wade mutters, running a hand through his hair.

"That's a good sign," I point out. "That doesn't happen often."

Jane and Marcus laugh. Her hand remains on his, but at some point, Marcus must have reached up to grab hers because now they're just holding hands on the table.

I sneak a glance at Wade, wiggling my eyebrows up and down. He rolls his eyes, but one corner of his mouth ticks upwards just enough for me to notice.

"Time is up!" Ryan yells. "Hold up those boards, people."

Wade lifts the whiteboard above his head. I search the crowd for the other boards poking up. Everyone wrote down a different answer, from Madonna to David Bowie. A pit forms in my stomach as I realize we are the only ones with our answer. That's usually not a good sign in trivia.

Ryan looks out over the crowd, expression unreadable, until he gets to our board. A slow smile appears on his lips. "It looks like only one team got this answer right. That's right, Bear Lake Monsters, the answer is 'Video Killed The Radio Star.' Which means the Bear Lake Monsters are tonight's winners!"

Our small table of four erupts in a cheer. We high-five each other, beaming, as the other teams groan and start to gather their belongings.

"Hell yes," I exclaim. "Marcus, you have to come to trivia with us every time!"

Marcus laughs, "Glad I could help make the game-winning goal there."

We gather our phones and wallets as the bar clears out for the night. Even Ryan is packing up his sound system for next week's trivia night.

The night air is cooler than usual for an August night in Juniper Ridge. The stars twinkle in the sky, and the quiet surrounds us like a blanket as we walk through the dirt parking lot.

"Thanks for going out with us, you guys," I say as we reach our cars. Wade drove us in my Bronco again.

"Thank you for inviting us. I had a really great time," Jane smiles.

Wade walks me to the passenger door to open it for me. Marcus and Jane stop next to his car, a couple of spots away from us.

"Hey Jane," I hear him say softly.

"Yeah?"

"Would you uh... I mean, if you want... Would you want to grab coffee tomorrow? With me?" he stammers.

"What are you—" Wade says as I stop dead in my tracks. I elbow him in the ribs, shooting him a pointed look. He looks at me, bewildered. I nod towards Marcus and Jane. A look of understanding passes through his features as he follows my gaze.

"Yeah, that'd be great," Jane says happily. A smile breaks out on my face. I can't help it.

Wade shakes his head, smiling. "Come on, let's go," he mumbles, opening the Bronco door.

Chapter 13

Wake Up Lovin' You

"I think I'd just like to hear you say it."

"Is that really necessary?"

"Yes."

Wade rolls his eyes, an exasperated sigh rolling out of his chest. "Fine," he concedes. He walks over to where I stand in the entryway of his upstairs apartment on the water, puts his hands on my shoulders, and looks me directly in the eye.

We checked the journal the minute we returned from the bar, and there it was. Another song. This time, it was the chorus of Billy Currington's "Wake Up Lovin' You." I didn't think it was Jane or Marcus anyway, but it still stinks to get confirmation that it couldn't have been.

Tired from our night out, we both decided to put it on pause until tomorrow.

"Hazel Mae," he says seriously.

"Yes, Waylon?"

The corner of his lips twitches slightly, but he schools his features back quickly. He clears his throat, dragging it out even further. "You were right. You are the reigning champion of trivia."

"And?" I press.

He shakes his head, looking to the floor, then back up at me. "And we should all bow at your feet. There. Are you happy?"

"Yes, very," I beam.

He chuckles, stepping back. I almost lose my footing at the lack of his arms steadying me.

"Are you staying here tonight or heading back up to Connor Ranch?" He asks, his back towards me.

"Staying here," I say. "Do you want to watch a movie?"

"Yeah, let's do it." He grabs a glass from the cabinet in his small kitchen, filling it with water.

"Gimmie," I reach my hands out, grabbing at the air for a drink of water.

Wade reluctantly walks over to the couch, handing me the glass. "Can't you get your own?"

"No." I hand it back to him after drinking a good third of the water.

He turns on an old western movie, and we snuggle into our respective sides of the couch. Wade's old wool blanket wraps around me. I use it in the summer more for the weight than the heat. Though it is a little chilly out on the water.

I'm not sure when, but at some point, we both fall asleep on his couch because I wake up to the soft glow of the sunrise peeking up over the mountains.

I'm no longer on my side of the couch. At some point in the night, I must have moved over to Wade's because my face is pressed up against his chest, his soft hoodie cushioning my cheek. His breathing is steady, and an arm is wrapped tightly around me. The other hangs off the side of the couch, brushing the wood floor. His chin rests on my hair.

It's cozy.

In all the times we've fallen asleep on the couch, I can remember only a couple where we've woken up in a similar position. Normally, I'd nudge him awake and make some sort of wisecrack about it, but today I don't want to spoil it.

I've felt off for the past few months, and somehow, lying here with my best friend comforts me more than anything else has in a long time. I let myself sink into him, closing my eyes again. Maybe if I fall back asleep, we can just lie around like this all day long.

Is this what it would be like if we were together? Falling asleep to a movie and waking up in his arms every morning.

My eyes fly open.

No. Nope. Absolutely not.

I'm clearly having some sort of quarter-life crisis. That's the only explanation for it. I've got to get out of here.

Slowly and carefully, I lift myself out of his arms, climbing over his tall frame until I fall onto the floor with a soft thud. I freeze instantly, looking up at where Wade is still asleep on the couch. No movement.

I pad over to the front door and slip my boots on. I still have his hoodie on from last night, but I decided to take it with me and wash it. I'll get it back to him later.

The guilt doesn't leave as I make my way out of Black Bear Rentals, though. It buries itself deep.

A warm summer breeze blows through the hair peeking out from under my sand-colored cowboy hat as my horse, Sage, and I trot through a small clearing in the aspen trees about a mile from Connor Ranch.

We're on the home stretch of today's trail ride with the Rodriguez family, who chose my absolute favorite week of the year to enjoy the beauty of the Rocky Mountains. The Rodriguez's are here from Oregon for the week, and their youngest daughter has been dying to ride the horses since they arrived.

We spent a couple of hours this morning warming her up to riding, and she took to it quickly enough to squeeze in a trail ride in the afternoon. Now, she rides a few paces behind me, a huge grin plastered to her face as we head back to the ranch.

Our ride today was up to the start of an old pioneer trail I love to take dude ranchers to in the summer. I start with stories about the trail when we start the ride. Then, as we get closer, I get to reveal that we'll be riding that same trail into the mountains for a bit.

All of the landmarks are familiar to me. Every rock and tree is like the back of my hand. I have a lot of fun sharing the history of the mountains with visitors.

Today was no different. We all spent the day chatting on horseback while the mountains showed off with late summer wildflowers, a perfect breeze, and light fluffy clouds against a blue sky.

I haven't heard from Wade today, but I don't expect to. Saturdays are usually busy at the rental shop, especially with the Summer's End Festival this weekend. He's had some help lately, but I know he's shouldered a lot of the work for the shop, with Wyatt slowly pulling away from the business.

I should check in with him when I get back to the main house to see if he needs any extra help, now that my dude ranch duties are done for the day.

A glint of light from the ranch below catches my eye as we round the last switchback. A burgundy Ford Ranger pulls up to the barn. My heart beats faster, thudding in my chest.

Why is Wade here?

I still don't know what to say to him after last night. How to... process how I was feeling. I had hoped to have more time to clearly think everything through. Down the mountain, he hops out of the truck, grabs something from inside, and heads into the barn.

It takes no time to wrap up the ride with the Rodriguez family and set the horses out to pasture. I find Wade waiting in the office of the barn, two coffee cups from Heidi's in his hands. A soft smile fills his features when his gaze finds mine.

"Hey," he says, clearing his throat and standing from the bench along the wall to walk towards me. He holds out the cup labeled *Hazel Mae.*

"Hi," I reply, taking the cup from his hands. I probably should have dusted off a bit before coming in, dust from the ride covers my jeans and button-up t-shirt. "This is a surprise," I add, before taking a sip.

"Thought you could use a coffee," he replies with a shrug.

"What makes you think that?"

"You always want a coffee."

I chuckle at that. "Yeah, I guess that's true."

He looks down at his feet for a moment. "I figured you must have been up early if you left without saying anything."

My chest tightens. "I'm sorry, Wade."

He nods, glancing up at me. "You always say goodbye."

We stand there frozen for a moment, unsure how to proceed. Uncharted territory again. Then, Wade smiles. It doesn't make it to his eyes. "How was your trail ride this morning?"

"It was good," I start, then quickly amend. I breathe a sigh of relief. "No, actually, it was really great. Everything went perfectly, and I'm pretty sure we all had lots of fun. I took them to the Pioneer Trail."

"Oh, really?" He says, eyebrows raising. "And you're sure they didn't fall into a trance from your never-ending story?"

"Uh, rude," I say with a smile, lightly batting him on the arm. "They loved my story, and it has a great ending. They had no idea we were on the pioneer trail until my big reveal. I should win awards." I tip my chin up with pride.

"I know you went and got a fancy degree, so this probably isn't what you had in mind, but you would totally thrive as like, some sort of history horseback riding tour guide," he laughs.

"I probably would if I could," I chuckle.

"Why can't you?"

"It doesn't really exist, I guess. Or at least I haven't heard of that," I shrug.

"Even better," he raises his eyebrows and smiles, "You can do whatever you want, because of who you are. You could literally rock any job. It just seems like you really love your history horseback riding tours you're doing now. Why not make it your thing?"

"Yeah, maybe." I haven't really thought about that. Would there even be enough clientele? Could I add it to the ranch? I never pictured myself sticking around and working on the dude ranch forever, but he's right, I do love it. It's my favorite place in the world.

"Hey, are you busy this weekend?" Wade asks.

"Nope, not really."

"I was thinking we could head up to Jackson Hole if you're up for it. Surprise Katie and Miles," he says.

"Yeah, that'd be great. Let's do it," I smile.

It's been a few months since we visited Miles's ranch, Lone Pine. It's just a couple of hours north, after all. Katie's rental cabin next to the ranch might even be open. It'd be nice for us both to get a break from cleaning out James's office.

Going through everything from the flood has started to become more of a fun task now that we've gotten past the overwhelming feeling of starting. Last time, I put on a playlist of 90's country music and sang along (horribly, I might add) to every song while Wade laughed. It was actually kind of fun.

"And what are you doing right now?" He says.

"Starving," I deadpan.

"Heidi's?"

One hour and a shower later, I pull on a nice pair of flared Wranglers, my least scuffed pair of cowgirl boots, and a lavender t-shirt with a black jean jacket over it in case it gets chilly at night. My dark brown hair lies in long waves over my shoulders, held back by a black headband.

One of the worst things about Katie moving away is the lack of fashion advice. I've never been one to care what I'm wearing, but I have to admit, some of her style definitely rubbed off on me over the years.

When I'm done in my room, I make my way down the stairs to find Wade on the phone, back towards me.

"Well, I need you too, Wyatt," he says in a harsh whisper. "I can't keep doing this all by myself." A pause. He runs his free hand through his hair. "Okay, I'll see you then. Yep. Bye."

I clear my throat as he ends the call, and he whirls around. His eyes widen just slightly as he takes me in. His gaze moves all the way up my body as I fidget with the buttons on my jacket.

"Are you ready?" I ask. It comes out shakier than I meant it to.

"Yeah–" he clears his throat, looking away, "Yep, ready when you are. You look, uh... nice."

"I think you're just too used to me caked in dust," I tease.

He lets out a loud laugh, then grabs his keys from the counter.

Chapter 14

Burn Out

"Chocolate or gummy?" Wade holds up two boxes of candy, one in each hand. I tap my hand on my chin with a hum.

"Gummy."

He tosses the other box back onto the gas station shelf, grabbing two more boxes of Swedish Fish.

We got an early start this morning, leaving Juniper Ridge around six to get to Jackson Hole around nine. Stopping at Heidi's on the way for breakfast, of course. We ate pancakes with the morning crowd of fishermen and truckers on their way north.

Usually, spontaneous road trips are reserved for the winter. When we're bored out of our minds and looking for an escape from the snow-covered peaks and cloudy January days. Both of us are too busy with work for the rest of the year, our limited free time spent relaxing at the lake or riding in the mountains.

This is a nice change of pace. Both of us could use a getaway, and I always miss Katie.

Miles and Katie live on Lone Pine Ranch, just outside of Jackson Hole, Wyoming. Katie went up there last summer to renovate a rental cabin that used to belong to the ranch, and never came back. She's been looking all her life for a place that feels like home, and Juniper Ridge just wasn't quite that.

Miles runs Lone Pine Ranch, taking it over due to his father's declining health. It's one of the largest cattle ranches in Wyoming, dating back a few generations on his father's side. He's tough to crack, but once you get to know him, he's one of the kindest people you'll ever meet. Next to Parker, his outgoing foreman.

Katie and Miles go together like a match and a flame, and I can see how much she loves it up in Wyoming. I've never seen her happier. So, if I have to drive a few hours to see her, so be it. At least I have Wade to keep me company.

Now, we're in the middle of nowhere, Idaho, at a truck stop to grab some snacks for the day. I wander past Wade to a carousel of t-shirts and hats near the back wall.

"Wade. Come here," I stifle a laugh.

"What?" He turns towards me from where he's squatting, reading the back of a bag of off-brand chips. A small piece of blonde hair falls into his eyes.

"Just come over here," I motion towards the display. "I found us matching hats."

He rolls his eyes, pushing to his feet. "We do *not* need any more hats, Haze–"

I hold up two hats, cutting him short. His mouth falls slack.

They're matching hats, alright. One is a bright, electric blue with 'TRUCKER' bedazzled across it in such large letters that they wrap around the hat. The other is hot pink, with 'TRUCKER'S WIFE' bedazzled in the same style. The best part is the bill, where the front of a semi-truck is embroidered on with flames coming off the sides.

"Who is buying these?" He exclaims. "Those are so..." he trails off, rubbing a hand down his face.

"Loud? Shiny? Glorious?" I try.

"I was going to say off-putting."

I close the distance between us, unceremoniously placing the blue hat on his head. "Wow, the rhinestones really bring out your eyes."

Wade rolls his eyes again as I giggle, straightening the hat. He knows better than to take it off, that'll just fuel me. It's too late. I'm committed to the bit.

"Is that all?" He deadpans. "Can we get back on the road?"

I nod, skipping past him towards the checkout. I throw the pink hat on my head, throwing a wink over my shoulder. "Sure thing, trucker."

Wade gathers our treats and treasures onto the counter as the cashier, an older man with a warm smile, starts to scan them.

"Can I scan those hats for you?" he asks cheerily, pointing to my head. Wade reluctantly hands over the tags he took off the hats. "I sure wish my wife would wear a hat like that with me, you've got yourself a good one there," he says.

"Oh, we're not–" Wade starts.

"Thank you," I interrupt. "We're newlyweds. Just got married last week!" I slip my arm through Wade's. He stiffens immediately, frozen in place.

The man's face lights up, breaking into a wide smile. "Oh wow, congratulations to the both of you!"

"Thanks," I say, looking up at Wade. He turns his head to me slowly, his eyes wide. I wink at him and turn my attention back to the cashier. "We figured after six weeks of officially dating, it was time to tie the knot. I just love my trucker!" I reach up and pinch Wade's cheek. Surprisingly, he doesn't stop me.

The cashier's eyes widen, his smile faltering. "Oh, that's... something." He bags up our snacks, handing them to us with the receipt. "Have a nice day."

"You too!" I exclaim. We make it about two feet out the door before Wade is wriggling away from me, apparently mobile again.

"What the hell was that?" He looks caught in between a laugh and a yell.

I shrug. "Just having some fun on our road trip, *husband*."

"You're incorrigible." Wade can't quite stop a smile. "Hey, did you hide that journal then?"

"Yep, it's safely tucked away in a lockbox under your floorboards," I nod. "With a camera pointed at it."

"Damn," he says. "You're not messing around."

"I'm getting to the bottom of this, Wade. No matter what it takes. No more Mr. Nice Guy."

Wade laughs, leaning an elbow out of his open window.

We decided last night to figure out this journal thing once and for all. Our matchmaking ways are clearly not working, so I found a little lockbox at Black Bear, slipped the journal in, and hid it under the floorboards.

Plus, Wade finally fixed his security cameras in and around the shop (not that he's ever going to check them), so I pointed the indoor one towards the hiding place. We'd have a clear, perfect view if someone came looking for it.

But first, they'd have to figure out where it is, lift the floorboard, and break into the lock box. It's pretty secure. I didn't even tell Wade where the journal is, just in case.

"I guess we'll see if anyone goes looking in the front desk," Wade says.

"I thought of that too," I say. "The camera has a clear view of the desk, too. So either way, we'll be able to catch the culprit."

"What if no one shows up?" He raises his eyebrows.

I shrug. "Then there won't be a song in the book, and we'll never know who's writing them."

"I *hope* we find out who's writing them. I kind of want to know," he says.

I squint, looking out towards the golden meadows passing by outside my window. "Me too, Wade, me too."

"I'm not wearing this in front of Miles," he says an hour later as we cross the state line into Wyoming.

"Aw, why not?" I pout, setting down my book. Wade reaches to turn the volume down on the radio, his forearm flexing. I rip my gaze back down to my lap.

"Because I'm not a trucker." He leans an elbow out the open window of my Bronco, his other hand on the steering wheel. Fields of green sagebrush, rolling hills, and the occasional black cow pass by. Johnny Cash plays quietly through the speakers. We don't usually see a ton of traffic going up to Wyoming, but it's even less today.

It feels like it's just Johnny out here and us.

"And, I'm not embarrassing myself again. He probably already thinks I'm a joke," Wade adds.

"Oh come on, that was one time," I say.

"Getting literally dragged through mud by a cow once is more than enough," he sighs.

"That could have happened to anyone."

"It was a *baby* cow, Haze. A baby," he throws me a pointed look.

I shrug. "Katie said it was at least eight months old. In cow time, that's practically an adult."

He looks over at me again, his lips pressed into a thin line. I shoot him a wink.

"I'm not wearing the hat on the ranch," he grumbles, cheeks turning pink.

I shift in my seat so I'm sitting almost sideways to face him, resting my head on the cool glass of my window. "That's okay, they can be our special hats just for when we're alone."

"Don't make it sound dirty," he laughs.

I take the hat off my head, placing it on my knee. God, it's even worse in the sunlight. "Why, are you hoping tomorrow I'll show up wearing the hat and nothing else?" I joke.

Wade coughs, his entire neck turning a bright, beet red. He tries to turn to the side, but I can still see the smile on his face. "Jesus Christ, Haze."

"You walked right into that one," I point out. "Hey, what hotel did you say we're staying at?"

He clears his throat again, shaking his head. Seeing Wade flustered is one of my favorite things. It's way too easy to push his buttons.

I'm half tempted to wear the TRUCKER'S WIFE hat the whole weekend just to bug him. I should have bought a big, ugly fake diamond ring, too. Missed opportunity.

"The Rustic Inn," he supplies, not taking his eyes off the road.

I hum. "Sounds cute." As it turns out, Katie's rental cabin is booked solid until Thanksgiving, and the bunkhouse the ranch hands usually live in is going through some renovations, so they're occupying all of the extra rooms in the big house, where we'd usually crash.

So, hotel it is. Wade booked it last night. We were only able to get it because of a last-minute cancellation, since Jackson Hole is right in the middle of their busy season.

The Snake River glitters out my window, a bright green as it lazily winds down the bottom of the canyon. Pine trees line the mountains like a blanket, gray cliffs jutting out at sharp angles at the peaks.

Wade looks over at me, a smile lighting up his face. The sun shines into his navy eyes, making him squint just a little bit. As usual, his hair is messed up, made worse by the ridiculous hat.

"What?" I smile.

"Nothing," he says, turning back towards the road. "I'm just glad we did this. We don't road trip nearly enough."

"I wholeheartedly agree," I say with a contented sigh.

Chapter 15

Rocky Mountain High

THE FIRST THING I see when we pull up to the big house on Lone Pine Ranch is Katie, standing on the porch with a hand blocking the sun. Her auburn hair burns brighter in the sunlight, the yellow dress she wears accentuating her curves.

I wave through the windshield as Wade throws the Bronco in park.

"Were you just waiting for us on the porch all day long?" I tease as we walk up the porch steps.

Katie pulls us each in for a hug. "No, I have your location, so I was stalking you."

"Creep," I say into her hair, pulling away. "How did you even know we were coming? It was supposed to be a surprise." My heart tugs a little as she looks me over. I miss the days when I could just drive ten minutes to her apartment, but I can practically feel the happiness spilling out of her whenever we visit her on the ranch.

"Miles told me immediately. He's weak to my power of getting information out of people. How was the drive?" Katie asks.

"Great–" I start.

"She made me buy matching hats at a trucker stop," Wade mutters at the same time.

Katie huffs a laugh. "Typical."

She motions Wade and me inside, leading us to the great room at the back of the house. The Teton Range shows off behind the wall of windows, grey peaks shining bright in the late morning sun, glaciers adding a dazzling white to the very tops. It's late enough in the year that the back few acres of Lone Pine behind the big house are full of tall golden wheatgrass, swaying lightly in the summer breeze.

We make our way out to the back deck that overlooks the breathtaking view. The house is built into a small knoll, so even though we walked into the ground floor, we're now a few dozen feet off the ground out back.

The side of the Teton Range shoots up out of the ground a few miles past the house, towering over the ranch. Sharp, jagged cliffs with bright white glaciers hidden in pockets near the tops of the peaks.

The wooden deck is wide enough that it fits a fire pit, grill, and smoker, and a host of tables and chairs. I know Katie spends a lot of time out here, and I don't blame her. It's breathtakingly beautiful.

Miles, worn ball cap pulled low on his head, stands next to a grill listening as Parker animatedly describes something about a problem bull. He cuts off when he spots us, breaking into a million-watt smile.

"Hey, you made it," Parker says with a wave. Miles turns, nodding a hello.

"Just in time for a lunch cookout," Katie says from beside me.

Parker wraps me into a hug, ruffling my hair a bit. "Good to see you again, kid."

Parker is Miles's right-hand man, the foreman of Lone Pine Ranch. He's always wearing a smile, a cowboy hat, and the occasional pair of chaps. The kind of guy that makes you feel like you've known him your whole life, even if you've just met. Not to mention, the life of every party.

Today, his chestnut curls are tucked under a brown felt cowboy hat. He's not in ranch hand mode, opting instead for a jean jacket over a rodeo t-shirt and dark Wranglers.

"You're barely two years older than me," I point out, but it's muffled by his chest. He pulls away, eyes squinting in the sun.

He leans an elbow on top of my head as if he's leaning on a counter. "Yeah, but you're smaller."

"I like the 'stache," I point to his new facial hair. A smug smile spreads across his face, but he's interrupted by Miles as soon as he opens his mouth.

"Please don't inflate his ego any more than it already is." Miles rolls his eyes.

He and Wade do some sort of man hug that's a mix of shaking hands and a firm pat on the back. Miles's tattoos peek out of the sleeves of his button-up shirt.

Aside from Miles, who stands near the grill, we all take seats on the log furniture near the other end of the deck. Katie and Parker snag the two rocking chairs, leaving a two-person seat for Wade and I to squish into. Parker opens the yellow sun umbrella above us with a small crank lever.

I relax into the chair, resting my sandals on the footrest in front of us. "How's the cattle business this time of year?" I ask.

"It's pretty okay," Parker says, "Branding is over, and we lost a couple head this year, but we persist. How's the horse ranch?"

"I can't complain. We're a little overwhelmed from the busy season, but it's a good thing."

"Hazel's being modest," Wade chimes in from beside me. The vibration of his voice rumbles through me. I shift away out of instinct, but there's nowhere to go. The armrest digs into my other side. "They're having a record year, and it's all her. She's made Connor Ranch a destination, more than even the lake."

I laugh, "I don't know about that."

Wade turns his gaze onto me, those navy eyes catching mine. My heart somersaults my will. "I do."

"That's great," Parker says, cutting through the haze. "We could use some of that here."

"We're a cattle ranch, not a dude ranch," Miles says from the grill.

Parker laughs. "I meant the good business energy, dumbass. I know what kind of ranch we are."

Miles raises an eyebrow, turning back to flip a hamburger. We fall into easy conversation about the summer and preparing for the coming winter. Somehow, out of all the careers we could have, all of us have extremely seasonal ones. It's nice to chat about it when we're all in the same boat.

Eventually, Miles brings us one heaping plate of burgers, one of brats, and another of bacon-wrapped jalapeno poppers. Katie brings out a couple of bags of chips from the house and some sarsaparilla sodas in glass bottles.

We cheers, clinking the bottles together before digging in.

"Do you think you made enough food there, Miles?" Katie jokes as he pulls up a lawn chair for himself.

"I didn't know if Parker was bringing anyone," he says with a pointed look at his friend.

"Aw, come on, Miles, that ended weeks ago," Parker winks.

"What ended?" I pry.

Katie takes a swig of her drink. "Parker went on three dates with a girl from town."

My mouth flies open. "Three dates? Did you propose?"

Parker rolls his eyes. "It's not that big of a deal, okay? She left town. It wasn't serious, just fun."

"Yeah, but three dates for you must be some sort of record," Katie teases. "I've never seen you with the same girl twice. What, are you holding out for someone else?"

The smile stays on his lips but falls from his eyes. "No."

"Speaking of dates, any news on that front for you, Hazel?" Katie asks. Everyone's eyes land on me.

"No," I hum. "Haven't had much time for anything of that nature this summer with the ranch picking up."

"Too bad you're so far away, we could fix that right up," Parker jokes. Wade stiffens beside me, mid-bite. He slowly sets his burger back on the plate.

"I need to use the restroom," he mumbles, leaving the side of me that was pressed up against him cold as he walks inside.

Parker and Katie exchange a look that I pretend not to see.

"So that's still going on," Katie says under her breath.

"Nothing's going on, Kate," I sigh.

"If you say so."

Parker, thankfully, changes the subject back to the shenanigans the ranch hands have gotten into this summer, and Wade returns after a bit, as good as new.

He chats with Miles about a fishing spot on the Snake River they want to go to while we're in Wyoming. His thigh pushes harder and harder against mine as he tells a story about a big rainbow trout he caught in the river last week. I'm hyper aware of everywhere we're touching, and suddenly the little couch feels a whole lot smaller. Heat creeps up my neck.

"Katie," I blurt. "We should totally do a hike while they're fishing."

"Yeah, I was talking to Codie this morning about a new hike in the park I haven't been on. How's tomorrow morning?" She pulls out her phone.

"Works for me."

"Great, I just texted her," she says. "Did Miles tell you about the bonfire tomorrow night?" I shake my head.

"It's nothing big, just the ranch hands and a few friends," Parker explains. "Y'all should come."

I look to Wade, who nods with a small smile. "We'd love to," I say.

"Everyone's leaving at ten o'clock, I'm serious this time," Miles grumbles.

Parker salutes him, "Yes, boss."

"I always forget how cute this place is," I muse.

"Me too," Wade agrees. We walk through the town square of Jackson Hole around sunset. We stayed at the ranch all afternoon laughing and talking with Miles, Katie, and Parker, until the foreman left to take care of something down at the bunk house. The four of us played Texas Hold 'Em, betting pieces of salt water taffy I brought as a gift for Katie.

Miles took us for everything we had.

Wade and I excused ourselves to check into our hotel in town for the night. We parked at the hotel, but as soon as I saw the horse-drawn buggy pass us by, I pulled him onto the sidewalk to take a photo. The golden light mixed with the magic of a western town summer night sucked us in, and we abandoned checking in for a walk around town.

We even stopped for ice cream cones from a little trailer parked behind a custom hat bar.

Now, as the sun hides behind the mountains surrounding the little western town, we walk back to the Rustic Inn, Wade's arm slung over my shoulders to keep me warm in the mountain chill.

"Today was a good day," I say, a shiver running through me caused by a breeze.

Wade pulls me in closer to his side. "It's nice to get away."

We round the corner, making our way up to the lobby of our hotel. He lets go of me once we're inside, and I feel a little hollow with the loss of contact.

"Can I help you?" An older woman behind the front desk beams at us. The lobby is small, just like the Inn. The room doors are all outside entry, like a motel. A huge moose antler hangs on the wall above the front desk, and burnished copper decorates the walls and fixtures, giving the lobby a high-end, western feel.

"Yeah, we have a reservation under Monroe," Wade says, leaning onto the counter.

The lady, Tilly from her nametag, types a few things on her computer before nodding. "Yes, I have you for two nights in a single king suite."

"No, that can't be right," Wade says quickly. "We need two queens. I double checked the booking online."

My stomach drops. *One bed?* By the look on Tilly's face as she looks at her screen, we're not going to win this one.

"I'm sorry," she frowns. "We don't have any other open rooms. I have in my notes that you booked this one on a last-minute booking site, and we can't guarantee what room you'll end up with." She gives us an apologetic smile.

Wade runs a hand through his hair. "Are there any other rooms? Or a pull-out couch or a cot or something?"

Tilly shakes her head. "I'm sorry, sir. I can check with our sister property, but they're a ways away up in Teton Village, and they're probably booked up as well. It's a busy week here."

I place a hand on Wade's arm. He jumps as if he forgot I was there. "Hey, it's not a big deal, Wade. We have sleepovers all the time. This one will just be... closer. Don't worry about it."

He turns to me, panic in his features. "But, I booked two queens, Haze."

"I know," I assure him. "It's not your fault. It's really not that big of a deal, right?"

There's a war going on behind his eyes. It's not like we've never shared a bed before. Sure, we were little kids, and a lot is going on this summer that makes me a little nervous to be in that close of proximity, but we can handle it. We're best friends. We know each other. It could be worse.

Sure, it's not the best timing. I'm not sure I'll ever get used to this pull between us that materialized out of nowhere this summer. Or, maybe it has always been there, under the surface. Waiting to break through into the sunlight.

That can't happen tonight, though. It's too fragile already. I'm not ready to lose him yet. It's like I'm holding onto him with a fraying rope, each day another broken thread between us. And, he can't see it.

The thought of leaving him had always felt far away. Like I would one day, but I didn't have to think about it too hard. Now, it feels like I'm leaving tomorrow. Everything is just moving way too fast, and I'm unprepared. I keep thinking that if I just spend a little more time with him, I'll feel better about it. As if I'll hit some limit of time spent with my best friend before I'm able to move on.

But I think the limit might not exist.

Five different emotions pass over his face before he sighs. “Right,” he whispers, turning back to Tilly.

She hands us two key cards, tells us where to find our room, and we walk right back out the front doors again.

“Cheer up,” I tell him once we’re alone. “I’m not a blanket hog.”

The fog in his eyes clears a bit. “You’d better not be,” Wade chuckles.

Chapter 16

Dream A Little Dream Of Me

THE ROOM IS NICE.

Very nice, actually.

There's a small kitchenette as we first walk in, across from the bathroom door. The room opens up into a small bedroom with a gas fireplace and a small balcony with a log railing, overlooking a street full of shops and restaurants.

The single king-sized bed stares right back at us as we take in the room, looming.

"Well," I clear my throat. "It's not as bad as I thought for a last-minute hotel room."

"There aren't bad hotel rooms in Jackson Hole," Wade mutters.

I set my duffel bag on the chair in the corner, pulling out my toiletry bag and my book. "Do you want to shower first?"

"No," he says, unzipping his backpack. "I'm gonna call Wyatt and see how it went today." Wyatt agreed to watch over the shop while Wade is gone this weekend, reluctantly.

"Okay, I'll see you in a few then."

Ten minutes later, I'm pulling the covers back, wet hair hanging down my back, dampening my pajamas. I settle in and open my book as Wade shuffles into the bathroom and turns on the water.

The same book I've been trying to get through all summer long, and I'm not even halfway. It's not the book's fault. Wade was right earlier, this has been a record year for Connor Ranch. Between that, cleaning out his dad's office at Black Bear, and the Arizona job, I've had a lot to focus on.

I'm not sure why I brought it on this trip either. I know I'm not going to be able to sit and read. Even now.

Back in the lobby, a king-sized bed seemed huge. I was sure we could set up a little wall of pillows and not even touch. But now that I'm in it, it's smaller than I imagined. I'm not exactly a dainty sleeper. In my own bed, I sprawl out sometime during the night and wake up each morning, taking over the whole thing.

I run a hand over the soft sheets. Should I try to separate us somehow, or would that make it weird? Wade was pretty freaked out already in the lobby. I'd hate to make it worse. I set my book on the nightstand and turn on the TV to an oldies channel.

He can't be anxious while watching *I Dream of Jeannie,* right? No one can.

The bathroom door opens, startling me out of my thoughts. Wade walks out wearing just a pair of shorts, drying his hair with a towel. He looks over to the TV.

"Good show," he smiles, setting the towel down. Water droplets drip down his neck onto his chest.

I've probably seen Wade without a shirt more than with a shirt. Lake days, hot summer nights at his apartment, fixing rental boats and jet skis. But here, in this little hotel room where we have to literally share a bed, it feels different somehow.

The room suddenly feels a whole lot smaller, and I swear the temperature just went up a couple of degrees.

I reach to my nightstand, fumbling for the fireplace remote. "Uh, yeah," I click the fireplace off swiftly. "It's a classic."

Wade arches a brow. "Are you too hot? Do you want me to open a window? Sorry, I turned on the fireplace because you were cold earlier."

"No, no, I'm fine." I shift around, trying to get my wet hair out of my face. "It's perfect now."

He nods, walking over to the other side of the bed where his backpack lies. He opens it, grabbing his toothbrush and toothpaste out of a small leather bag. I tear my eyes away from the muscles flexing in his biceps.

I shouldn't have set my book down. At least I could pretend to read it.

"I was thinking, there are enough blankets in the closet, I could just sleep on the floor," I stammer. "I can fall asleep anywhere, I don't mind."

Wade sets the backpack on his nightstand, turning to face me with a look that pins me down. "You're not sleeping on the floor, Haze."

"But–" I start.

"No. You were right, I don't know why I was so worried. It's not that big of a deal. I just... I don't like a change of plans. But

I'm good now. Let's just forget about it." He runs a hand over my arm, sending a chain of goosebumps in its wake. I nod, averting my gaze back to my lap.

He finishes up in the bathroom, switching the lights off. I'm still staring absentmindedly at the TV when he pushes the covers back on his side, climbing in. The bed dips, sheets rustling as he lies down next to me. Not touching, but close enough that his warmth seeps through.

I turn the TV off, then switch out the light, lying on my side to face away from him. I can do this. If he's chill, I'm chill. It's two nights.

Darkness engulfs the room, the only light peeking through the crack in the curtains from the streetlights. Somehow, the lack of noise and light charges the room even more. My skin prickles in awareness. I can't see Wade over my shoulder, but I can feel his presence, heavy in the air.

I won't be asleep for a while, I know it. I should have left the curtains open so I could stare at the stars at least.

I like that he's so easily able to fall asleep around me. It makes me feel like he feels safe with me. I know it's probably not that big of a deal, but it makes me happy. I like that he wakes me up when I sleep over on his couch with a freshly brewed coffee, exactly the way I like it, because he pays attention to what I like.

I like that we spend the mornings laughing and watching TV together in his tiny apartment on the lake. I like it when he shucks off his sweatshirt, opting for the t-shirt underneath when we unlock the shop and step outside into the sunlight.

I like spending time with him doing mundane things.

Which probably isn't something I should be thinking about. It's dangerous, this thing between us. Wanting something I absolutely cannot have.

Do I want that?

"Haze," Wade whispers from behind me. He must be facing towards me.

"Yeah?" I turn over to face him in the dark. I can just make out the outline of his silhouette. Our knees knock together. Neither of us makes any effort to pull away. That small bit of contact puts me at ease, grounding me.

"Thanks for helping me clean out my dad's office." His voice is thick with sleep, an octave lower. "It really means a lot to me. More than you know."

I reach across the bed to find his hand. He must do the same, because we meet somewhere in the middle. He wraps his fingers around mine, giving me a squeeze. My breath hitches before I can hide it.

His other hand grazes my waist, a ghost of a touch that sends a shiver through me. I'm hyper-aware of every place we are touching, and it feels like I'm drowning in this feeling. I let my eyes flutter closed, sinking into it. I'm too tired to fight it right now. I'll fight the pull between us again in the morning.

His thumb traces patterns onto the back of my hand, lulling me into a relaxing feeling like I'm floating on a cloud. Just this once, I let myself enjoy it. I let myself pretend that we are more than what we are. What we'll ever be.

I let my heart take over, feeling things that would not only be dangerous but absolutely devastating. It's so easy to get lost in his touch, his presence, his heartbeat. It'd be so easy to scoot just a little bit closer. Close the gap between our lips. Pull his hips into my waist.

Would he let me do it? Does he feel this between us, too?

Of course, he doesn't. You're making it weird, the little voice in my head chides. Of course, my subconscious is right. It's not worth the risk to find out. I couldn't live with myself if I ruined my friendship with the most important person in my life because I'm feeling all hot and bothered from one platonic sleepover.

He needs friend-Hazel right now. He needs friend-Hazel always. I need to stay in my lane here, especially when he's trying to thank me for cleaning out his dad's office with him. That's certifiably a non-sexy task.

"Of course," I whisper. My voice comes out gravelly and low. "I can imagine how hard it is for you. I'd never let you do it alone."

"I know," he says on a contented sigh.

It only takes me a couple of minutes to fall into a dreamless sleep.

I wake up slowly, and then all at once. It starts with a glimmer of sunshine through the window, then the muffled sound of a door closing. A horn honking.

I shift to turn to my back, but something is holding me in place on my side. Something warm, wrapping me up like a teddy bear.

That's when it all hits me. I'm in a hotel room in Wyoming.

With Wade.

Wade is the something.

My eyes fly open. I'm suddenly aware of all the places we are touching, which is, well... everywhere. His arm is wrapped around my waist, *under* my pajama shirt, his palm splayed against my belly. Our legs are tangled together beneath the covers, his breath warm and steady in my hair.

Shit.

I must have scooted over towards him in my sleep sometime during the night, causing him to latch onto me like a koala. This is exactly what I was afraid of. I can't be trusted in my sleep. I'm a snuggler at heart, and I run hot. It's something my past boyfriends have complained about.

I try to wriggle away a little bit, testing his grip. He sighs in his sleep, pulling me in even closer against him. There's no more space between us.

And definitely something poking me in the back.

My pulse races. I've got to find a way out of this... precarious situation before Wade wakes up. I'd be mortified. I try another wiggle, and again, his arm flexes against me.

Okay, so moving away isn't going to work. I'll have to wait it out then. Pretend I'm asleep until he either wakes up or moves.

The butterflies in my stomach are flying in a full-blown swarm. I guess if I'm stuck here for now, I might as well enjoy it. I haven't woken up with someone in... wow, a long time, I guess.

I relax back into him, evening out my breathing and closing my eyes. That just makes it worse. Wade's hand flexes on my stomach, the movement sending goosebumps scattering all over me. He murmurs something incoherent and then rolls his hips against me softly.

Oh my god.

I've got to wake him up and put a stop to this before he–

A loud knock at the door startles us both.

"Haze?" Wade says, his voice like gravel. "What's happening?" He untangles our legs, but keeps his hand on my skin.

"I don't know," I whisper, shifting so I can see the door. Another loud knock.

"Hazel? Wade?" Katie's voice yells from the other side.

I glance at the clock on the nightstand. Ten o'clock. *Shit.*

"Shit," I hiss, shifting away from Wade. He doesn't pull me back this time, but his hand leaves a trail of heat across my side as I slide away.

I run to the door, unlocking the deadbolt and the chain. Light floods in the room when I throw it open.

"What the hell are you doing? We had a hike, remember?" Katie says. Her hair is braided in two braids that fall down her back, topped off with a Lone Pine Ranch hat. She's dressed for a hike, alright, in a long-sleeve SPF shirt and khaki shorts.

"I must have slept through my alarm," I yawn. "We'll hurry."

"You'd better, Codie is waiting at the trail," she pushes past me. "What room is Wade in? This is the only one you texted me–" She stops dead in her tracks.

"It's not what it looks like..." I start, trailing off. It certainly looks like something. Wade sits up in the bed, rubbing a hand over his face. The blanket falls from his bare chest.

"Really?" Katie spins back to face me, beaming. "I don't see how it could possibly look any other way."

I roll my eyes, picking up Wade's shirt from the dresser and throwing it at his face. He doesn't catch it in time. "We booked this place literally two days ago. They had one room left. We checked everywhere else in town. This was it."

"I booked two queens," Wade says.

Katie nods, still grinning like the Cheshire cat. "Right. I'm sure. I'll forgive you for not waking up on time, but only because you've given us so much to discuss on our hike." She turns on her heel, marching out of the room. "We're leaving in ten," she throws over her shoulder before slamming the door.

Chapter 17

Ruin The Friendship

I'LL NEVER GET SICK of going on hikes at Grand Teton National Park. Never. Even when I'm old and wobbly and Wade and Katie have to carry me up the hill, I'll still be here smiling at the other-worldly peaks covered in evergreen trees and purple, yellow, and red wildflowers.

It just happens to be convenient that Katie lives so close, so I have a reason to visit Jackson Hole. It also doesn't hurt that she lives on the prettiest cattle ranch I've ever seen.

We hop out of her car and onto the side of the road. Unfortunately, with how late Wade and I got up, we didn't make it into the park early enough to beat all of the hikers to the parking lot. Luckily, another group was leaving when we pulled up, so we aren't that far from the trailhead.

"Ready?" Katie says, strapping on her hydration pack.

"Ready," I nod.

We're hiking up to Bradley Lake today, a hike I haven't done yet. It's not an all-day strenuous hike, just a smaller one to a secluded lake. It's wildflower season, and apparently, Katie heard that this was one of the best trails to see fields of blooms.

We make our way to the parking lot where Codie is waiting for us, perched on a gray rock. She doesn't notice us at first, focused solely on the book in her hands.

"Codie!" Katie calls. Codie looks up, shielding her eyes from the sun. Katie waves as we get closer.

"Took you long enough," Codie teases with a smile. She stands from the rock, stuffing the paperback novel into her hip pack.

"That's my fault," I admit, tugging my hiking socks up on my calves.

Katie laughs. "Yeah, wait until you hear about what I walked in on this morning."

I roll my eyes, "I told you, Kate, it was nothing."

"Sure looked like nothing."

We make our way onto the trail, immediately ducking into the tall aspen trees lining the base of the hill. A small creek trickles by to our left, the sound filling the air with a peaceful melody. Birds sing over the music of the water, and trees whistle in the breeze. Nature's song.

Interrupted by Katie MacPherson and her meddling ways. "You should have seen it, Codie," she repeats. "Hazel was half an hour late, so I went to her hotel room and guess what I found?"

Codie shoots me a knowing smile. I shake my head.

"She's not alone in her room," Katie continues.

Codie gasps sarcastically, her eyes practically twinkling at me. "No, you don't say? A consenting single adult wasn't alone in her hotel room on a summer vacation?"

"It's not like that," I laugh. "It's just–"

"Nope," Katie interrupts, waving me off. "None other than *Wade Monroe,* her supposed *best friend,* was lying naked in her bed–"

"He wasn't naked, he just didn't have a shirt on," I interrupt.

"–after what I'm to assume was a wild night of passion–" she presses on.

"Oh my god, the drama," I say.

"–and they didn't even have the decency to try and hide it," Katie finishes, a smug smile on her lips.

"We don't need to hide anything because nothing happened!" I exclaim, throwing my hands into the air.

"*Nothing* happened? Nothing at all," she asks with a suspicious glance.

"Well, there was a little–"

"Hah!" Katie points a finger at me. "I knew it."

I sigh, taking a step over a large boulder in the trail. "I'm not going to tell you anything if you're going to use it against me."

We turn around a sharp switchback in the trail, making a single-file line with Codie in front, me in the middle, and Katie at the rear. A field of purple flowers shines in the sunlight to our right, swaying gently. I stop to take out my phone and open the camera app. Wade will love seeing this.

"Fine, fine," she concedes. "I'm done teasing. Go ahead, give us the tea."

I finish snapping a few shots of the meadow, putting my phone back into my pocket. We continue up the trail, gaining a bit of elevation. The trees go from groves of green-leafed aspens to lodgepole pines, towering over us like skyscrapers.

Pinecones litter the forest floor, a couple of squirrels dart out from behind their trunks.

I take a deep breath, steeling myself. The fresh mountain air fills my lungs, and it feels like taking a drink of water in a desert. "First of all, Wade booked a double queen room, but it was so last-minute that the app he used said we might not get the exact room we picked. We figured it'd still be the same type of room, but it wasn't. All they had left was a single king suite. It's really not that big of a deal. I sleep over at his place all the time. We're best friends," I explain, running a hand over my braids.

"You don't share a bed at Wade's place," Katie points out from behind me. "Right?"

I turn around to shoot her a glare. She just smiles at me, her ponytail swishing behind her, a fan of red. "No, we don't share a bed. But we've slept in close quarters before, it's fine."

"Okay, but what happened?" Codie says over her shoulder.

"Nothing happened!" I say.

"You were about to tell us about something," she points out.

I sigh, kicking a rock off the trail at my feet. "The bed was just a little smaller than I thought. I didn't really think it all through. We kind of ended up getting closer than we meant to in the middle of the night, and I woke up in his arms."

Katie gasps from behind me. Codie hums in approval.

"It's not like that!" I exclaim again. "We didn't mean to, I can't be held responsible for what I do in my sleep."

"That's your subconscious talking to you, babe. It does what you really want deep down, and you want Wade. Just ruin the fucking friendship already," Katie says.

"I do *not* want Wade," I say. "We are friends, and that is it."

"Whatever you say," she sing-songs.

We come up to a clearing in the trees and stop to take a drink of water. The meadow is filled with yellow wildflowers and light green sagebrush.

"Look," Codie whispers, pointing to the far edge of the meadow. A brown figure emerges from the trees, far away but walking slowly in our direction. I squint to make it out. "Elk," she says.

We watch in silence as the elk makes its way to the middle of the field to chomp on some sagebrush. It's huge. Large antlers grow back from his head, his hooves making a quiet clomping sound on the rocky ground. Light brown fur covers his body, with a tuft of white poking up from his tail.

"Oh, cool," I whisper in awe. "That's a big one."

We take our time watching the elk from a distance. I snap a few more photos, then we keep making our way up to the lake.

It sneaks up on us, coming into view after a particularly steep hill of switchbacks. I'm torn between the view behind us of the green valley stretching all the way to the smaller mountains surrounding Jackson Hole in the distance, and the smooth, glassy lake in front of us. The reflection of Grand Teton a perfect image on the water, glacier peaks and all.

"Wow," I breathe.

"Yeah," Codie whispers. Katie just nods.

We find a fallen lodgepole trunk near the edge of the water to sit on and take in the view of Bradley Lake. The water is so clear, I can see all of the rocks, moss, and sticks resting on the bottom.

"Thanks for taking me on this hike, you guys," I say. "I'm really glad Wade and I decided to come."

"Of course," Codie smiles. "You should visit more often. There's plenty to do, especially in the summertime. Or, if you're here in the winter, you can always come up for one of our book club meetings."

"I might have to take you up on that," I say. "I read everything Katie throws my way anyway."

Codie laughs. "She's got some good recommendations, that's for sure. We read the exact same books. I'd love to come visit your way too. I'd love to go on a trail ride at your dude ranch."

"You ride?" I ask.

"Yep," she nods. "I used to jump horses when I was a teenager. I miss it."

"Wow, how was that?" I gasp.

Codie smiles, looking over at the grove of pines beside us. "It was fun. Hard work, but worth it. Pretty intense."

"I bet," I say.

We wind around the lake, chatting about all of the books we've read recently. Even though I miss Katie, I'm happy she has a good group of friends up in Jackson Hole, especially Codie. I know she can handle herself, but I'm glad she doesn't have to be alone.

I find out Codie is coming to the bonfire tonight up at the ranch. The bonfire I almost forgot about in all the craziness with the hotel mix-up.

"Parker texted me about it last week," she says. "I wouldn't miss a chance to see whatever he has cooked up."

"There's always something with Parker," Katie agrees.

"Codie, have you ever, I don't know, thought about dating Parker?" I ask. Codie and Katie both dissolve into a fit of laughter. "Okay, I guess not," I say.

"No, it's just," Codie starts between laughs. "He's like my brother. He's cute and all, but so not my type. I've known him, like, forever."

"Not like he ever dates anyone anyway," Katie says.

"Makes sense," I smile.

We make our way back down the mountain, talking about our plans for the rest of the summer. By the time we get back to the parking lot, I'm ready to lie right back down to sleep again.

"Hiking in the high elevation really gets you," I point out.

Codie nods. "Yeah, I live here, and it still kicks my ass sometimes."

"We'd better check on the guys," Katie says. "We'll see you tonight, Codie."

We say our goodbyes and trek back to our car under the heavy rays of the midday sun. Katie's mention of seeing Miles and Wade puts a spring in my step. I can't wait to show him the photos I took of the trail.

"Good hike?" She asks as we fall into our seats in her car.

"Great hike," I beam. "I really like Codie, she's so funny."

Katie takes a long swig of water, pulling back onto the road. "She's the best. If I can't bring you up here, I'm glad I have her." I laugh. "Are you sure you don't want to move up to Wyoming?"

"I'm sure," I smile. "I'm right where I belong." A warm feeling rushes through my chest at the thought of Juniper Ridge.

"Really?" She asks. "Does that mean you're not moving to Arizona?"

A pit hollows out in my stomach. "No, no, I'm still deciding, I just... I don't know, I love Juniper Ridge, but I can't stay there forever," I rush out.

Katie presses her lips together with a hum. She's quiet for so long that I think she's let it go, but she breaks the silence a few moments later. "It just seems like you're trying to convince yourself of that, babe. Like you've decided that's what you're supposed to do, but it isn't what makes you happy."

"It does make me happy," I argue. Blood rushes behind my ears. "I worked really hard for that job, Katie. It's what I've always wanted."

"I know you worked hard," Katie says, her tone softening. I take a deep breath. "All I'm saying is I want you to be happy. I'm not saying that has to be Juniper Ridge. It didn't make me happy. I just don't want you to do what you think you're supposed to do in your head and miss out on what you're actually meant for.

"I did that for a while. It didn't work out for me. Do you think I wanted to meet Miles and settle down at his ranch in a state I had barely set foot in?"

"No," I grumble.

"Correct," she says. "I wanted to travel forever and never have a real relationship. But I would have been miserable eventually, Hazel. The happiness and comfort I feel here is something I never thought I'd have. I get to keep my career and my purpose, and also have that once-in-a-lifetime great love with

Miles. You can have it all. I know it. I just don't want you to settle."

"I know," I whisper.

"Alright, soapbox over," Katie says, pulling her water bottle back up to her lips. "Make sure you hydrate. It's gonna be a late night if I know those cowboys."

Chapter 18

Baby, I'm Burnin'

KATIE DROPS ME OFF at the Rustic Inn, grabbing a coffee from a local cafe while I shower and change clothes. I opt for a short denim dress that splits into a V at the neckline and clings to my hips, landing at the tops of my thighs. Paired with my longest pair of heeled, brown cowgirl boots, of course, the ones I brought just in case Katie wanted to go out.

I quickly throw my hair up into a pair of braids, and finish the look off with a white denim jacket in case I get chilly. Way up here in the mountains, it's bound to be cold once the sun sets.

I tidy up the room a bit, putting away the pajamas and hair-brush I threw on the bed this morning in my rush to get out the door. Wade left after me, but he must have stayed a bit to make the bed and clean up a bit, too.

A soft knock sounds at the door as I zip up my duffel bag. I make my way over to the door, adjusting my jacket one more time.

"Whoa," Katie says as I swing it open. "You look hot." She leans an elbow on the doorframe, holding out an iced coffee to me.

I take the coffee, trying a sip. "Whatever, I barely did anything. Hey, this is great, what is it?"

"Iced mocha. Figured we could use some sugar and sweetness after that hike."

I nod. "You're absolutely correct."

I follow her out to her car, swiping my small clutch from the table by the door on my way out. The sun is high in the sky by now, a few puffy clouds lingering like pillows. The sidewalks have filled up with wandering tourists carrying various combinations of drinks, paper bags, and cameras. A busier version of Juniper Ridge in the summer.

I hop in Katie's passenger seat, pulling a pair of sunglasses over my eyes. We'll be meeting the guys back at the ranch for dinner and the bonfire. Wade took the Bronco this morning, so we'll drive back to the hotel together and leave for Juniper Ridge in the morning.

One more night next to Wade. That's all I have to make it through.

"Parker has been up since about three this morning, smoking various meats for the bonfire tonight. At my house. Ask me how I know that," Katie says, unamused.

I laugh. "Seriously?"

"Yes. He woke me up at three in the fucking morning by shaking me awake in *my room* to ask if I had any black pepper he could borrow."

Tears prick the corners of my eyes from laughter. "Why didn't he just go looking in the kitchen? I'm sure Miles loved that."

"Sometimes I think he has a death wish," she muses. "Luckily, Miles is a deep sleeper, so he didn't wake up. I, however, have been up since an ungodly hour, so I might need a nap if I'm going to make it through this bonfire." She turns onto the small road that leads out to Lone Pine Ranch, through a pair of sagebrush-covered hills. "I'm not sure what's gotten into Parker lately. He's nervous about things. He never gets nervous. And, he asked Miles for a couple of weeks off work later this month."

"That is odd," I say.

She sighs. "Who knows with him, though. He'll probably just smile right through whatever is going on, and we'll be none the wiser."

Katie pulls up to the ranch house, throwing her car into park. We head inside, through the heavy wooden door, and into the kitchen.

"Are Walt and Isabella around?" I ask.

Katie shakes her head, handing me a soda bottle from the fridge. "No, they're on their first vacation together in years. Now that Miles has taken over Walter's ranch responsibilities and Parker has stepped into the foreman role, we did a little bit of scheming and sent them up to Alaska for a few weeks."

I take a sip of the cola, slipping onto a barstool. "Oh wow, that's really great. I'm sure they'll have a great time."

She nods. "They've always wanted to go." She drapes her Camelbak over the barstool next to me, taking her ponytail out.

"I'm going to go clean up; you're welcome to hang wherever. I shouldn't be long, then we can start on season six."

"Sounds good," I say. Katie and I used to watch a western drama together when she lived in Juniper Ridge. It just doesn't feel right to either of us to watch it without the other, so we save up episodes and binge them when we're together.

I wander over to the big bay windows overlooking the front of the house. I can see all the way to the barn and bunkhouse where all the ranch hands live, but not quite to the Old Cabin that Katie spent last summer renovating. It's a couple of miles down the road.

That's where Wade and I would have stayed if it hadn't already been booked. We'd be guaranteed to have separate rooms there.

Deep down, a small voice in the back of my head is disappointed by that. I shove it down. That's the last thing I need to get through our last night here.

A moan escapes my lips as I bite into the brisket sandwich Parker has handed me. I don't think I've ever tasted a better sandwich in my life. Maybe it's the hike and the lack of any real food yet today, but this might be my new favorite food.

Wade laughs from beside me, guiding me to a seat next to the bonfire. His fingertips brush the small of my back, sending a shiver through me. "That good, huh?"

"Parker, you should own a restaurant. Seriously," I say, sitting on the chair next to Wade's.

Parker smiles, his entire face lighting up. "I'm not sure who would go to a restaurant that only serves brisket, pulled pork, and cheap beer."

"I would," Reed, one of Miles's ranch hands, says from across the bonfire. I can barely even make out his straw cowboy hat, shoulder-length hair poking out from the bottom. The bonfire is huge. I'm told they 'go big or go home' with fires here, and I believe it now. Wade and I are sitting probably around five or so feet away from the fire, and I'm already burning up.

"You little shits already eat all of my food at the bunkhouse, I should just start charging you," Parker laughs. "Too bad Miles moved out of the bunkhouse a few years back, he misses out on all of our cookouts."

Miles huffs. "Yeah, I'm all broken up about not having to sleep in that cramped bunkhouse with all of you fuckers. That's totally worth the one night a week you don't eat hot dogs for dinner."

"It's at least twice a week now, you'd know that if you ever visited us," Parker smiles.

Miles rolls his eyes. "I don't need to visit you, you're always here. And don't think I didn't hear you rummaging through my kitchen in the middle of the night last night, keeping Mac up. I should start waking you all up at four with an airhorn like the good old days."

"He did not keep me up," Katie attempts. "I was already awake."

Miles looks between the two of them, eyeing Parker suspiciously. "I know you had something to do with it. Stay out of my house."

"If I had stayed out, we wouldn't be eating this lovely meal," Parker gestures to the heaping pile of brisket on his plate.

Miles rolls his eyes, resting a tattooed arm on Katie's armrest. She threads her arms through his, giving him a reassuring smile.

"How was your hike?" Wade asks softly, leaning towards my ear. We haven't seen each other for very long since he and Miles got back from fishing. He showered as Katie, and I took a walk to the wildflower patch out back. His dark blonde hair is still a little damp, glowing a brighter yellow in the sunset and firelight. The linen button-down he brought is just a little wrinkled, and it makes me want to snuggle into his chest.

I clear my throat, setting my sandwich on the paper plate on my lap. "It was good," I answer. I focus on the baby pink color of my nail polish. "The lake we hiked to was gorgeous, and the whole trail was filled with flower fields. We even got to walk past the trail horses at the start of it."

He chuckles. "Leave it to you to find the horses in a national park."

We've migrated closer, leaning over to each other so our shoulders are touching. My bare skin against the soft material of his shirt. We watch the coals burn bright at the bottom of the fire as the twilight around us turns into pitch-black night, stars twinkling all around us.

We might be surrounded by cowboys, but somehow it feels like it's just us.

"How was fishing?" I ask.

"Miles kicked my ass," he sighs. "I didn't have the right flies."

I try not to, but a smile breaks out on my lips anyway.

"Hey," he says. "Stop smiling. It's not fair, he doesn't even fish."

"Right, I'm sure it was just beginner's luck," I tease.

Wade's eyes seem to twinkle. He smirks, "You're supposed to be on my side."

"I'm always on your side, Wade." I nudge his knee with mine. "That's what friends do."

"Friends," he repeats under his breath. He turns his attention back to the fire.

Parker is on his fifth totally-real-not-exaggerated ghost story by the time Wade and I excuse ourselves to head back to our hotel for the night. Since we are leaving early in the morning, we say our goodbyes to everyone.

"I'll miss you, but I'll see you soon. I have to be back down there in a couple of weeks," Katie says when she pulls me into a tight hug.

"I'll still miss you either way," I say.

Codie and I hug next, her emerald green sweatshirt soft on my arms. We haven't known each other very long, but we've gotten to spend some time together in the past year, and I consider her my friend, too.

"Thanks for coming on a hike with us," she says. "Next time Katie comes down, maybe I'll hitch a ride with her and see your neck of the woods."

"I'd love that," I smile. "Let me know when you visit, and I'll see if I can snag a cabin for you at the dude ranch."

Miles sends us off with a rare smile as everyone makes their way back to the fire. The cold night swallows us as we walk through the darkness to the car.

"I'm glad we came," I say to Wade as we walk through the starlight.

"Me too," he agrees. "I just wish we had had more time together."

I playfully smack his shoulder. "*More* time? More than the pretty much every day we already spend together? I figured you'd be relieved to get rid of me for half a day."

"I like spending time with you, Haze." We come to a stop at the passenger side of my Bronco. Wade turns to face me, his features half illuminated red by the firelight and half blue from the light of the moon.

It hits me that he looks kind of beautiful in this light. I allow myself the thought, out here in the dark wilderness where no one can hear it. Then I tuck it into my heart and bury it for good.

His blue eyes bore into mine, searching for something in my gaze. He must find it, because the corner of his lips twitches up the smallest amount, his eyes crinkling at the side.

"I like spending time with you, too," I say, but it comes out breathier than I meant it to.

Wade steps in closer, reaching his arm around me. I brace for whatever he's about to do, and surprise myself by staying put. If he reaches for me, would I lean into him? I can't remember why it'd be such a bad idea.

The click of the door handle startles me out of the spell. The door swings open to my left, and the moment has passed. I clear my throat and mumble a *thank you* as I climb into the seat.

It's an effort to stay awake on the drive from Lone Pine to our hotel. I start to drift off a few times, shaking myself awake. The parking lot is full when we get back, cloaked in complete darkness.

"Why aren't there any streetlights here?" I whine.

"I'll help you," Wade says, offering me his elbow. I wrap my arm around his, and he leads us to our door, letting us in. He flicks the light switch, illuminating the room in a soft, yellow glow.

I don't even bother taking my braids out. Changing out of my dress and into my pajamas, I brush my teeth and fall onto my side of our shared bed. Wade crawls in next to me, switching the lights off.

The sheets feel scratchier tonight, colder somehow. I toss around for a few minutes trying to get comfortable, but nothing works. My cheeks heat, still warm from the fire. The rest of my body shivers underneath the covers, a chill taking over.

"Haze," Wade whispers. "Are you okay?"

"M'fine," I say, trying not to let my teeth chatter. His hand reaches out, making contact with my arm.

"You're warm." He runs the other hand over my cheek. "Do you have the chills?"

I nod, but realize he can't see me. "I think so."

"Come here," he says. His low voice in the silent darkness causes my stomach to do a flip.

I don't have the energy to fight it anymore. I'm worn out from today, from worrying about the job, from waking up in his arms this morning.

So I don't.

"Okay," I whimper, sliding over to him. He wraps his arms around me, pulling me into his chest. My head rests in the crook of his neck, his chin in my hair. I let myself melt into him as he warms me up. Our legs tangle together just like this morning, but now it's on purpose.

I force my breathing to steady out, suddenly conscious of every move I make. It's hard not to be with Wade so close. I can feel *everything.*

His chest rising and falling at my back, the warm breath tickling the back of my neck, his arms wrapped around me, holding me tightly to him. Another shiver racks through me, and he tightens his grip, tucking me further under his body.

"I'm s-sorry," I whisper.

"Shh," He buries his face in my hair. "Stop apologizing. You'll feel better in the morning. Let's just get some sleep."

I nod, nuzzling into my pillow. The contrast of the soft covers and Wade's hard chest at my back is enough for me to be the most comfortable I've been, probably ever.

I don't last very long, especially not wrapped up in Wade. But it's the best night of sleep I've had in months.

Chapter 19

When Will I Be Loved

HAIL FALLS ONTO THE hood of the car with loud taps as we wind through the canyon on the border of Idaho and Wyoming. When Wade and I got going early this morning, it was sunny and clear in Jackson Hole. The further we drove away from our hotel, the worse the weather became.

Now, we're smack in the middle of a summer hail storm on a narrow canyon road.

"We should stop in the next town and wait out the storm," I say.

"What?" he asks, not turning his head from the road.

"I said let's stop and wait out the storm in Alpine," I yell.

He nods. "We're gonna have to stop and wait out the storm."

"I know, that's what I said."

"What?"

"Never mind," I throw my hands up, exasperated.

The mountains in front of us open up into a small valley. Usually, we'd be able to see a lake right about now, and the

Snake River emptying into it. But today, it's all black clouds and gusts of wind.

We still haven't talked about last night. Or the night before. It's probably for the best. For all I know, I'm blowing things up in my head to matter more than they actually do. Wade probably didn't think twice about it.

He's so calm and collected, driving with one hand on the wheel and the other propped up on the door. He adjusts his glasses, squinting through the glass at the road through the drenched windshield.

Every once in a while, I'm hit with the thought that he's this whole other person. We're almost always together, and I tend to just think of Wade as an extension of me. I've grown used to having him around whenever I need him, to talk or joke around, or just exist in the same space.

But today, he feels different. We've had all of these new experiences lately that we haven't encountered in our many years of friendship, and it's like I'm seeing a brand new side of the Wade I thought I knew everything about.

I hate thinking about him having a separate life outside of the time we spend together. It's selfish, but I want to be there for everything. Even during college, when we weren't together quite as much, the divide between us felt so big. A deep cavern that I couldn't jump across.

And after this summer, that cavern could grow into a full-on trench. Sure, we'll have phones with all-day access to contact each other, but it's just not the same. We'll start to grow apart, and there will be nothing I can do about it.

He'll have new experiences I won't be able to be there for, and so will I. We won't be able to pick up and take a weekend drive up to Jackson on a whim. Those things will have to be meticulously planned months in advance. I won't be able to stop by Black Bear after a tough day at work and vent to him on his couch. We won't be at Cisco's every week for line dancing, trivia, or anything else they come up with for the busy season. And all winter, I won't be able to invite him to the ranch in the middle of a blizzard to sit by the fire and read and talk all day long.

I'll miss him, and he'll miss me, and then one day, he'll forget that he misses me at all.

It's a depressing thought for a depressing, rainy day.

Wade pulls into the parking lot of a diner, the only building in this tiny town with any lights on. He cuts the engine, turning to me. The hail has turned to a downpour of rain in town, quieter than the canyon but stormy nonetheless.

"Here," he takes his jean jacket off, handing it to me across the dash. "Hold it over your head. Let's just go quickly."

I nod, fanning out the jacket above my head. We count down from three, whipping the doors open and running towards the covered porch of the diner. My boots splash in puddles on the muddy parking lot, a cold wind cutting into my skin.

Wade catches me as I tumble into the door after him, slipping on the tile floors.

"Careful," he says, voice low. His hands squeeze my arms, straightening me out.

"Thanks." I lower his jacket, wrapping it around my shoulders.

Wade leads us to a booth in the corner next to a tall window. About five different colored lightcatchers hang in the window. I can only imagine how colorful this little corner is when the sun is out.

Wade slides in next to me on the bright red leather seat, resting his elbows on the table. "I'm starved," he says.

"Me too." I flip open a plastic-coated menu from the end of the table. "Good news, the menu is seven pages long."

He hums, reaching around me to grab his own. He's still wearing his glasses, tiny little raindrops sticking to the lenses. "I feel like that's probably not a good sign, but I really don't care as long as they have a decent burger."

"There's a page of burgers, alright." I turn his menu to the middle, pointing at the extensive list. "They also have clams, what do we think about that?"

Wade takes a look around the diner. "We're in the middle of the Rocky Mountains at a diner in a town that literally has one stoplight. What do you think about them?"

I nod. "Probably not a good idea."

Wade laughs, closing his menu. An older man wearing a red apron greets us and takes our orders. A burger for Wade, a club sandwich for me.

I take a sip of water from the plain, plastic cup on the table. "I should have gotten the pad thai."

"You're ridiculous," Wade chuckles.

"What if every single thing they have is actually really good? How would you know?" I ask.

"I guess I wouldn't."

My gaze catches on a poster of Rosie the Riveter behind him. This whole place is covered floor to ceiling with 1940's movie posters, framed photos of Elvis and Hank Williams Sr, and more clocks than I've ever seen in my life.

Cat clocks, boat clocks, clocks shaped like almost all 50 states, and cuckoo clocks. You name it, it's here. The ticking is drowned out by an oldies country station playing from the speakers. About half of the tables are full, mostly older couples that I assume live in the small town.

"I love it here," I grin. "It's like Heidi's but more chaotic. I'm gonna take a photo and send it to her."

"The last thing she needs is inspiration," Wade laughs. "She's got enough going on in that cafe."

I whip my phone out anyway, snapping a few photos and sending them to Heidi. "This is whimsical, Wade. We could all use more whimsy."

He smiles, "I think you're about as whimsical as you could be. You literally spend your days riding horses in the mountains above a little lake town."

"Exactly, you should be more like me," I say. "That's what I've been telling you."

He chuckles, looking out the window at grey sheets of rain, blowing in the wind. "This storm really isn't letting up, huh?"

"Doesn't look like it," I shake my head. "That's okay, I was hungry anyway."

He runs a hand through his drying hair, a little wavier than before from the rain. "Are you ready to be home?"

“Not really,” I shrug. “I kind of wish we had more time. This trip has been so fun.”

“Me too,” he agrees.

I love Juniper Ridge, but I also love road trips with Wade. Seeing Katie and Miles at Lone Pine Ranch. Hanging out with Parker and Codie.

To be honest, I’ll even miss having to share a hotel room with Wade. And bed, for that matter. It’s like having a sleepover with my best friend every night. Sure, we can do that when we get back to Juniper Ridge, too, but it’s not the same. I’ll go back to sleeping on his couch once or twice a month after a late night in town.

How is it possible to miss someone when they’re sitting right next to you? For your heart to ache for a version of someone you’ve had glimpses of, but that’s all it’ll ever be?

My heart breaks for a life I’ll never have and for the one I have now, but will one day have to give up.

Group Chat

No Scrubs

Katie: Hey, Hazel, do you remember that one time Wade took his pants off at the lake?

Wade: Okay, hang on, I didn't take my pants off. They fell off when I was wakeboarding. And I immediately jumped in.

Katie: Same thing.

Wade: That is not the same thing!

Hazel: That was a great day.

Wade Monroe renamed the chat to "Wade's Bullies"

Katie MacPherson renamed the chat to "Wadey's Babies"

Wade Monroe has left the chat

Hazel Connor added Wade Monroe to the chat

Katie MacPherson added Miles Autry to the chat

Katie: Wade, stop being a baby.

Miles: How do I remove myself from this chat?

Hazel: I forgot how old you are, Miles.

Hazel: Turning 90 this year?

Katie: 95

Miles: Please remove me from this chat.

Chapter 20

Meet In The Middle

I WAKE UP THE NEXT Sunday morning already tired. I yawn as I drag myself out of bed to get ready, doze off for a couple of minutes during breakfast, and struggle to keep my eyes open getting the horses ready for another Sunday family ride with my parents and Wade.

I shuffle into the barn around six in the morning, my boots dragging in the dirt as I make my way over to the very last stall. Before our ride this morning, I need to fit in another training session with our newest horse, Fern. She'll be a trail riding horse for the dude ranch guests, so we've been retraining her brain from her racehorse past. Fern is in her golden years, but as much as I can tell, she needs rest, she still has a few race-horse tendencies that have carried over. I'm hoping to get her ready for next summer.

We've been making great progress lately, learning to stay tied without moving and trotting at a leisurely pace. I'm so proud of how far she's come this summer.

It also means I can't take more than a few days off from her training schedule to make sure it all sticks. Since we spent the weekend in Wyoming, I can't afford to sleep in this morning and put Fern off to another day.

Even though I'm barely standing, I'm so exhausted today. Truthfully, I haven't slept well since sharing a bed with Wade, but that's not something I want to unpack right now. Or ever, for that matter.

I lead Fern out to the pen on the backside of the horse barn, reins in hand. Today, we're working on reteaching her that leg pressure doesn't mean go fast, as she's been conditioned to do. She's going to need all new controls taught to her so she doesn't race off with a dude ranch guest on her back.

Fern shakes her mane when the early morning sun hits her face. Horses may not be able to talk, but I swear sometimes I can *feel* what they're trying to say. I like to think Fern likes basking in the sunlight.

I bring her to a trot around the perimeter of the pen, hanging on to her reins in the middle. She trots slowly, just as I've signaled. The corners of my lips tug upwards into a smile.

A light summer breeze blows through my braid as she circles around me. There's no better feeling than this. Horses are so smart, it feels like we're somehow connected. Fern takes my new commands so easily, looking like a natural trail riding horse.

Dust kicks up from my boots, spinning around on the loose dirt of the pen, coating the bottom of my jeans. White, fluffy clouds spin around my head. I breathe in a deep breath of fresh pine-scented air, and it comes out as a laugh as Fern picks up her speed, taking my cues.

She'll fit in so well with the other horses next summer with the dude ranch guests. I bet she'll be a new favorite. It'll be fun to tell her history, too. How many races she's won, that she traveled across the country to be here to live out her retirement in the mountains at our little ranch.

I'm smiling from ear to ear when I slow her down, going to pet her neck and give her the treat I've been keeping in my pocket. She scarfs it down, her teeth lightly scraping my palm.

"Good girl, Fern," I praise, scratching her neck. Her white mane falls over her brown coat, a beautiful contrast. She really is such a pretty horse. No wonder she had so many adoring fans.

Reins in hand, I turn to lead her back to the barn. My heart skips a beat when I see Wade standing on the bottom rung of the corral fence, matching my grin.

"Hey!" I exclaim, running over to the edge.

"Hi," he smiles from the other side of the dark green metal bars. "You looked great out there."

"Did you hear that, Fern?" I turn to scratch the side of her neck. "Wade thinks you're great, too."

"I was talking about you, but she's great too," Wade says.

"Oh," I stammer. Butterflies threaten to rise. I shouldn't take him too seriously, but after this weekend, I'm all tied up in knots. It's not fair. "Thanks. You're here early," I get out.

"I brought you a coffee from Heidi's," he winks. "I thought you'd be dragging, but I guess I was wrong."

"Oh, don't let this fool you, I'm still tired," I say. I lead Fern to the opening, swinging the gate out. Wade catches it, closing it after we walk through. "I skipped training with this girl all weekend, so I thought I'd fit a session in before I'm even more exhausted from the family ride."

He nods. "Makes sense."

Once Fern is untacked and safely back into her stall, I follow Wade to the barn office, where an iced coffee waits for me on my desk.

"Oh my god, you have no idea how badly I need this," I say, grabbing the little cup and taking a sip. The perfect blend of hazelnut and vanilla. "Thanks, Wade."

"Of course," he says, taking a sip of his own coffee. His eyes shine as he plays with a hair that has found its way out of my braid already. "Fern looks like she's fitting in well already."

"She's going to be great," I nod. "I can feel it. She's a natural."

"*You're* a natural," he says. "This is what you're made to do, Haze."

I turn my focus to my boots on the wooden plank floor. I *do* love working with horses. I love going on trail rides. I love managing the dudes. But I don't know if it's what I'm *made* to do.

How will I know? I guess that's the million-dollar question. I know I love history too. I know I worked so hard to get my degree, and even enjoyed it along the way. If there were a way I could do both, I'd be there so quickly.

But, there's not. And even if there were, I don't think I could ever work on any ranch besides this one. It'd feel wrong.

I take another sip of Heidi's coffee and grab my cowgirl hat off the rack next to my desk. It's time for another family ride.

When Wade first turned sixteen and could drive up to the ranch all on his own, we started going on rides a lot more often. I was just so excited to have my best friend around more often, I didn't care what we were doing, but Wade loved horses. I'd get so annoyed with him for waking me up at five in the morning on weekends.

Every Friday night when we'd talk on the phone about our grand weekend plans, I'd beg him to come over at eight instead. He'd say, "The sun is up at six, so why shouldn't we be?" By then, I was an awkward thirteen-year-old, and I couldn't figure out why he'd want to hang out with me in the first place. He had cool high school friends and hockey teammates to spend time with. I had convinced myself it was the horses, so I took every opportunity I could to go on rides with him.

One Friday, he asked if we could just hang out at the main house the next morning. Confused, I asked him why he didn't want to go on a ride.

"We always go on rides," he replied. "I just want to hang out this time. Maybe we can play a card game."

"Why do you want to hang out with me? Don't you have better friends in high school?" I laughed to pass it off as sarcasm, but the question had been nagging at me.

"You're my best friend, Haze. I don't come up here to ride horses. I come up there to spend time with you," he had replied matter-of-factly.

I smile at the memory, setting my saddle onto Sage's back.

"Good morning, Waylon, you look especially nice today." Mom walks into the barn with her signature sweet smile and a pat on his shoulder.

"Morning, Mrs. Connor," he says with a smile. "Brought you a coffee from Heidi's."

Wade *does* look especially put-together today. He's wearing a navy blue button-up long-sleeve shirt instead of his usual graphic tee and jeans that look new. His hair almost looks like it has some sort of gel in it, holding it in shape, instead of his usual messy waves. Even his smile is brighter than usual. He looks... kind of cute.

Does he have plans today that he won't have time to change for? He didn't mention anything to me when I texted him yesterday about today's ride.

He catches my glance, eyebrows furrowed. *What?* He mouths.

I shoot him a shrug and turn away to saddle up as my cheeks heat.

Our ride consists of Wade talking to my parents and me, mostly staying quiet. My mind is buzzing with everything going on.

The Arizona job, this past weekend in Wyoming, training Fern, Wade's dad's office. This summer has been a blur of everything happening at once. I'm not afraid of change or anything, but it sure feels like it's creeping up on me quickly.

It's... uncomfortable, to say the least. I've always had a plan for my life. I know exactly what I need to do at all times. Now that I'm at a turning point, even one I planned on, I feel uneasy. I know I've got to get out of my comfort zone. I know I've got to find out who I am and what I want out of life. I just wish I had a few more years of this little bubble I've created for myself.

But I know bubbles don't last forever.

I'm in the middle of overthinking my entire life trajectory when Wade slows Thistle until we are riding side-by-side.

"What's up? You've been extra quiet today, and it's starting to really freak me out. I've never told so many mediocre stories to your parents in one day," he says, quietly enough for only me to hear.

"I'm sorry. I'm just tired, I think. You don't have to entertain them, they're fine on their own," I say, managing a small smile. We pass by a grove of green-leafed aspen trees, opening out into a clearing. The late-season wildflowers cover the mountain hills, a spattering of purple, red, and yellow. If I weren't on a horse, I'd be running through the field as fast as I could, reaching out to touch the blooms.

"Haze, I'm joking. I don't mind talking to your parents. I'm just worried about you," he says. My heart tugs at that.

"Really, I'm fine. I've just had a lot on my mind lately, and I didn't get a lot of sleep last night."

"If you say so." He turns back towards the path in front of us.

I love this part of the ride. We are surrounded by quaking aspen trees and beautiful late-season wildflowers. It feels a little like an enchanted forest. Mom and Dad ride side-by-side ahead of us, laughing and talking as they ride through the trees.

"So, I actually wanted to ask you something," Wade says, breaking the silence. He stares ahead, fidgeting with the reins in his hand. His jaw ticks once, twice. I feel myself leaning a little bit closer. "You know the Summer's End thing that's happening tonight downtown?"

"Yeah," I reply warily. The Barn, a local wedding venue, throws a Barn Bash for locals every year right before the Summer's End Festival. It mostly consists of some swing dancing, a small open bar, and the best kettle corn in the world. One time, we just went to grab kettle corn and left right afterwards, heading over to the dock for a late-night swim. To be honest, I had completely forgotten about it this year.

"Well, I was thinking we could go together. I know it's last-minute, but I really want to go this year. With you. We'll get lots of kettle corn, I promise," he smiles.

"Sure, that sounds fun. I can't say no to kettle corn," I reply. Relief spreads through me.

"Okay. Cool," he says. "I know we haven't been in a while, but I miss going with you. And everyone."

"I've missed it too," I say. It's not a lie.

"I'll pick you up at nine," is all he says about it for the rest of the ride.

Chapter 21

Why Don't We Just Dance

A soft knock comes on my bedroom door at exactly nine o'clock. He's so infuriatingly punctual. "One second," I call out, unwrapping a piece of hair from my curling iron. It's been a long time since I've styled my hair with anything but a hairbrush. I've already burned my fingers twice today. I switch it off, taking one last look in the mirror.

I decided on distressed jeans, my trusty dark brown cowgirl boots with blue stitching, and a black blouse with ruffle sleeves. It's finally cool enough to wear jeans at night after the heat waves earlier this month, and I'm taking advantage of it.

"Come in," I yell. The door creaks open hesitantly as Wade steps inside my room.

He's dressed in dark, ironed jeans, boots that look like they've been polished or something, and a gray sport coat over a dark button-up shirt.

A tucked-in shirt.

His blonde waves are gelled back into a different style than usual, which looks like it took some effort, and he smells faintly like cologne. A smile creeps up on the right side of his mouth, and I can't help but smile back.

Perhaps the most surprising thing is the bouquet of purple and white flowers in his hand that he's holding out to me with a big grin.

"Oh, for me?" I say, still a little confused. "Thank you, Wade."

"I saw them at a booth on my way over here, and I thought you might like them. They're lilacs. You sometimes mention bringing home lilacs because they smell good. If you don't want them, you can give them to your mom or something. Or I can get rid of them–" he rambles.

"Wade," I interrupt. "I love them. They smell amazing. Thanks for thinking of me." My heart flutters. There's an unfamiliar pull in my chest, an insatiable itch to have his arms wrap around me, pulling me close. I plant my feet into the carpet instead.

"Okay, good," he says on an exhale.

I set the beautiful flowers on my bedside table, making a mental note to get some water for the bouquet later.

"Wanna drive?" I ask, following Wade out into the hallway.

"Always," he nods. I toss him my keys, unable to stop myself from smiling when he catches them with one hand.

He opens my door, helping me in before rounding the Bronco to hop in the driver's side. I take him in while he fiddles with the ignition.

Wade is dressed up. He's wearing a sports coat. I didn't know he owned a sports coat. He looks... good.

Really good.

And on top of that, he brought me flowers.

How am I supposed to deal with this? I've already been in my head way too much about him, and now it's like he's trying to break me.

Does he know how I'm feeling? God, that'd be so embarrassing. If Katie is to be believed, I'm not as subtle as I think. That needs to change.

Wade pulls into a dirt parking spot at The Barn, throwing the Bronco in park. There are a ton of people here already, cars parked in every available spot outside of the front entrance, and some in some... less traditional parking spots. The wildflower field next to the barn has started to fill up, too.

The sound of fiddles floats out of the barn doors and through the air, spreading across the fields. Cotton candy skies surround the little valley of Juniper Ridge, framed by steep green hills that give way to gray rock cliffs at the peaks.

The white wood of the barn, freshly painted, stands out and brightens up the twilight. String lights fall from the roof, arching up onto posts surrounding The Barn. Whiskey barrels filled with periwinkles hold the posts up.

"Ready?" Wade says, helping me out of the car. I nod, my boots hitting the gravel with a thud. I adjust my blouse, taking a deep breath. He grabs my hand and pulls me to the bar just inside the door.

Heidi stands across the room running a small refreshments stand with coffee and snacks. A small bar stands across from her, a crowd of customers standing in between the stands.

Bar might be a loose term for the four-foot-wide table that Eric, our high school friend who now teaches at the middle school in town, is tending by himself.

"Waylon, Hazel, so great to see you guys!" Eric smiles, drying a shot glass with the towel hanging from his apron. "Can I grab you something to drink?"

"Hey man, can we get two Jack and Cokes?" Wade asks, leaning one arm on the bar.

"Sure thing," Eric smiles.

All of the tables are bar height, with dark, metal saddle stools surrounding them. Wade takes the seat right next to me instead of across, our elbows bumping together on the unfinished wood.

I check my phone, taking a sip of my drink. Nothing from Katie yet. She mentioned she and Miles might be able to swing by, but I'm not counting on it with how busy she has been lately. I'm not sure if they even made it out of Wyoming this morning.

"I missed this," Wade says, staring out into the crowd of people dancing. A small smile plays on his face.

"What?"

"Going to the festival with you." Those navy eyes sparkle in the soft lighting of the barn. "I forgot how much fun it was. We used to have such great times here."

"We've had some fun times for sure," I laugh. "Remember the night you and Katie had one too many whisky sours, and I had to drag the two of you off the dance floor at 2 am?"

He nods, swallowing another sip. "I do remember that night. That was the night you were with that asshole, what was his name?"

"His name was Cole, and he wasn't–"

"Cole, right. What an ass," he repeats. A frown forms on his lips. "That dude was really on my nerves. I swear to god he was looking at every other girl in the barn," he says, shaking his head and taking another sip of his drink.

"Well, I wasn't that into him anyway. He was really cute, but that was probably the best thing about him. I'm pretty sure going to the festival was the most exciting thing he ever did," I shrug.

"That guy didn't deserve to even look at you, Haze. You are so out of his league. Same with Shawn," he spits.

"Who is in *my league,* Wade?" I tease, nudging his arm.

"Not them." His gaze hardens.

My breath catches. For a split second, I glance at his lips and back up to his eyes. If I'm not imagining things, I can almost see red creeping up his neck. I force myself to break eye contact, pulling myself away, reaching for my drink.

My hand comes to a halt right before grabbing the whiskey glass. Jack and Coke probably isn't the move with this energy passing between us. Especially since I'm certain it's just on my side.

I need something else, something to bring me out of this.

I grab the water pitcher from the center of the table and bring it to my lips, gulping down as much water as I can until I start coughing.

"What the hell was that?" he says. Wade takes the pitcher from me as I wipe water off my lips. He searches my eyes as if he'll find the answer there.

"Just thirsty," I shrug.

He narrows his eyes at me. I almost drop my gaze as if he can see into my head, but I hold strong. Eventually, he seems to accept it with a small nod.

The Barn is packed with people line dancing, throwing darts, and talking over the loud country music. Everyone is soaking up the last bit of summer fun before a quiet, snowy winter. We run into other locals we know all night, chatting about the busy season and fall activities. Connor Ranch isn't the only booked-out place to stay in Juniper Ridge. Allie, a bubbly blonde I went to high school with, tells a similar story about her luxury yurts just outside of town.

"Wanna dance?" Wade asks once we're alone again.

"Always." I take his hand as he walks me out towards the crowd of people.

His arm wraps around my waist with a gentle firmness. We rock back and forth to the sound of the guitar, surrounded by all of Juniper Ridge.

The song changes into a slower ballad not long after. I turn to sit back down, but he spins me back around, into his arms. Closer than we were before.

I tilt my chin up to look into his eyes. There's something there that I haven't seen before. I can't quite place it. His hand tangles into the ends of my hair at my waist, sending a shiver up my spine. We stay like that for a while, swaying slowly, not saying a word.

At the end of the song, his lips brush against my forehead just slightly before he lets me go.

It's something he's done before, but like everything lately, it feels different. Comfortable, but less familiar somehow.

The music picks up again as we slowly separate.

After two more line dances, I'm twirling around in my boots, Wade laughing as I catch myself from falling. I've always had two left feet, as my dad says. Wade makes up for it with his sense of rhythm.

"I think I needed this," I grin.

Echoing my thoughts, he replies, "Both of us needed a breather." His eyes crinkle at the sides as he smiles and takes a sip of beer.

"So," I start, "Do you think whoever is writing in the journal is here tonight?"

Wade hums, surveying the room. "We can't be sure, but I'd say pretty much everyone who lives in Juniper Ridge is here tonight, so probably." He's right. Juniper Ridge may be a small town, but it sure looks big when we're all in one barn.

"Anyone looking particularly in love? Enough to write love song lyrics in a journal that isn't theirs at least."

His gaze falls back on mine, and his eyes do that sparkling thing they've been doing lately. Or maybe I'm imagining things. "I haven't noticed."

"Wade," I chastise. "You're supposed to be keeping an eye out, we still haven't solved the great mystery of Black Bear Rentals."

"Okay, okay," he waves a hand in the air. "Who do you think our suspects are tonight?"

I scan the room again, seeing if anyone catches my eye. Usually, my rule is to go with my first instinct. Although that's been extremely hard for me lately.

"What about Tom and Megan over there?" I point over to the bar where they stand, Tom listening eagerly as Megan tells a story, talking mostly with her hands. They went to school with Wade and me, Tom carrying on his family's shake shop in town, and Megan working for a marketing firm virtually.

"As far as I know, they're both single," Wade says, bored.

"Exactly!" I exclaim. "But they seem to know each other pretty well."

"Hazel, *we* know each other pretty well. We've been here together longer than they have." Wade tilts his head down, hitting me with a pointed glance.

"Well, yeah, but we're... us."

"Right." He straightens, his lips pressing into a thin line.

I sigh. "Do you have any better suspects? What do you think?"

Wade laughs, adjusting his sleeve. He takes a long sip of his drink before leaning over the table on his elbows and looking at me with those eyes that see everything I try to hide.

"I think–"

"Hey, you two, thought I'd come say hi before I head out," Heidi says from behind us, interrupting Wade's thoughts. We whirl around to see her standing a few feet away in her usual apron and a cornflower blue dress. A few wisps of her grey-blond hair wisps from out of her bun. "Are y'all having a good time? I think this year is the best yet."

"I'm so happy Wade asked me to come, I've missed Summer's End," I say.

"I used to love coming to this with James," she says. A twinge of sadness paints her features. "He hated to dance in public, but he loved to grab a drink and talk to everyone in the town. I'm so glad Wade has you around, Hazel. It's been tough the past few years without James, but I can rest easy knowing Wade has someone to guide him through." She presses a hand to her heart, a sad smile on her lips.

"Thanks, Heidi." I place a hand on her arm.

"Well, that's enough of that. I'll let you get back to your fun. We'll see you next weekend for a family dinner, right?" she says with a wave of her hand.

"I'll let you know if we can make it, Mom," Wade replies as she turns to walk away.

"Family dinner next weekend?" I say to Wade as soon as she's out of earshot, eyebrows raised.

"Yeah, she wants to start them up again and insisted I invite you since you used to be at almost every single one before my dad died," he explains. "No pressure though, I can just tell her you have work at the ranch if you don't want to go."

"But you want me to go?" I ask.

"Well, yeah, of course."

The warm feeling in my chest spreads a little further. "Okay, I'm in."

“I’ll let my mom know,” he nods towards the door. “Do you want to head out? Seems like things here are wrapping up.”

I glance past him. Heidi isn’t the only vendor to have packed up. Eric, the bartender, has a last call sign out, and The Barn is slowly starting to empty.

There aren’t any other cars around the Bronco by the time we make our way out to where we parked, about two blocks from the Barn. The moon is shining brightly enough tonight that I can pick out the small white wildflowers in the field next to the road, blowing in a light breeze. Stars twinkle from above. All of the summer constellations on full display.

Juniper Ridge is magical at nighttime.

“I think I’ll walk home tonight,” Wade says softly. “Are you okay getting back to the ranch?”

I nod, pausing with a hand on the driver’s side door.“Thanks for inviting me out tonight. This was really fun.”

“Thanks for going with me.” He shoves his hands in his pockets.

“I love summer, but I have to admit, I’m excited to be celebrating Summer’s End already. I don’t think we’ve ever been this busy at the ranch. I’m ready to watch the snow fall outside as I sit next to a fireplace,” I sigh.

“Next summer, let’s take some more time off. More boat days and visits to Jackson Hole,” he suggests.

I’m not going to be here next summer. The thought surprises me. Of course I’m not.

Or this winter.

I didn't think about it like that. Our first summer apart. He'll probably keep busy enough with the rental shop. But I'll be alone in a state where I don't know a single person. I push the thoughts away again, burying them deep inside.

"Deal," I plaster a smile on my face. "On second thought, let's just run away and live in the mountains somewhere. No more responsibilities. We can follow Katie and Miles. All we need is an ice cream machine to make brownie batter shakes, and like, a few horses in case we need to run to the nearest town for food."

"I'll run away with you any day, Haze," he whispers. The laughs die on the tip of my tongue. Something crackles between us, sending a shiver down my arms. For a moment, neither of us moves.

Get it together, Hazel, I think to myself. *Wade doesn't need his best friend looking at him all googly-eyed.*

Something flashes across his face. The intensity of his full attention sends butterflies to my stomach again. I must be crazy, because at this moment, if he kissed me, I'd probably kiss him back. I don't want to admit it to myself, but this is the second time I've been close to throwing caution to the wind and ruining seventeen years of friendship.

This is a bad idea, the tiny voice in my head whispers.

My heart doesn't care about that. It just wants him.

"Hazel, I've been wanting to ask–" he starts, eyes down.

I interrupt before he can say anything else. "I should probably get going, make sure everyone makes it into their cabins safely, and all. I think most of our guests were planning on coming tonight."

"Right. Okay then. Text me tomorrow?" Wade says, looking a little deflated. He regains his composure a bit more before adding, "I was thinking we could tackle the 2001-2002 file cabinets if you're up for it."

"Of course." He stays for another beat, opening his mouth like he wants to say something else, then turns on his heel and heads back towards the barn.

I watch him walk away into the night, harder and harder to see as he makes his way back to his apartment. I lean back against the Bronco, letting loose a sigh.

I'm not used to this feeling.

Usually, I'm pretty much a live-in-the-moment-type person. If I want to ask a guy out, I do. If I want to kiss him, I'll go for it. If I get rejected, yes, it hurts, but not enough to devastate me. I'm confident I can brush off and try again another time with someone else.

But this thing with Wade terrifies me to my core.

This is not something we can do and come back from easily. If I kiss him, and he's not into it, it could ruin everything forever. If we dated for real and broke up, I'd not only lose that relationship but also my best friend in the world. I don't know if I can come back from that kind of loss. It's too much.

I fumble with the key, trying to find the ignition. I drive home as fast as I can without majorly breaking any laws, windows all the way down to let in the cool mountain air. Tomorrow, I'm getting my shit together. No more messing around. This is way too important. I refuse to ruin what we've built just to see what it's like to kiss him.

Not to mention the guilt I feel for hiding the Arizona job from him. I don't know why I didn't just tell him right off the bat. I know he'd be supportive. He'd probably help me move without me even having to ask. We'd make it work, video calling and texting as often as we are able. But deep down, I have a tiny sparkle of hope that we could be something else, and that's what's holding me up.

I can't let that guide me. I'd rather never know than start something with him that just ends in heartbreak. I'm not sure I could recover from that. I nod to myself as I wind up the dirt road to the ranch, building my walls back up slowly with every inch of space I'm putting between us tonight.

Chapter 22

Say Don't Go

"Hang on, back up. What did you say happened?" I whisper into my phone.

Wade's heavy sigh comes over the speaker pressed to my ear. "I said Earl was in here this morning, and I didn't think to check the journal before he came in. But when he left, BAM. Another song."

"No, I heard that part. I meant the other part."

"Jesus, Hazel, are you serious?"

"As a heart attack."

Another sigh. There's some rustling on the other end before Wade's voice is back. "I said you might have been right about Earl and Mary."

"Hah!" I whisper-shout. "Damn it, I wasn't recording. Could you say it one more time?"

"Shut up," he laughs. "Why are you whispering anyway?"

"I don't know, because it's six in the morning and the sun isn't even warm yet." I can feel his eyes roll all the way from the ranch. "That still doesn't explain how he managed to get the journal without showing up on the camera, get into the lockbox without damaging it, and put everything back."

I checked the camera footage as soon as Wade texted me this morning and found nothing. I saw Earl, sure, but he just came in, restocked the bait fridge, and left. Granted, it was pretty dark out, so maybe he somehow pulled an international spy-caliber move and snuck through the shadows.

Knowing Earl, he didn't. But sure enough, another song. I had Wade check it this morning on a video call.

"Just put it back into the desk," I say. "We're no closer to figuring it out when it's hidden away. Maybe this will tempt whoever is writing in it to write more."

"Yeah, I guess," Wade says. There's some shuffling on his end of the call, then the sound of a door shutting.

I had planned to get up and get some chores done around the dude ranch, but all I got to was the horse barn before I ran into my mom turning down cabins. She was on the last one. An entire half day of work, done between four and six in the morning.

That has to be some sort of record.

So now, here I stand. Alone in the quiet barn after I called Wade to ask what his plans are for the day. As it turns out, he planned to see what mine were. We agreed on gameplanning at the ranch.

"What time should I come up there?" He asks.

"Probably around nine. My folks are doing breakfast at eight, and for some reason, it's a whole sit-down thing. Text me when you're on your way. And we will absolutely be discussing this whole Earl and Mary situation."

"I'm not sure it's at the situation-level, but there's definitely something there," he agrees. I pat my horse on the neck softly, then walk out of the horse barn into the purple morning light.

"You weren't there, Wade. At the feed store. You don't understand. It was the cutest thing ever!" I exclaim. "I'm telling you, this could be it."

He laughs on the other side of the line. "Don't get too excited, it's still pretty far-fetched. I seriously doubt Earl is writing song lyrics in a random journal."

"Well, someone is."

"Yeah," he sighs. A pause. "It's just not adding up."

"We'll figure it out." My boots clunk against the wooden porch steps as I make my way into the main house. "If you're lucky, I'll save you a breakfast burrito."

"How about I pay you for it with a coffee from Heidi's?" he asks.

"Deal."

A smile spreads on my lips. I can't help it. My best friend is back to being my best friend. Maybe I'm not going insane after all.

The smell of crisp bacon fills the air of the house. Sunshine spills in through the tall windows in the den as I pad over to my usual leather chair, laptop in hand. Mom is in the kitchen, finishing up breakfast prep as Dad flips an omelette at the stove.

When you work on a dude ranch all day, you tend to eat pretty hearty breakfasts.

I curl up in the chair, pulling a light blanket over my lap. My laptop pings with a few notifications the second I get it open, catching my parents' attention.

"Good morning," my dad says over his shoulder.

"Morning," I call back. My attention is immediately taken by my overflowing email inbox. Vendors for the ranch, new client inquiries, bookings, and some mailing lists I've been unable to shake for years.

There are a lot of moving parts to running this place, and most of them go through me. Dad shares some of the responsibility, answering new bookings as he's able and handling most of the financials.

I know he feels bad about how much responsibility I've taken on at the ranch, but I wanted it. It was the perfect job to get me through college and the years after.

"Come eat, Hazel Mae!" Mom's voice cuts through my bubble of focus after updating this week's marketing reports. I close my laptop and set it on the pile of blankets, walking into the kitchen. r

We sit at the island for breakfast, my spot always the closest to the window. I've always had a thing about being near windows. I can't stand being somewhere I can't see the outdoors, especially on Connor Ranch. Wade teases me about working on a computer with the sun in my eyes, but I don't care how much I have to squint. It's worth it.

"What are everyone's plans for the day?" Dad asks as he pulls up a stool.

"I'll be on a trail ride this morning and at the feed store this afternoon," Mom smiles.

I pop a piece of bacon in my mouth, tearing off a bite. Perfect. "I'm planning on heading to the barn and doing some admin and marketing work today, then I'm headed to Black Bear tomorrow to help Wade with some more flood damage," I say.

Mom shakes her head. "It's such a shame about that flood. All of James's old things... I just feel so bad for those boys without their dad around."

"We're getting through it all pretty well," I assure her. "A lot of it wasn't damaged too badly, the important things at least. It's all of the paperwork from the old tackle shop that's too far gone. I don't think James ever digitized any of it. But, it's not like they really need it anymore."

Mom nods. "It's nice of you to help."

"It's Wade, I'd help him no matter what. Plus, Wyatt isn't really around much anymore, so he needs the extra hand."

"And how is the job hunt going? Have you thought more about the Arizona museum?" Dad asks. My parents' eyes land on me.

I swallow, setting my fork down on the table. "They actually invited me down there for a sort of trial period in a few weeks. I'm thinking about it."

"That's wonderful, honey," Mom beams. She clasps her hands together with a grin. "When do you leave? How long are you going for?"

"I haven't decided if I'm going yet," I admit. The pit in my stomach drops.

"Oh," she says. Her face falls. "Is there a reason you wouldn't go? You really wanted this job, right?"

I pull a string from my shirt in my lap. "I don't know. I think I'm just getting cold feet or something, I guess."

Dad reaches out, resting a hand on my arm. "It's a big decision, it's normal to be a little nervous. You'll feel a lot better when you're there. If you don't, then you know it's not right for you."

"You wanted this so badly, Hazel. I'm sure when you go do your trial, it'll make you feel a lot better about it. That's a very nice thing they're offering you," Mom chimes in.

I nod, taking a deep, shaky breath. "Yeah, I know. You're probably right. I'm sure it'll be great."

Mom smiles at me, but it doesn't quite reach her eyes. I don't blame her for being concerned. She's right, I tried so hard to get my degree. To apply for jobs. I was ecstatic when I got an interview at the Arizona History Museum.

But then, it hit me. I'd be leaving Idaho. Maybe for good.

Each interview, I felt a little worse about the whole thing. I didn't even celebrate when I got the job. I've been feeling one thing for the past few weeks.

Afraid.

Is this how it's supposed to be? Is there any way it's supposed to feel when you're leaving the only place you've ever known as home? I can't shake the feeling that I should think about it just a little bit longer. But where will that get me?

Maybe the problem is that I'm thinking too much. Maybe Mom and Dad are right. Maybe I'll land in Arizona, and all of my nerves will melt away in the desert heat.

"I know it'll be great, I can feel it," Dad says. He takes a bit of his eggs, shooting me a wink and a smile.

"Thanks, Dad," I say. "Fern is doing great."

My mom nods, not reacting to my change of subject. "I'm glad. I knew she'd do well working with you. You're a natural with horses, Hazel Mae. You always have been."

"I love working with her. She's so easy to teach, I can tell she loves it here," I say. "I think she'll be more than ready for trail rides next summer as long as she stays up on her training schedule. She's still a little jumpy with her legs sometimes, but overall, she's adjusting well. I'll make some detailed notes."

"That's wonderful," Mom smiles. We're planning on picking up at least two more horses before next season. With all of the extra growth at Juniper Ridge lately, we're about at our limit with what we have now.

I'm sure Dad will have to build another cabin here soon, too. Not over the winter, of course, the elements make it way too hard to do any sort of outdoor project until about March.

Mom and Dad fall into conversation about a few of the cabins' air conditioning units that were repaired this week. My attention falls on the dark green mountains outside of our windows, climbing up towards the bright blue sky. It's a beautiful day to be outside.

The first time I saw that view, I remember thinking it looked painted on. Like nothing could possibly be that majestic. Green in the summer, golden in the fall, white in the winter.

I've now explored most of that on horseback. The aspen groves that turn into thick pine tree forests. The clearings that open up, deer lying in the tall grass. The rocky cliffs that look like they could fall at any moment, but never do.

There's not a piece of Connor Ranch I haven't explored. Not a single corner that I haven't played a made-up game in with Wade and Katie, or ridden past with my parents on a summer afternoon.

After breakfast, I wander around to the back of the house, the morning sun beating down on my face. Golden grass blows in the wind behind our small lawn, like waves on the lake. A small, yellow butterfly flits by me, heading for a tree in the backyard. Tall, evergreen pines shade the back porch from the summer heat.

There's something magical about these mountains.

Chapter 23

Slow Dance In A Parking Lot

A SOFT KNOCK ON MY bedroom door startles me as I pull a sweatshirt over my head. It may be the heat of the summer outside, but the Connors sure love their air conditioning.

"Come in," I say, adjusting my hair. Wade's head pokes into my room from the doorway.

"Hi," he says, grinning. The door opens the rest of the way, revealing his tall frame. He's wearing jeans and a Black Bear Rentals shirt, his light hair even lighter from the sun.

"Hey," I say, plopping into my office chair at my desk.

He makes his way over my bed, throwing himself onto it like he owns the thing. I can't remember a time when Wade came over and sat anywhere else. He says it's comfier than anything he has at home, and I believe it.

"Please don't ever get rid of this mattress." He settles into my pillow, closing his eyes and putting his hands behind his head. "Actually, on second thought, please give it to me. It's not very comfy, you should get a new one anyway."

I roll my eyes. "Yeah, I can see that. You look really uncomfortable right now."

He hums. "It's awful. I'll take it off your hands for you."

I nudge his feet, the only part of him I can reach from my desk. "Get up, weirdo. We've got work to do."

He kicks at my hands. "Can we work after nap time?"

"You can nap in your own bed."

He cracks one eye open. "Yours is better."

"I'm not selling you my mattress, Wade, get your own," I say.

He sits up with a sigh, running a hand through his already messy hair. He's not all that much taller than me, but he looks huge on my twin-sized bed. Strangely not out of place, though. He fits in my life naturally. Like he's always been here.

"Take a look at the new song," Wade tosses the journal over towards me.

I flip to the next page, and sure enough, there are more song lyrics scrawled onto it. This time it's a song I recognize. "Slow Dance In A Parking Lot" by Jordan Davis.

"Another fairly modern song?" I raise an eyebrow, looking up at him.

He nods. "Yeah, at this point, it seems like they're all over the place. Some old, some new, mostly country but not always."

"Sounds exactly like your music taste, are you sure it's not you?" I huff a laugh.

"I think I'd know if I was writing random songs into a journal, Haze. Plus, I didn't even know where you hid it."

"Maybe," I hum. "Or maybe it's a new form of sleepwalking. Sleep-writing. Maybe you have a condition."

He rolls his eyes, falling back down onto my pillows. My fluffy comforter puffs up around him. "If anyone has a condition, it's you. What's it called when someone comes up with nonsense on a daily basis?" He teases.

"I don't know, ask your mom."

He laughs incredulously. "Wow, a your-mom joke? That's all you've got? You must be overworked. Also, I'm telling my mom you said that."

"Don't you dare!" I pick up a discarded throw pillow and chuck it at his head. He catches it about an inch away from his face, grinning. "I meant because she's dealt with your nonsense longer than any of us have."

He chuckles, his Adam's Apple bobbing. "You love my nonsense."

I do. "If you're not sleep-writing, then it's gotta be Earl. He's our only prospect left. He's been at the shop around the time of each song showing up, and we know for a fact that he's crushing on Mary–"

"We do *not* know that for a fact," Wade interrupts.

"– plus, we have no other possibilities. And *someone* is writing songs in that journal. I'm gonna get to the bottom of it and prove that it's Earl." I clap my hands together.

"And how do you suppose we do that?" he asks.

"I'm so glad you asked, Waylon." I rifle through my desk drawer.

"Don't call me that," he mumbles.

"Why? Everyone calls you that. It's your name."

"*You* never call me that. I feel like I'm in trouble." He shivers, frowning.

"Here it is!" I pull a small business card out of the drawer, handing it to Wade.

He turns it over in his hands a few times, the gold foil lettering glinting in the light. "Styled floral arrangements? What's this?"

"That is our key to getting Earl and Mary together. Once we get them together, we'll see if the songs change. I've noticed there's a theme to all of these songs. Unrequited love, yearning, the works. If you read it as a story in order, it's the beginning of a love story. It just hasn't hit its peak yet. Once they're together, I suspect the songs will either change tone or stop completely. Then, we can carefully ask him about the journal, and he'll have to admit to it. Mystery solved," I explain.

Wade lays the business card down, his brows furrowed. "How does a floral shop play into this?"

"We're going to order some flowers from them and place them on her porch. From Earl. If she has feelings for him, which I think she does, this will be all she needs to admit it." I open my laptop, typing the name of the floral shop. "The thing about Mary is, she loves flowers. A lot. All of the gardens surrounding her shop are planted every year by Mary herself. Each year on my mom's birthday, Mary comes up to the ranch to hand-deliver her a bouquet of lavender wrapped in brown paper straight from her flower garden. And, because she's friends with my mom, I happen to know her favorite flower. Violet hyacinths."

I scroll through the custom bouquet flower options on their website. Everything from daisies to roses to wooden flowers fills the screen. I type the flower name into the search bar at the top of the page. Dozens of options in all the colors of the rainbow show up. I scroll until I get to the perfect one. This is going to be the most beautiful floral arrangement Mary has ever seen.

"Wow," Wade breathes.

"What?" I ask without looking up.

"Nothing, just the level of creepy shooting through the roof."

"It's not creepy, it's just good research and observation," I level him with a glare.

He laughs, walking over to see my screen. "Doesn't make it any less creepy. I bet you don't know my favorite flower, and you see me all the time."

"Your favorite flower is yarrow," I recite.

"Wh– what?" He stammers, tripping backwards over his own feet. "How could you–"

"You point out yarrow in the mountains every time we see it on a trail ride, or out by the barn. You always say you love it. You don't comment on other flowers. I used my magical powers of deduction to figure it out," I tap my head, then turn back to the screen and press order. Done. "Now we wait."

I look back up at Wade and find him looking at me. His eyes wide, lips parted. He stands towering over me in my short desk chair. "I'm very observant, you know this," I say.

"I'm just confused because *I* didn't even know that was my favorite flower and somehow *you* did," he mutters.

"Well," I shrug. "Now you know. The flowers are ordered, and the plan is in motion. We can pick them up anytime tomorrow and take them to Mary's. I have a good feeling about this. I think this is the key."

He nods. "I've heard the third time's the charm."

"Shh," I hiss at Wade. "Keep it down."

"I can't keep it down when you're stepping on my foot," he whisper-yells.

"I'm lightly nudging your foot *because* you're being too loud."

Branches of an overgrown bush poke into my skin. I push my hair out of my eyes, peeking around the corner again. We're posted up across the street from Mary's house, Wade holding the floral bouquet behind me.

"Oh, there she is, there she is," I whisper, pointing to the car pulling into Mary's garage.

"I can see, Haze." Wade shifts around me, getting into position. The plan is to wait until she's inside, drop the flowers on the porch, and run. Nothing fancy. Wade can run faster, so we decided he'd run the flowers up while I keep watch.

The garage closes with a loud squeak. I count to thirty in my head, then make a hand signal.

"What's that supposed to be?" Wade whispers.

"I don't know, it just seems like we should have some sort of signal."

"That signal doesn't mean anything, it looks like you're swatting away a bug," he says.

"Oh my god, just go!" I whisper-yell.

Wade stands, walking carefully across the street as if it's made of glass. He steps up to the porch with the flowers, setting them softly onto Mary's welcome mat, then backs away just enough that he can reach the doorbell.

He looks over his shoulder at me, a smile starting on his lips. I give him a thumbs up, and he nods. When he presses the doorbell, everything is a blur.

He runs back to me, hand reaching out to grab onto mine. He pulls me behind the old mill building we were hiding next to, caging me in against the cinderblock wall.

The sound of our heavy breathing fills the air, both of us grinning.

"That was–" he starts.

"Shh," I interrupt, looking over my shoulder. "That was her door." The sound of Mary's screen door opening echoes across the small street. There's some shuffling, a small chuckle, then the screen door closing again.

I breathe a sigh of relief, turning my head back to Wade. Our noses accidentally bump together, sending a shiver down my spine.

"Sorry," he mutters, stepping back. He rests his hands on his hips, catching his breath. "Holy shit, we did it."

I nod. "I really thought we'd get caught."

"I knew we wouldn't," he winks. Actually winks at me. My brain conjures about twenty dirty jokes to quip back.

Instead, a curt laugh escapes my throat. "Well," I say. "Now we wait and watch for results."

"You were right, this is fun," Wade smiles, and I swear his eyes twinkle just a bit. "Just like when we were kids."

He's right. I always feel like a kid again around Wade. It's my favorite thing about him. Everything is easy.

Chapter 24

I Wish You Would

DO YOU EVER HAVE a moment you wish you could just bottle up and hide in forever? No responsibilities, no decisions to make, nowhere to be.

When I was little, my dad used to call those snow globe moments. I'm pretty sure that at some point, my little kid brain didn't know how to communicate that I wanted to keep a memory forever, so he made it into something I could understand.

I used to stare into our Christmas snow globes for as long as my attention span allowed, making up little worlds in each one.

This one has a bakery, and the baker is secretly a former North Pole elf who loves to make chocolate chip cookies infused with Christmas magic. That one has three skiers going down a snowy slope. They're all best friends who meet up once a year to ski and sit around a fire for a week, then go back to their far-away lives. That one is a small, snowy town at night. If I could jump into it, I'd live in the cabin on the far edge and make lots of snowmen in the yard.

My parents always encouraged my overactive imagination and helped me come up with scenarios that became bigger and more far-fetched over time. My dad started bringing home snow globes for me from the places he traveled to for auctions and other ranch-related work trips, and to this day, I have an entire collection now somewhere in my closet.

I'm not sure exactly when snow globe moments started, but now whenever I want to bottle up a memory to return to later, I label it in my mind and put it into a little mental snow globe.

Days like today.

My feet splash in the cool, turquoise water as I sit next to Lainey Monroe on the back deck of the boat. The sun warms my skin and the dark blue fabric of my bikini as a whisper of a breeze runs through my hair. A toddler's laugh fills the air as his dad and uncle throw him around in the water. The smell of the lake and sunscreen calms me like nothing else can, besides maybe the smell of sagebrush in the mountains.

I close my eyes to take it all in, and when I open them, my best friend in the world is climbing up the ladder next to me. Wade plops down next to me on the deck mid-laugh, still dripping water, his sandy blonde hair a mess of a mop on his head. He wraps an arm around my shoulders, and I feel the cold water droplets pricking into my skin. I cringe away.

"Hey, you okay?" Wade says, jokingly ruffling my hair with the hand that isn't burning into my left shoulder blade. It makes me chuckle.

I look up at him, taking in his grin. "Yeah, I'm good. You're just freezing."

"You're all warm from the sun," he observes. "You've gotta jump in." He plants a soft kiss on my forehead, which calms me down a bit. It's something he's done thousands of times before. Familiar. But for some reason, goosebumps pop up on my arms.

"Want to go for a swim?" He asks so softly I can barely hear him. His eyes trail from my eyes to my shoulders, and back up to my lips as he reaches out and places a strand of hair behind my ear. Before I have a chance to answer, he stands, adjusts his swim trunks, and jumps into the cool water.

Wade makes a funny face from the water, splashing around. I laugh and follow right after, jumping off the boat. The cool water surrounds me, waking up every nerve ending in my body.

"Hi," Wade's voice comes from behind my head. I push around to face him, treading water. Sunlight glints off the turquoise water, small waves rolling past us. The sky is a little bit hazy. It always is this time of year in the mountains.

"Hey," I smile. His leg brushes against mine in the water.

"I'll miss lake days once it gets cold," he says. A drop of water runs down his cheek, then his neck.

I'll miss you, I think, hoping my face doesn't give anything away. I try my best to smile and nod, looking down at the water. It's clear enough to see my legs with just a slight blue-green hue to them, but the water is way too deep to see anything else. Wade said it was a couple of hundred feet once, I think.

"Uncle Wade," a tiny voice calls from the boat. We turn to see Drew standing on one of the leather seats. "Come play a game!"

"Duty calls," he says from beside me. I start to shiver as he swims away, towards the ladder on the back of the boat. The water is the warmest it'll be all year, but when I'm out here by myself, it's frigid.

Wade waits for me at the ladder, motioning for me to go up first. I step on the first rung, then the second, before a few big waves hit the boat from a nearby wakeboarder. Wade's hands find my waist as I start to wobble.

"I've got you, just hang on," he says from below.

"Okay," I muster, gripping the handle on the boat. His hands rub against my bare skin, turning my brain to mush. Is this what it's like to be touched by him? His firm grip keeps me upright. This is dangerous.

"I'm good," I call down over my shoulder. I catch a glimpse of his mess of hair, darker from the water. Turning forward, I grip the handle with all my might and pull myself up onto the back deck.

"Haze, wait–" he says, reluctant to let me out of his grip.

"I'm fine, Wade, I can make it up," I interrupt. The waves are still coming, so I practically have to roll myself onto the deck. Standing isn't an option. Out of the corner of my eye, Lainey, Wyatt, and Drew are holding onto the handles at each of their seats at the front of the boat as it rocks back and forth.

Surprising me, Wade makes his way up the ladder despite the waves, falling over half on top of me. "Why did you do that? You should have waited. You could have fallen off the boat," he says.

"You did the same thing," I point out, rolling onto my side to face him. His eyes are wide, his hair wild, and he's gripping onto my shoulder as if he can hold me right here safely. I didn't even notice when he grabbed onto me.

"Only because you did!" he exclaims. We're both still breathing heavily, from swimming to the boat, I think. It must be.

The waves have calmed, so I push to sit up. The checkered floor of the deck digs into my palm. It's great for non-slip, but it hurts like hell to lie on. Wade follows, helping me up with him. We climb into the boat, sitting on one of the bigger seats in the back to catch our breath.

Wyatt tosses us our towels. I wrap mine around me, grateful for the warm, dry fabric. My hair is dripping wet and a tangled mess, I'm sure. I usually braid it when we go for swims, especially when it's this long.

"Ready for games?" Drew says, bouncing up and down in his seat.

"Drew, Uncle Wade and Aunt Hazel might be tired from swimming. Let's give them a break," Lainey warns.

"It's okay," I smile. "We are so excited to play games. What do you want to play?"

"Truth or dare!" Drew yells as loud as his little lungs allow.

I raise my eyebrows, looking up at Lainey. She shrugs. "He learned it at daycare from one of the older kids. It's his favorite game now."

"Okay, Drew, truth or dare?" Wade says, rubbing the towel on his hair. It smacks me on the back of my head. We haven't moved from the seat we plopped in on, and I don't really want to. I pull the towel tighter around me as Wade sets his on his lap.

"Truth!" Drew yells around the goldfish he's snacking on.

Wade pretends to think. "Hmm..." he hums.

"You're slow, Wadey," Drew says. Wyatt huffs a laugh from the captain's chair.

"Fine, here it is," Wade says. "Did you sleep during your nap today, or did you play with your toys? You have to tell the truth."

A sly smile spreads across Drew's face. "I played," he says quietly, as if only Wade could hear.

Wade laughs, leaning back in our seat. His left arm wraps around the back of the seat behind me.

"Drew–" Wyatt starts.

"No, no, he gets immunity during truth or dare. Isn't that right, Drew?" Wade interrupts.

"Yeah!" Drew exclaims.

"I've never heard that rule before," Wyatt mumbles.

"My turn," Drew declares, already onto the next.

"Okay," Lainey looks around at us. "Who do you pick?"

"Dad!" He yells, pointing a tiny finger at Wyatt.

Wyatt crosses his arms, raising a brow. Lainey just winks. "Dare," he says.

Drew thinks for a long moment. Then suddenly, he smiles, clapping his little hands together. He smiles, proud of himself, and says, "I dare you to jump in the water."

Lainey laughs, "You *are* the only one who hasn't been swimming yet."

To my surprise, Wyatt shrugs, standing up from his chair. "Easy," he says.

He pulls his shirt over his head, folds it neatly on the chair, and climbs up to the back deck. Before I can even turn to see, he jumps into the water with a huge splash.

Drew runs to the side of the boat to see, squealing with laughter. Wyatt surfaces near the ladder, shaking the water out of his hair.

"Water's nice today!" He yells.

"I told you that earlier," Lainey yells back.

Wyatt climbs the ladder, water dripping onto the deck and rolling right back off into the lake. He grabs his towel from the boat and dries himself off, wrapping it around his swim trunks before stepping into the boat.

Wade is so close to me, his laugh rumbles into my chest, vibrating my arm. Despite myself, I lean a little closer into him. The arm that's behind me has relaxed a little, brushing against my shoulder.

Drew wanders into the cabin of the boat to play with a toy car, bored with the game already.

"I think," Lainey says. "It's my turn. And, I pick Wade."

Wade laughs. "Hit me. I pick dare," he says, adjusting in his seat. He inadvertently pulls me another inch closer. Our thighs are pressed together on the seat.

Lainey's smile is only what I can describe as premeditated. She pretends to think a bit, looking around the boat. "Kiss Hazel. On the lips."

My heart drops to my feet. I feel my cheeks instantly heat. I look over at Wade and expect the same panic that I'm feeling, but he's smiling.

Laughing.

His sister-in-law just told him to kiss me, and he's laughing. He looks down at me, a question in his eyes. I'm having an out-of-body experience. I feel my head nod, but it's heavier than before. That's all the confirmation Wade needs, apparently.

"What's one kiss between friends?" He says, not taking his eyes off of me.

Maybe Lainey replied. Maybe not. All I can see is Wade's blue eyes dropping to my lips. I part them on instinct. He shifts in the seat, facing me, running his hand through my wet hair.

"Right, Hazel?" he whispers.

"Right," I nod. My voice comes out shaky. "Friends. Yeah."

I don't have time to process or brace myself before his lips are on mine. Neither of us moves at first, and the kiss should end there. He should pull back, laugh, and move on with the game.

But he doesn't. We don't.

Instead, his lips brush against mine, working them further apart. He grips my hair tighter, pulling me closer to him. I finally snap out of whatever trance this put me in and kiss him back. A soft groan escapes his throat, and I reach for him, any part of him, and end up finding his forearm. I grip it hard.

Every nerve ending in my body is on high alert. A wave of need rolls back and forth in my chest, knocking my bearings off. *Wade is kissing me. We are kissing right now. For real.*

"Alright, *friends,*" Wyatt's voice cuts through the haze. "This is a family show."

I feel Wade chuckle against my lips before I break our kiss, jumping back like I touched a live wire. It kind of feels like I did.

"Sorry," Wade winks at Wyatt, who turns the key in the ignition. The splash of the propeller is loud behind me.

"I think we've had enough fun for one afternoon," Wyatt says. Drew protests with a loud yell from the cabin.

I barely process what's happening.

What was that?

Wade sits next to me, unaffected, letting the breeze run its fingers through his hair. We cut through the turquoise waves, the wind loud enough to drown out the buzzing in my head.

But not loud enough to quiet the beating of my heart.

Chapter 25

Feels Like

I CHECK MY MAKEUP ONE last time in the mirror in Wade's tiny bathroom. After Wyatt pulled the boat in for the day, we walked over to Black Bear Rentals to shower and freshen up for dinner later tonight. In true Wade fashion, he's currently over at the public showers using the worst public soap imaginable, letting me have the apartment to myself so we aren't waiting on each other.

We didn't say anything else about The Kiss, but Wade seemed just as relaxed and care-free all the way home. I can't say the same for myself. I've been a bundle of nerves ever since. I tripped while getting off the boat, falling against him. I fumbled with his key in the apartment door so long he eventually stepped in and unlocked it himself, and I got tangled up in my bikini top trying to get ready to wash up.

Even now, as I brush my blow-dried hair, my hands are shaking.

I brought a denim sundress with me for dinner, paired with my dressier cowgirl boots and ruffled lace boot socks. My long hair falls down my back in natural waves, and I've pinned back the shorter front pieces with white clips that match my socks.

I'm impressed I was able to pull together any sort of look after that lake day. I'm usually too exhausted and sun-baked to care. But now, I'm grateful for past-Hazel, who had the fore-thought to pack nice clothes for dinner. After The Kiss, I'll take anything I can get to keep my confidence from faltering.

Packing up my makeup bag, I gather everything into my beach tote and head out into the living room just as the front door opens. Wade walks into the apartment still in his swim trunks, dripping wet.

He doesn't see me at first. He heads over to his laundry corner and towels off his hair one more time before dropping the towel in the washer and turning back towards his room.

Finally, his eyes land on me. They travel up slowly, assessing every part of me. When he catches my gaze, there's no smile on his face. Only determination and something I can't place.

"What? Is something wrong with my dress? Is it my hair?" I run my fingers through my waves, turning to go back to the bathroom.

"No, no, nothing's wrong," Wade says quickly, blinking. "I just–, well, you... I like your dress. And your boots."

I can't help but smile as I say, "Thanks, Wade."

He changes in his room as we talk through the wall. Since this wasn't built as an apartment, the walls are paper-thin. We can pretty much talk as easily through rooms as we would in the same room.

"Did I tell you I found more about that fishing spot my dad wrote about near the Ambretta Caves? He wrote about it a couple more times in his notes," Wade says loudly through the wall.

"No, you didn't, anything good?"

"It looks like he did go there a few times and caught some pretty nice trout. It sounds like it's really pretty. I'd love to fly fish it sometime," he says. I can hear clothes rustling as he hurries to get ready. "I'm just surprised he never took me up there. I wonder if he ever brought Wyatt, I should ask him when we see him tonight. I know it's just a random fishing spot, but I went to all of his spots with him multiple times and never heard of this one. Maybe it's a dud."

"Could we head up there this week? That'd be really fun. We could plan it on a day we can bring the horses, it shouldn't be too far of a ride from the ranch. We can pack lunch and spend an afternoon up there," I suggest.

"Let's do it," he emerges from his room wearing a navy long-sleeve fishing shirt, light colored jeans, and a backwards Colorado Avalanche hat. My pulse speeds up.

How have I not noticed how attractive he is? Is this what happens when you kiss your best friend once? You immediately notice everything you didn't notice before? This is going to be a long night.

He saunters over to me, throwing his arm around my shoulder. "Ready?" He smiles widely, eyes twinkling again.

"Ready," I say on a deep breath. I'm fine. If he can pretend nothing happened, I can too.

Walking along the dock, Wade chats my ear off about some new tackle he's stocking in the shop that's apparently flying off the shelves. I know he likes lake rentals, but it's clear he's much more excited about fishing tackle in the shop. I can't help but think about years ago, when the entire shop was tackle and fishing guide services. I wonder if he misses that.

I toss Wade the Bronco keys, and we hop in. I'm pretty sure he drives my car more than I do, but I'm okay with that. I love driving, but I love being a passenger even more. I turn on the radio immediately, and we sing along to "All Your'n" by Tyler Childers as loud as we can on our way to Heidi's house.

I lean out the window, letting my hair blow wild in the breeze. It's that time just between dusk and night that I love so much, when you can see the outlines of the mountains, some dark blue light reflecting off the lake, and the signs downtown are all lit up. Vacationers line the streets waiting for shakes in their swimsuits.

I look over at Wade singing along to the song, smile on his face, wavy hair poking out from under his ball cap, and think about how rare it is to have two snow globe moments in one day.

Our little snow globe shattered into a million pieces the second Wade pulled the Bronco into the driveway at his childhood house, and I instantly started to panic. I've done this a million times before, I should be fine. I should be able to walk in there and act like normal.

But it doesn't feel normal anymore. Not after today. *We* aren't normal. He kissed me, and it was...

It's all I can think about.

Thinking about it all night isn't going to help, though. It happened. I'll process it later.

I smooth out my dress and step out of the Bronco when Wade comes around to open my door. He smiles at me, and I feel instantly at home. The same feeling I get walking around Connor Ranch.

From the noise I can hear before the door even opens, it seems like everyone is already here. Wade and Wyatt may be quiet, but the rest of the family sure isn't. Especially his mom.

Heidi knows everyone in this town because of her outgoing personality. If Heidi decides she wants to get to know you, you'd better buckle up because she always gets her way in that regard. I can remember several occasions when I was growing up that Heidi marched up to the ranch, knocked on the door out of the blue with a loaf of banana bread or a casserole, invited herself in, and talked with my mother for hours.

I've always been grateful for her ability to always make my mom feel included in the community, even when we were brand new to Juniper Ridge.

Wyatt answers the door with a nod, Drew attached to his side with a tiny racecar in his hands. He invites us in, and we step into the Monroe house.

Wade reaches for my hand, giving it a squeeze of reassurance as we make our way towards the dining room.

The Monroes' dining room sits at the back of the house, just past a sitting room and stairs to the bedrooms on the second level. The deep oak dining table overlooks large floor-to-ceiling windows with a perfect view of the mountains above the town.

Heidi always used to laugh at all of the new homes being built. The papers that bragged about lake views in their listings. She always said the mountains were much better to look at. I'm inclined to agree. If I look closely enough, I can just barely see the lights of the ranch up on the mountain bench.

Heidi is busy with two pots on the stove and one dish in the oven, Lainey sitting at the kitchen island, talking to her about baby number two's nursery. If she weren't so pregnant, I know she'd be in the kitchen helping Heidi with dinner.

Wyatt and Wade have slipped into a conversation about a big lake trout Wade caught a few weeks ago on the boat, so I unlatch our hands and head into the kitchen to help out with dinner. I'm not much of a cook, but Heidi teaches me something new every time I visit.

"Hazel Mae, honey, hello! I'm so glad you decided to come!" Heidi says, happily stirring away at a stew on the stove. It smells heavenly in here.

"Of course, I always love a good Monroe family dinner. Anything I can help with?" I ask.

"The mashed potatoes are just about done, if you'd like to take them off the stove and start mashing. They probably need some butter and salt, that's over there in the corner," Heidi says, handing me a hotplate for the boiling pot of potatoes. "The masher is right next to the pot. Yep, that's the one."

I grab the pot off the stove, drain the water, and let the butter melt a bit before starting to mash the potatoes.

"How is the ranch, honey? I've heard great things from Elyse lately."

"It's great! We had an awesome, busy season this year. I think we'll need to hire another ranch hand next year if things pick up as much as they did this season. It was a bit overwhelming, but we got it done."

"That's amazing. I'm so happy for your family. They've done such a great job with that property," she smiles with pride.

"I think next summer Wyatt and I are dropping the kids here and heading up to one of your cabins for a weekend. Baby will be big enough, and I already need a parents' weekend out. No phones, no monitors, just sleep. Lots of sleep," Lainey says dreamily.

"You drop those babies off over here whenever you want to, Lainey dear," Heidi laughs.

I laugh, stirring the potatoes a bit. "If you know a month you're interested in, I can block off a weekend in our best cabin. The one with the hot tub. But we are already booked out for most of July," I mention.

"Wow!" Lainey gasps. "At that rate, you are going to need a few more cabins!"

"Tell me about it. I never thought we'd need to expand, but there aren't any other dude ranches in the area, and we get booked out pretty solid during the busy season. I've had to send a few families to Katie's vacation rental cabins this summer because we haven't had room, but it just isn't the same as a full-service dude ranch. Sometimes I'm jealous of Black Bear Rentals for having competitors to share the load with," I say.

"Speaking of Wade, he mentioned to Wyatt that he's been cleaning out the back office with you. I'm so happy he's finally going through all of those records his dad kept over the years. Has he been doing okay with it?" Heidi says as she turns the heat on the beef stew off, reaching into the oven to grab the rolls that are baked to a perfect golden brown.

"It's been going well. We aren't quite done yet, but we've gotten through the biggest chunk of it. I think it probably felt a little weird for him at first, but we've been having fun with it lately. We even found a new fishing spot to check out on the river from one of his journal entries," I reply.

Lainey grabs a roll straight from the rack to snack on as Heidi turns to give me a sympathetic smile.

"I'm glad he has you, Hazel," she starts, "You've always had a gift for pulling him out of his own head. And he lives there far too often."

Wade is almost *always* in his head. We are the same in that way, always overthinking everything when we shouldn't. I can practically hear him thinking about every situation as it's happening. The only time he's truly relaxed and not overthinking everything is when it's just us.

I guess that's why we are such good friends; he helps me think things through when I need to, and I help him loosen up and live in the moment. It's nice to think that Heidi has also noticed this.

Heidi and Lainey fall back into a conversation about the restaurant and if chili is soup-like enough to be considered in the running for soup of the week.

Wade saunters into the kitchen from wherever he and Wyatt had gotten off to, and as if we've done it a thousand times before, he wraps his arm around my waist in a hug and plants a soft kiss on my temple. His hands find the counter on either side of me, boxing me in. Butterflies erupt in my stomach, overtaking the discomfort.

This is different.

Heat rushes to my cheeks, and my voice comes out high-pitched and weird when I turn my head over my shoulder to say, "Hey."

"Hey, yourself," he says with a grin. I look up and catch his eyes. They're full of happiness, crinkling at the sides.

I'm not sure what's gotten into him, but I'm not about to ask about it now. Not after the day we've had.

"I'm mashing. It's going pretty well, although I'm sure if you asked the potatoes, you'd get a different answer," I reply, clearing my throat and shoving the butterflies away once again.

"Oh, I'm sure the worst part is over for them, they've already been peeled and boiled," he nods.

"You think that's the worst part? I look at it more like a deep exfoliation and dip in the hot tub. Then just when they think their day at the spa is over, BAM. They get crushed by a masher and covered in butter."

"You continue to shock me, Haze," Wade laughs as he takes the masher out of my hands and mashes the last few stragglers himself.

"That makes two of us today, *buddy*," I tease.

Wade's cheeks turn red this time as he turns his attention to the very important task of mashing potatoes that are already plenty mashed as it is. Interesting.

Heidi's yell makes me jump. "Lainey, tell the boys it's time to eat, will you? I'll dish up Drew's plate so he can get started."

In just a few minutes, food is piled onto plates, and we are sitting at the dining room table. Sometimes I wonder if the Monroe boys know how lucky they are to have a restaurant owner and chef as a mom. My mom is a great cook, but Heidi is just on another level.

I'm not sure what I was so nervous about tonight. The conversation is easy like always, I'm sitting next to Wade like always, and Heidi is regaling us with tales from her youth as she usually does during family dinners. Sure, Wade's hand hasn't left mine, and that's a bit different than usual, but I can't complain.

I probably like it a little too much, and it's getting exhausting trying to force myself not to. So I decided to just go with it. I let my stomach flutter when he starts tracing small circles with his thumb on my leg. I let myself blush when he looks at me like I'm the most important person in the world. I let myself laugh and enjoy his family.

I catch him looking over at me more than a few times, and after a while, I start looking back. He gives me a small smile and squeezes my leg on one occasion, and my heart does a little flip. Must be the wine. Speaking of the wine, once it goes to my head a bit, I'm fully leaning into him between our chairs.

At some point, his arm landed around my waist and pulled me in a bit, and I caved. I'm close enough now that when he talks, I can feel his voice vibrating through my head. Just like earlier on the boat.

After dinner, Lainey and I are cleaning up in the kitchen while the boys are outside helping Heidi take down a few of her outdoor swings for the season. Drew runs around on the lawn, his racecar now turned into an airplane.

"So how is the firm?" I ask.

"We've been a little slow this year, but nothing unusual. Plenty of clients to keep me going," she says. Lainey is a lawyer for a firm based in a bigger city in Utah, about an hour away. Luckily for her, most of her work is done from home in her gigantic study.

"You know," Lainey says as she dries off a plate, "I didn't believe it at first, but I'm so glad Wade got out of whatever hole he fell into after their dad died and finally let himself love you. He's just about back to his old self."

"Oh, I don't know about that," I say nervously. I know Wade loves me, but to hear that he might *love* me is a bit too much to wrap my head around. She's just making assumptions after what happened on the boat.

"I do," she continues, "That boy has been head over heels for you since he was nine years old. Wyatt claims he didn't know, but I saw it for myself the first time I ever saw him around you.

He's just different. Lighter. I love the kid, but he's just not as fun on his own. I think you pull that out of him," she laughs.

"Oh," I sputter out, not sure what to say.

"I just wish I could go back to that night he was so messed up about not being able to take you to your senior prom and reassure him it's all going to work out. Maybe it was homecoming. Either way, he was distraught. Had a whole plan to go and ask you with flowers and some sort of little trinket, I'm not sure what. When Katie told him you had already said yes to someone else, I thought he was going to burst into tears right there," she chuckles, "Poor kid. But, he finally got there."

My ears ring. Some invisible ghost has taken a sledgehammer to my chest. I have absolutely zero idea what she's talking about. I just nod.

I turn back to the sink to finish up the dishes, schooling my features into something I hope resembles neutral. What is she talking about? Which dance? It has to be prom, I skipped out on my senior homecoming dance in favor of helping out at the ranch during the busy season. I think I went to prom with Hayden. Yes, that was his name.

I remember not wanting to go with him necessarily, but I didn't have anyone else to go with, and Katie had a date. We were so excited to be going in the same group that I didn't really care who my date was.

Had I known, I would have much preferred Wade. But, he was newly twenty-one, in college, and I was sure he wouldn't even consider going to a high school dance with me. Apparently, I was wrong.

Clearly, Wyatt and Lainey had interpreted it wrong. I'm sure he wanted to ask me out of duty, or out of nostalgia, since we had never gone to a school dance together. Either way, I feel an overwhelming sense of guilt. Had I known, I probably would have canceled on poor Hayden and jumped at the chance to go with Wade.

What a missed opportunity. I wish I could go back in time and fix it. I bet going to a dance with Wade would have been a blast.

Once the kitchen is cleaned and everyone is back inside, Wade and I say our goodbyes and head back out to the Bronco. He reaches for my hand again, resting our interlocked fingers in my lap. As if he has to be connected to me at all times.

I glance over at him more than I should during the car ride, thanking the universe for planting the idea in his head to wear that backwards hat today. I'd love to blame my attraction on the wine, but it has long since left my system.

I wonder if I'll be this happy in Arizona, all on my own. Or wherever I end up. Maybe I can convince my family and all of the Monroes to go with me.

But I can't see Wade anywhere other than here.

Chapter 26

Just In Case

It's been exactly four days since dinner at the Monroes' house, and Wade and I have texted more than we have in our entire lives. And that's saying a lot, with the amount we usually text every day.

Four days of sending funny gifs back and forth, inside jokes, sharing about our days, and planning our fishing day trip up to the caves.

I fire off another .gif in response to his latest text, this time of a Cisco fish flopping in the air. I'm grateful he'll understand what I'm trying to convey (see you at Cisco's later), because we are telepathically linked when it comes to humor. I take my attention off my phone for the thirtieth time since I started on this spreadsheet and get back to work.

We still haven't discussed The Kiss, and I'm happy not to. Any time I start to think about it, my stomach sinks, and I feel like I might go find him and do it again.

That, obviously, cannot happen.

So, I'm happy for the distraction of his extremely good mood, and chalk it up to the consequences of truth or dare. That's all it was anyway.

Today, I'm planning out the schedule for the fall at the dude ranch. We have a good amount of bookings for fall, but not nearly as many as in the summer. It'll give the ranch hands a good opportunity to get everything reset and ready for another season after the chaos of summer. We could all use a little bit of a break around here.

Plus, there's always lots to get ready for the wintertime. Funny how up here, the world revolves around summer and winter. In the fall, you're getting ready for winter, putting things away, closing out the summer craziness. In winter and spring, you're preparing for a busy summer season and everything that comes with that. In summer, you're surviving through the chaos, and it all starts over again in the fall. I kind of like the clockwork of it all. It feels comfortable and stable. Two things I'm all about.

I'm about to finally close out of this spreadsheet to avoid an impending headache, when I notice I have some emails in my inbox to check on.

One in particular catches my eye. It's from Deborah Makar, and the subject line says only "Communication from the Arizona History Museum." I take a deep breath and open the email.

I skim over the email a few times until I get the gist of it. It's longer than their other follow-ups, probably because we are getting closer and closer to the deadline for me to give an answer and move forward in the process.

From the email, it seems that although she is still the poster child for patience, Deborah would like to know if there's anything she can do to move my timeline up. She politely reminds me about all of the benefits that come with the job, that there are other applicants they can look at if I'm no longer interested, and to let her know if I have any further questions.

I've been so caught up in things here that I've neglected saying yes to the trial run.

Before I can lose my nerve, I shoot off a quick reply asking for the details of the trial period.

I've only been to Arizona once before, and never to Tucson. All of my interviews were over video chat. I've never been an archivist before, though I did work on campus at the museum while I got my degree.

But this is a big museum in a major city. One of the biggest history museums in the West. I could get a taste of the job and have confidence when accepting instead of hesitating like I am now.

I snap my laptop shut and look for flights on my phone. If I'm going to do this, I want to be absolutely sure.

It's perfect timing, really-the dude ranch is in a bit of a lull after the Summer's End rush, and we are in between seasons. I'll have to leave the office organizing to Wade for a couple of days longer than we had planned, but I'm sure he'll be fine with that.

Shit.

Wade.

I know I should have told him by now. The longer it goes on, the worse I feel about keeping something so huge from him.

Based on Deborah's email, they are going through a festival of their own right now, so I wouldn't be able to visit for two weeks anyway. That gives me about a week and a half, if I'm being realistic, to tell Wade about the job. I want to give him a few days before I up and leave for Tucson, even though it's just a short trip. He deserves that at the bare minimum.

I run my hands through my hair, thinking everything out. I should probably start another spreadsheet. That would make me feel better. I'm probably overthinking this anyway. Maybe I'm the one who will care the most about leaving, and Wade will be fine. After all, his family is here, and it's not like I'm his only friend. I'm sure he'll miss me, but we'll still talk all the time.

Hell, maybe it'd be good for him.

He'd actually have time to hang out with other people, maybe even date more often. I shove down the twinge of jealousy I feel about Wade spending a lot of time with anyone but me, especially dating someone else.

I groan, letting my head fall into my hands as I hunch over my desk.

I'm in way over my head.

Wade grabs my hand, leading me out to the wooden floor, now busier than earlier. Everyone is line dancing to an older country song. We slip right in, our boots stomping on the ground with the beat. I'm grateful for the simple tank top and jeans I'd chosen earlier tonight; the air is starting to get a bit stuffy with all of the movement.

The room moves around me in a blur. I'm caught up in laughing and dancing with Wade, both of us grinning so big I'm not sure why my face doesn't hurt yet. This is where we fit the best. Dancing in our boots, eyes watery from laughter.

When I arrived at Cisco's earlier, Wade was already here, sitting alone in a corner booth. He spotted me the second I walked in the door, a grin spreading across his face. I hadn't sat down for five minutes before he was pulling me out to the dance floor.

Tonight is live music night at Cisco's with the same local band that plays every summer weekend. They mostly do covers of old 60's country songs.

After two more songs, the music slows, and for a beat, we just look at each other, not sure what to do. My chest is still heaving, out of breath from dancing, when Wade grabs my waist and pulls me into him, swaying to the music. My heart is racing, and I'm not sure if it's from the dancing or how he's looking down at me.

He's always finding excuses to dance, as if he just can't sit still for more than a few minutes with music on. Is this how it would have been if he'd asked me to my senior prom? I can't imagine it would. We were both a bit more awkward back then, especially Wade. Now, he's so sure of himself all the time. Confident and grown up.

No longer the gangly, awkward kid he used to be. I almost can't believe how far he's come. When I look at him now, under the dim lights of Cisco's, my cheeks heat.

"What are you thinking about?" Wade asks into my hair, his words brushing over my ear and sending chills down my back.

"Nothing," I say too quickly. "Well, actually, I was thinking about something Lainey said to me at your mom's house the other night." He stays quiet, encouraging me to continue. "She said... well, she said that you were going to ask me to a dance when I was in high school, and you had a whole plan, but Katie told you I was already going with someone else, so you decided not to. Is that true?"

A beat of silence. He looks like he doesn't want to answer.

"You know what, never mind, it's nothing anyway," I wave it off.

"No, it's okay," he starts. "Yeah, it was something like that." I try to hide my surprise as he continues, his eyes locked on something behind me. "I just thought it would be fun if I took you to your senior prom. I felt kind of stupid for never asking you to go with me when I was in high school, but you were younger then, and I don't know, it just felt like it was time," he shakes his head. "But it was kind of a dumb idea. Why would you want to go to your senior prom with some twenty-one-year-old guy?" A dry laugh escapes his throat.

"I would have loved to go with you, Wade," I say, catching his eye. "Do me a favor, and next time you want to do something with me, just ask. I feel like we missed out on that experience."

"Okay," he whispers, tucking me back into him.

We are taking a few too many liberties, standing this close, swaying to the music. It's like we're locked in some sort of game, seeing how much we can get away with without the other calling us out. His thumb is making lazy circles on my back, slowly moving down. My hands make their way into his hair, twisting his soft waves between my fingers.

His breath is hot on my neck. We lean into each other until our chests are touching, and it feels like we're alone, not in a bar full of people.

Like all good things, the band's set comes to an end, and we separate, cool air rushing to fill the space between us. We settle our tabs and walk out into the night, hand in hand.

Our cars are parked together, but we came here separately, and we'll leave that way too. I have an early morning at the ranch tomorrow, so I can't crash on Wade's couch another night.

Plus, it feels different now. Like crossing some sort of line.

I stand at my driver's side door as Wade leans up against his truck, still playing with my hand. He starts to let go, then grabs my fingers, running his thumb along my knuckles, gaze trained towards the ground.

"Haze–" he starts, but he's immediately interrupted by another voice.

"Mary, I swear," Earl says from the feed store across the street. "I didn't send them."

Mary and Earl stand on the front steps of the hardware store, far past closing time. She holds the vase of purple flowers out to him.

"Oh, Earl, it really was a kind gesture, and they're beautiful flowers. I'm afraid I just don't feel the same way," Mary's soft voice dances through the night air.

I glance over to Wade, whose eyes are as wide as mine. We break apart, crouching down behind Wade's tailgate until we can just see over the top.

"No, Mary, you don't understand," Earl pleads. "I agree with you."

"You do?" she asks.

"Yes, that's what I'm trying to tell you. I don't know who sent those to you, but it sure as heck wasn't me. I've always thought of you as a great friend, nothing more," he says.

"Well, that's a relief," she smiles. "Come in and have a coffee, won't you?"

The door to the shop closes behind them, and a lamp in the front window switches on.

I turn to Wade, who is staring at the shop, mouth ajar.

"Well, shoot, I guess I was way off base," I whisper.

He turns back to me, running a hand through his already messy hair. "I thought for sure it was him."

"Yeah," I say, staring back at the shop. More than just the journal, I thought they'd be great together. "Well," I sigh, pushing off the truck. "Back to square one."

Group Chat

Wadey's Babies

Wade: A cat visited the shop today.

Hazel: ... and?

Wade: It was cute.

Hazel: Wow.

Katie: Stop the presses!

Wade: It was orange.

Hazel: Are you fucking with us? I don't get the joke.

Katie: He just wanted to see "Wadey's Babies" pop up on his phone.

Wade: Will you please change that name back? To literally anything else.

Katie: No.

Hazel: No.

Miles: Someone please remove me from this chat.

Katie: No.

Hazel: No.

Wade: Sorry, man. There's no way out.

Chapter 27

Save A Horse

The road winds lazily up the canyon, through groves of pine trees and across golden meadows. My hand cuts through the cool mountain air rushing by my window.

Wade leans an elbow out of his, already a little pink from the sun. He always gets this lopsided tan by the time August rolls around each year.

I adjust my swimsuit top under my sweatshirt. We're headed up to Lilac Creek, more specifically, our favorite swimming spot on the creek. A little hole of slack water, separated from the current by a little wall of rocks that Wade and I put there years ago.

When the lake gets crowded, or the days get hotter, we head up to the cold creek for a quick swim. Only late enough in the year that the water is warm enough not to give us hypothermia.

"Oh, hey, I wanted to show you something." Wade reaches into the pocket in his door, pulling out the leather journal. His hair glows lighter in the sun, like it's illuminated from within.

"Look at this," he says, turning the journal towards me. "Another song popped up. I'm not sure exactly when, but it definitely wasn't Earl. He hasn't been at the shop and... well, just take a look."

He hands me the journal, open to a new page. Written in dark, neat ink are the lyrics to "Save A Horse" by Big & Rich.

I can't help it. A laugh bursts out of my chest, tears pricking at the sides of my eyes.

"Are you kidding me?"

"I pretty much had that same reaction this morning," Wade smiles.

I close the book and hand it back to him. No reason to have to read into the lyrics of this one to catch the meaning.

I lean back against the leather seat of his truck, hot on my back. "Yeah, definitely not Earl. That was not the vibe when we saw him and Mary."

"I'd say not," he says. His gaze catches mine, blue eyes as light as the water of the lake when the sun is shining directly on them.

"Who else could it possibly be?" I ask, not expecting an answer. Wade shrugs, looking down the road. He turns off the main highway onto a dirt road that leads down to the little creek. The truck bounces as we drive over rocks and ruts in the road.

"I think from now on I'm just going to keep it in my backpack. See if anyone asks about it. It might be the only way," he says.

I nod, grabbing my towel from the back seat and setting it on my lap. The creek comes into view, green water rushing by in white rapids, a small pool built into the side.

Part of me is hesitant to let Wade keep it. I kind of like seeing the songs pop up mysteriously. It's exciting. That won't happen if it's always in his backpack.

But, he's right. Maybe this will finally expose who's been writing in the journal all this time.

I kick my jeans off, setting them on top of my boots next to the bank. I do the same with my sweatshirt, reaching up above my head to shimmy out of it, setting it on the pile. The sun warms my skin. I adjust my pink bikini, one of the thick tank top straps falling just slightly off my shoulder.

"Ready?" I say, looking up at Wade. But he's already looking at me. His gaze travels down my body, raking over me with an intensity I've never seen. I shiver under his attention.

"Yeah," he grits out, snapping his eyes back to mine. "Yeah, after you." He clears his throat, reaching back between his shoulder blades and yanking his t-shirt off in one quick move.

I allow myself one small glimpse of him before tearing my gaze away. His abs flex as he reaches down to take off his boots, setting them next to mine. I take one deep breath, then step into the cool water.

The cold bites into my skin as I step down the rocky bank, further and further into the creek. It's just as we left it, rocks stacked up under water as a barrier between us and the much-colder current.

Water splashes behind me as Wade makes his way into the pool. The shade of the Aspen trees surrounding the creek banks casts us in a shadowy light, with sparkles of brightness moving with the wind. Leaves create little windows of sunlight that kiss the water, sending beams of yellow to the murky bottom.

I finally make it to the wall, to the boulder I use as a make-shift bench. Behind me, Wade gasps as he gets to where the water meets his waist.

"Shit," he hisses. "I forgot how cold the creek is."

I laugh. "Colder than the lake, that's for sure."

He slowly makes his way to the rock as I watch the current snake past us, disappearing into the grove of trees.

"Hey," he says as he sits next to me. His thigh floats below my knee. I rest my leg on him, scooting closer. His warmth pulls me in like the tide.

"Hi," I say. I know I'm smiling too much, leaning into him more than I usually do. But I can't bring myself to care. "It's a perfect day for this."

Wade nods, looking up at the trees hanging over our heads. "Remember when we built this? God, that must have been at least ten years ago."

"Yeah," I smile. "Your dad was so surprised when he saw it." My memories surface: Wade carrying the biggest grey rocks we could find from dry ground into the creek, creating a little dam that lasted all these years. Me standing in my jeans in the water, placing smaller rocks in the cracks between the big ones, making sure the wall would hold up. We did that all day, completely entertained by the mountains and the creek.

He laughs, the movement sending ripples across the surface of the calm water. "I think he was too impressed to be angry about it."

"I'm kind of impressed we did it that quickly. He was just upstream fishing for a little while," I muse.

"The creek was smaller back then," Wade says. "And, you know how he got when he was fishing. He'd be out for hours longer than he planned. I'm sure he lost track of time that day."

I nod, resting my chin on my knee. "I miss him," I whisper.

"Me too," Wade says with a sad smile. "I'm glad we can still come here and see our handiwork."

His arm rests on the rock wall, hovering around my shoulders but never touching me. He's there, but still just out of reach.

The combination of the cold creek and the hot sun must be going to my head. I lean back into his arm, nudging it onto my shoulder. At first, he doesn't take the clue, looking at the rapids just past my head.

But then, when my hand grazes his thigh under the water, he looks at me.

Really looks at me.

His eyes travel across my face, cataloging me as if he wants to remember what I look like at this exact moment. I jump when his fingers graze my outer thigh, drawing tiny circles on my skin. We're under a spell, and I'm afraid to break it. Taking more than we should, as if the water of the creek is hiding this thing between us. This magnetic pull.

"Haze–" he starts. His features shift, something deeper traveling across his face.

"Come on," I interrupt, blood rushing behind my ears. I reach for his arm, pulling him away from the rock and into the deepest part of the pool. The water is up to my shoulders here.

He sighs, opening his mouth to say something, but closing it a moment after. He follows me out to the middle, water rippling around us.

I turn to face him, angling my head up to meet his gaze. He smiles softly, pinching a piece of my hair on the surface of the water. It fans out around us like a shield.

"I'm going under," I say.

He laughs, "Okay, let's do it."

I grab onto his forearms, pushing myself under the water. It lasts all of three seconds before I'm shooting up to the surface, gasping from the cold. I open my eyes to Wade doing the same thing.

"Way too cold," he breathes out, catching his breath. I giggle, moving my hands up to his biceps to warm him up. Not that it will do anything since he's still submerged in a freezing cold creek.

"It's refreshing," I lie. "Aren't you awake now?"

"Why do we do this?" He asks.

I shrug. "For the thrill, I guess."

"Thanks for coming with me. And thanks for all of your help at the shop this summer," he says earnestly. There's a soft tone to his voice that makes my heart squeeze. "I really don't know how I would have gotten through it without you, Haze. Seriously. Thank you."

My nose stings. "Of course. I'd do anything for you."

Something passes across his features. Something I can't read. Then, he reaches for me.

He pulls me towards him so quickly I don't have a chance to react or stop myself from wrapping my legs around him, my ankles crossing behind his back. His arms circle my waist, holding me up. Wade pulls me even closer until our chests brush. His eyes are just inches from mine, pupils blown out.

My breath hitches. My pulse speeds. My thoughts seem to stutter, not sure where to focus.

His hands tracing my sides, my thighs wrapped around his warm skin, our lips so close that if I were to lean in just a tiny bit, would touch.

Why is it so much harder to resist now that I know what those lips taste like?

A shiver runs through my entire body as I lean a little bit closer, closing the distance between us. Urging Wade to do the same.

"You're cold," he whispers, stopping me in my tracks. "We should get out and warm up."

I want to tell him I'm not cold at all. In fact, the opposite.

I want to tell him I have a few good ways he could warm me up that don't involve ever leaving this creek.

I want to keep leaning forward until his lips are on mine again, a ghost of the memory of last time urging me on.

But, I don't. That's not us. Wade and I are best friends, and nothing more. We can't be anything more.

So I nod, detaching myself from him, letting the frigid water flow into the space between us. The spell is broken, and while I should be relieved, I'm anything but.

Chapter 28

Crazy

THE SUN HAS GONE down by the time we make it back to Connor Ranch. There are just a few things I need to do in the barn to get ready for tomorrow, and Wade sticks around to help.

Luckily, we don't have any dude ranchers this week on the ranch, so there aren't as many chores to finish.

It's nice to give the horses a break from trail rides with guests, but I have a sneaking suspicion that they get bored easily. I don't know about other horses, but these ones love people. Horses are pretty much just really big dogs.

Sage is always nestling into my shoulders, asking me to pet her. It's adorable. I can't imagine a life growing up without horses. I think back to when Wade first came up to the ranch to see our horses.

He's a great rider now, but that wasn't always the case. The horses scared him at first. It took him a while to warm up to how big they were before he'd get within ten feet of them. Once he started riding, he turned out to be a natural.

Now, he's hanging my saddle back up, already looking at me with that classic Wade smile. Wide. Happy.

I look down at myself. Like usual, I'm covered in dust, hair stringy and damp from the creek water, my cheeks are hot, likely sunburnt, and my jeans choice today was made purely out of practicality. The easiest to slip off for a swim.

I shouldn't care. Wade has seen me in my unofficial ranch uniform for years.

When we started the clean-up process, I had turned on my speaker to a country oldies playlist. Now, "Your Cheatin' Heart" by Hank Williams comes on, and Wade laughs.

"I love this song," he beams.

He starts dancing awkwardly, trying to do some sort of lasso move, but the song isn't quite fast enough for it to look right. He gets crazier as I giggle, adding in disco moves that make no sense at all.

"What are you doing?" I laugh. He just shrugs, pulling me into a swing dance.

Our shoes kick up dust on the dirt floor of the barn, my hair flying through the air like a curtain. A horse barn might not be the first place I'd pick to dance, but Wade will dance with me anywhere. He's always been like that.

Until the song changes again, and the opening notes of Patsy Cline's "Crazy" echo off the wooden walls. We step apart, catching our breath. There is no possible way to swing dance to this song, even for Wade.

But, before I can step away to go back to brushing Sage, he tightens his grip on my hand and pulls me in for a slow dance.

I try to hide my sharp intake of breath. Another fleeting moment that I lean into, unable to stop myself. Another gaze I'll try to catch and keep forever.

Twice in one day, we've found ourselves in this situation. Alone, closer than we should be, and doing something that could change the course of what we have.

No one around to dare us, no plausible deniability.

No more excuses.

Just him and me.

And he's looking at me with a longing I haven't seen before.

I'm afraid to say anything and break the spell. If we talk, we might have to acknowledge the entire room buzzing around us.

His throat bobs as he swallows. His eyes move down to my lips again, staying longer than before, and I feel heat rise up my neck. I can't help but wonder what he's thinking.

Is he feeling the sparks that I'm feeling? He has to, right? His hand moves up to cup my cheek, and I'm frozen in place. The pad of his thumb brushes against my bottom lip. The only thing I can think about is how much I want this.

Want him.

We stay like that for a moment, stuck between our friendship and something that will change it forever. Nothing has happened yet. If we break apart now, we can chalk it up to a day in the sun, the song, or just ignore it completely. But as soon as we cross this line, things change for good.

We may have kissed on the boat, but not like this. This would be a choice.

I'm studying a single navy blue speck in his eye when he leans in, and his lips land on mine. The butterflies in my stomach turn into a wave I can feel all the way to my toes.

Then, there's no more thinking. There's only the softness of his lips on mine, my lips parting and his tongue sliding tentatively into my mouth.

My hands are frantic, looking for something to grab onto. I thread my fingers through his belt loops and pull him closer until we are pressed up against each other. My arms brush against his skin. His lips move against mine as a moan escapes from the back of his throat.

A small sigh escapes him, and I melt into his arms. The hand that was on my cheek is on the back of my neck, tangled into my hair, the other one gripping my waist so hard I'm sure it'll leave a mark. It's pure magic.

My back hits something hard, and I realize we're moving. Wade's hips roll into mine, pressing me into the cool wood beam. His hands move from my hips to my neck, angling my head to the side to deepen the kiss.

I try to swallow a moan, but it gets out anyway, answered by one from Wade. The sound travels all the way down my spine. I run my hands over his shoulder blades, feeling the muscles in his back flex as he leans over me.

It's thrilling, this new permission to touch him. I've known him for most of my life, talk to him every day, but this is a side of him I've never seen.

"Fuck," he murmurs against my mouth, tangling his fingers into my hair. I reach up and mirror him, grabbing onto his hair, which elicits another groan from deep in his throat. He rolls his hips into me again, his hardness pressing onto my stomach. I wrap my arms around his neck as he peppers kisses along my jaw, to my ear, and back again to my lips.

I've never kissed like this, so all-consuming. So devastating. I'm sure I'll be thinking about this for the rest of my life. It just feels so... right. So much time we have wasted not doing this.

I didn't know it could be like this. Every single nerve ending in my body feels like it's on fire, lighting up as he traces his fingertips over my shoulders, down my arms, across my hips. I'm aware of every place we're touching.

Wade pulls away, resting his forehead on mine, both of us out of breath.

"You have no idea how long I've been waiting to do that," he laughs. "You're so perfect, Haze." I suppress a shudder at his words. A grin escapes onto my lips.

He turns back into me to kiss me again, but both of us jolt at the sound of the barn door rattling. We jump apart like we are on fire as my dad enters the barn. I smooth my hair as quickly as I can before he looks our way.

"Oh, hey kids," my dad says with a smile, "I'm glad I found the both of you. I need your help, are you busy?"

"N-no," I choke out, "We're not busy at all. Just cleaning up the bar, that's it."

"Is everything okay?" Wade asks. How is he so calm? *Damn him.* He crosses his arms, furrowing his brow. My cheeks start to heat when I notice his hair, slightly mussed from me running my fingers through it.

"It's the sprinkler out in the pasture," my dad says. Some of the fog clears from my mind, and I notice Dad's shirt is covered in water. His pants too.

"What happened to the sprinkler?" I demand. "Are you okay?"

Dad shoots me a reassuring smile, "I'm fine, Hazel Mae. The sprinkler head broke off, and it's shooting water into the air. I need Wade's help turning the water main off. And probably yours tomorrow, we'll need to dig it up and replace the broken piece."

I nod. "Okay, we can do that." I turn to Wade, trying my best to hide the panic in my eyes. "Right?"

Wade reaches for my hand, rubbing his thumb along my palm. "Right."

"Thanks, Wade," Dad says. Wade jerks his hand away from mine.

We follow him outside and to the nearest pasture to the side of the barn. Sure enough, water shoots from the ground like a geyser. Off to the side, Dad crouches next to the shutoff valve, Wade following his lead.

I can't hear what they're saying over the rush of water, so I hang back a bit. This is going to be a beast to clean up tomorrow. Mud, chunks of grass, and sloshy pools of water scatter across the pasture.

"Haze," Wade yells. "Hold onto this knob right here."

"Okay, coming," I reply, crouching next to him. He turns a spout as I hold the other knob in place as steady as I can.

Oh my god. We just kissed for real.

How do we come back from this? How am I supposed to act around him now?

All I can think about is his thigh pressed up against mine, the way his forearms flex as he turns the valve, his floppy hair falling into his eyes in the moonlight. This is not supposed to be happening. We're supposed to be best friends. Best friends don't kiss. Right?

Wade cranks the knob shut, the tiny geyser slowly shrinking until it's a trickle in the mud.

"Thank goodness you were here, Wade. I really appreciate your help," Dad says.

Wade nods, wiping his wet hands on his jeans. "Of course. I can come back up tomorrow and help you fix it, too. I'm sure Lake Supply has new piping."

Dad waves him off. "Don't you worry about that, I'm planning on heading there in the morning anyway. I've got a couple of ranch hands from the dude ranch that'll be able to help. I'm sure you've got plans with Hazel, right, honey?"

"Uh, yeah, right," I stammer.

"Alright," Wade nods. "Give me a call if you need an extra hand. I'm happy to help out, Mr. Connor." He stands, pulling me to my feet with him, my legs a shaky mess. Wade snakes an arm around my waist, holding me up.

"I'd better head back home," he says, turning towards me. He's so close I can feel his breath skirting through my hair. "I'll talk to you soon, Haze, okay?"

Wade smiles at me.

He smiles, and my stomach drops like a rock.

I'm leaving.

In a few weeks, I'll be moving away, and Wade will be here. He'll be devastated, even more so after tonight. I'm making it so much worse than it needs to be.

How could I do this to him?

"Okay, talk to you soon," I whisper.

Tomorrow. I'll sort out everything tomorrow.

Chapter 29

Boot Scootin' Boogie

"Hazel, what's wrong?" Katie's voice, even over the phone, brings me back down to earth.

I twist a piece of hair around my fingers as I work up the nerve to tell her about last night.

"Not to be dramatic, but everything is wrong..." I pause. "Last night after our ride, well, Wade and I– He.. We kissed."

There's a faraway laugh, like she pulled the phone away. "Seriously? That's your SOS? Y'all kissed? No shit. That's been coming for years."

"Katie, this is serious. I kissed him. Or he kissed me. On the lips. There was tongue," I whine.

"Is that it? There wasn't any more?" She asks.

"Of course there wasn't! He's my best friend! Are you crazy? This changes everything. I just ruined our seventeen-year-long friendship because I have a stupid crush. I'm sure this is your fault somehow," I narrow my eyes, as if she can see me. "You suggested this, and it planted a worm in my brain, whispering at me all day long to kiss him, and now look where it got me. I've ruined everything."

"Whoa, there, cowboy, calm down," Katie says. "Let's start over. Was it a bad kiss? Did you hate it?"

"No, that's the problem," I sigh. "I loved it. It was the best goddamn kiss of my life," I sigh. "We were in the barn, dancing and messing around after our ride. Then we started slow dancing, and it was like I was in a trance. I think maybe he leaned in first, but I definitely kissed him back. A lot. I've never kissed like that before; it's like I was drunk on it. I think I blacked out for some of it. I'm so embarrassed." I cover my face with my hands.

"So what's the problem? Was it bad for him?"

"I don't know. I guess not, he seemed into it," I admit.

"Well, there you go," she says, matter-of-fact.

"There I go, what?"

"You're two consenting adults who kissed, you both liked it, and you both have clearly been harboring feelings for each other for years. I just don't see the issue here. Go kiss him again, see what happens," she says with glee.

"The problem is that he's my best friend. I like him way too much to be in a relationship with him. When it goes south, which it will, I'll have lost my best friend in the world."

"Sounds like you're already there, babe. You can't take it back. And even if you could, I don't think either of you wants to," she says. I scoff at that. "You wouldn't, and he wouldn't, Hazel. That boy has been pining after you for years. I know you refuse to see it, but believe me. He's totally in love with you."

"He is not in love with me," I mumble.

"I appreciate your tenacity, but he is. And don't think I didn't notice you aren't denying you wouldn't take it back. It sounds to me that if it's meant to be ruined, it's already too late. So why not just go with it and see what happens?"

"Well, maybe because my dad interrupted us, we had to fix a broken sprinkler, and then we left without talking about it at all," I cringe.

"Okaaaay," she drags out. "Well, that changes things a bit. Your dad, huh?"

"Yes, it was awful," I groan. "The sprinkler in the pasture was shooting into the air, and he came to get us to help. I don't think he noticed anything, or at least he didn't say anything. Wade fixed it, but my dad was there, so we couldn't talk about it, and he said he'd talk to me 'soon,' but I haven't heard from him yet."

A pause on the other line. I press the phone against my ear, blinking my eyes shut. "Well, it hasn't even been a day. He didn't say anything about the kiss?"

"My dad was right there. Feet away," I deadpan.

"You've just got to talk to him. Communication is key," Katie assures me.

"Yeah, you're probably right. But not yet. I'm not ready," I whisper.

"Do you remember when I told you about the first time Miles kissed me?" Katie asks.

"In Salt Lake City?"

"No, in Wyoming." Katie met her boyfriend, Miles, four years before they actually started dating. They had a one-night stand when Wade and I took her to the city for her birthday and didn't talk again until she saw him again in Jackson Hole.

"It was the fourth of July," she continues, "and we were so mad at each other for some reason or another. I had gone back to the cabin to turn a light off, and he followed me. I remember arguing with him, and winning, and then all of a sudden it was like he set my heart on fire." Her dreamy sigh is so unlike the old Katie. The one who swore she'd never have a relationship. "But I was also really scared."

"Really?" I whisper.

"Of course. You'll remember we didn't exactly like each other." I laugh. "But it turns out under all of that, we loved each other. If we'd just sat down and talked at that moment, it probably would have saved us a lot of heartache later on."

I nod, knowing she can't see me, but she lets me sit in my thoughts anyway.

Katie has always been great at comforting me. I don't know what I'd do without her. She's my rock. There's not a single thing I haven't told her, and that goes both ways.

Best friend isn't a person to me, it's a level, and she and Wade are both on it.

"So," she starts, breaking the silence, "Ol' Wadey is a good kisser, I take it?"

I cough out a laugh. "I never thought I'd say this, but Wade is such a good kisser, I don't know how anyone else will ever compare. Ten out of ten. Easily the best kiss I've ever had in my life."

"Maybe no one else has to compare. You can move into his teeny tiny little floating apartment and spend all day kissing him until your lips fall off," she giggles.

"You joke, but after last night, that doesn't sound all that bad," I grin.

"Oh, Hazel, you're so down bad it's not even funny. Except for me, it's hilarious to me. I predicted this a millennium ago," she says.

"Shut up." I sit up. "Please tell me you're still coming to town this week."

"I sure am. I'll be in tomorrow afternoon. And I'm taking you straight to Cisco's, because I'm sure you need to get out," she says.

I look around my room, littered with piles of printed off spreadsheets, a half-drunk bottle of Gatorade, and blankets piled in a heap on the floor.

"Yeah," I sigh. "I probably do."

Katie picks me up as twilight sets in over the valley, casting the evening in a glow of blue and purple. Even the mountains seem to soften, as if falling into a peaceful slumber.

"Oh, wow," she yells from her open car window as I walk down the porch steps. "Bringing out the big guns tonight, huh?"

"Just for you," I wink, opening the passenger door and sliding in. I'm not sure what possessed me to, but I threw on the official going-out dress that I only wear to very fancy occasions.

A little black dress with slim spaghetti straps and ruffles along the bottom, brushing my knees. My favorite dress.

Katie, on the other hand, went with bell-bottom jeans that hug her curves and a slim-fitting red t-shirt with the words "cowboy butts drive me nuts" written in a swoop vintage font across the front.

She's my idol.

"I hope you're ready to line dance with me, I won't accept no for an answer," she says over the sound of the wind rushing by as we drive through the small canyon.

I laugh, lazily swinging my arm out the window, feeling the breeze rushing against my skin. "I'm up for just about anything. Just excited to have a night out."

Katie nods, her long, copper-tinged hair flying out the window. "We need it, we work too goddamn hard in the summer. I could really use an off-season right now."

"I'm almost there, but I don't think you'll be getting an off-season any time soon," I point out.

She sighs, turning onto the main road that leads to the center of Juniper Ridge. "Nope. But I'll have maybe a month between summer tourists and skiers."

"How is Miles doing with the ranch?"

"Same old, same old. Getting ready for winter, pretty much like he does all summer. Parker has been gone the past few weeks, so he's had a lot more fall on him," she says.

"He's gone? Why?"

"Something about going back to his hometown for a few weeks to take care of some things. He was very vague when I asked him about it, so I didn't pry. But he's been gone longer than we expected. Miles hired him to be the foreman because he didn't have time to, and now he's juggling both jobs," she says.

"I hope he's okay," I reply. "Is he going to hire someone in the meantime?"

She shakes her head. "I don't think so. He's headed into winter; hopefully, Parker will be back before snow falls. At this point, I wouldn't be surprised if he drove up to Washington to help him out with... whatever it is he's doing up there."

Katie throws the car in park, turning to face me. "Look. I know you've been stressing and overthinking a lot lately with the job and Wade. I also know that's just your personality, so I'm gonna let you do that. But not tonight. Tonight I just want to hang out and have a good time with my friend, whom I don't get to see nearly enough anymore. Deal?"

"Deal," I nod.

We make our way into the crowded bar, finding a small booth toward the back. There may only be one choice when it comes to nightlife in Juniper Ridge, but at least it's a good one.

With the slowdown of the tourist season already, Cisco's is packed with locals who may not have had time all summer to spend on a night out. It's a relaxed, upbeat energy that I love to be surrounded by.

Saturday night at Cisco's is line dancing night. In the summer months, an instructor teaches a free line dancing class before the evening rush, then the dance floor is open the rest of the night.

Usually, that means hordes of vacationers on the dance floor. But classes ended weeks ago, so it's just locals tonight. And boy, do we like to dance in our boots in this town.

Katie orders a whiskey sour for her and a huckleberry vodka lemonade for me. Our go-tos at Cisco's.

"So," Katie starts after taking a long swig of her drink. "When do you leave?"

"Five days." The number sits like an anchor on my chest.

"How long are you down south for?" She asks.

"Just a week." I stir my drink with my straw, watching the deep blue of the huckleberry mix with the light yellow lemonade.

"I'm excited for you," she smiles, running a hand through her hair. "Take a picture of a cactus for me, will you?"

I laugh. "I think I can manage that, I've heard they have a few."

"Oh no, wait. Actually, bring me one of those cactus fridge magnets. The ones in cute little terracotta pots. Are those things actually alive?"

"I always assumed they were, but I'm not sure how they live," I say.

She hums. "I must know. Bring one back for me so I can sus it out."

I laugh, taking a sip of my drink. The band setting up when we walked in kicks off their set for line dancing with a loud string of words that no one can quite understand, with the terrible acoustics at Cisco's.

I take it to mean they're ready to play.

Sure enough, the first notes of "Boot Scootin' Boogie" by Brooks & Dunn fill the hot, dry air.

"Ooh, good one!" Katie exclaims over the music. She grabs my wrist, pulling me up and to the plywood dance floor.

We twirl and stomp our way through five songs before I need to sit down and take a break in the middle of a Pitbull song that I didn't even know you could line dance to.

Katie follows me back to our booth, collapsing on the faux leather bench. Her hair is wild, about two times the volume as when we got here.

"God, I missed this," she pants. I can only nod back, gulping down the glass of water our waitress left for us.

"Hey, did you invite Wade? I thought this was a girl's night," Katie teases.

"No," I shake my head. "Why?"

Katie nods toward the front door. My gaze follows hers, cutting through the neon lights of beer signs and dance floor spotlights until I see a familiar face.

A very familiar face.

Walking in the door with his ex.

My heart rises in my chest when I see Wade walk in, and crashes right back down to the ground when Sabrina walks in behind him.

They walk right to the bar, taking the last two stools, and order their drinks. The bartender brings Wade a beer, and Sabrina something clear. My head swims. Heat starts in my cheeks and spreads down my neck.

"Hazel, are you okay?" Katie says. She places a hand on my arm, but I barely feel it.

"Why is he here?" I grit out. "With her? I thought..." Tears prick my eyes. I don't know what I thought. Did I actually deep down think that he'd want to be with me? Ridiculous.

"Hazel, I'm sure it's not what it looks like–" Katie starts.

"It doesn't matter what it looks like," I cut her off, gathering my purse. Where did I put my phone? "I just – I don't know, I thought that maybe when he kissed me in the barn it meant something. Clearly, it didn't. He hasn't so much as texted me, and I thought it was because he was busy or something." I throw my arms up in exasperation. "It's fine. I'm fine. Or, I will be. But, can we please just go? I can't be here anymore."

Katie's gaze searches mine, a flicker of sympathy passing across her face. "Oh, babe." She takes my hand. I try taking a deep breath, but it's shaky. "Are you worried he's going to move on from you if you leave?"

A tidal wave of emotion floods my vision. I don't have to respond. She can see it written all over me.

Katie hooks her arm through mine, pulling me to my feet. Walking out of Cisco's is a blur. All I can hear is an echo of her words in my head, playing on repeat.

He's going to move on from you if you leave.

Chapter 30

Friday I'm In Love

HALF AN HOUR LATER and a cab ride from Juniper Ridge's one and only taxi driver, Katie and I are finally back at Connor Ranch. Cricket chirps fill the night air, the moonlight illuminating our path to the door.

"Are you sure you don't want to cuddle up on your gigantic couch and watch a rom-com?" Katie nudges my shoulder as we walk up the porch steps.

"I'm sure. I'm pretty tired." It's an understatement.

She nods, pulling me in for a hug as we walk inside. We have the whole ranch house to ourselves this weekend.

"Maybe we can go for a ride in the morning then?" She asks.

I force a smile. "Yeah, that sounds great."

"Please come get me if you need me. Seriously, Hazel."

I promise her I will, even though I won't, and head in the opposite direction. Katie stays in the guest room when she visits, on the first floor opposite my room. I'll admit I miss the days we were little enough to fit in my room for sleepovers.

I don't bother turning the light on in my room. The full moon is bright enough. I change into my silk pajamas, braid my hair, and sit by the window. The lights from Juniper Ridge twinkle in the distance. The moonlight shines across the lake and outlines the mountains behind it.

I usually love nights like this. I'd open the window and sit on the bench beneath it, reading a book or listening to old country songs until the lights in the town turn off, one by one.

But tonight, I don't feel like doing any of that. I can't sleep, either, so I'll just watch the night pass by in silence.

I've never felt this lost before. I've always had something to work towards. School for a large part of my life, then internships, then building up the dude ranch in preparation for me leaving one day, and finally interviewing.

It's a wonder I even got an offer from the history museum. Archivist jobs are not easy to get. I'd be a fool to let this opportunity pass. I may never get another one.

But now, I'm not sure what I want.

If I stay, I'm losing out on all of my potential. The best job offer I'd ever get for a career I worked so hard for. A new life I might love. My parents would be so disappointed.

If I go, I'll have to leave a huge part of my heart in Idaho. The ranch, my parents, the mountains I grew up exploring, and my best friend. I'm not sure how I'll live without those things. Even losing one feels like losing a piece of myself.

But how can I stay and never know what could have been?

It was hard to see Wade tonight. Sometimes we spend so much time together that I forget he has a life outside of me.

But that's selfish of me. It's a good thing he's going out again. As difficult as it is, he deserves happiness. The last thing I want is for him to be lonely when I leave.

Any logical person would be happy for him. And I would be too. If he hadn't kissed me.

Why did he have to kiss me?

It was bad enough on the boat. Sure, we both knew deep down that wasn't a normal kiss from a friend, but we still had plausible deniability. We could have played it off if we wanted to. For years.

He just had to go and kiss me again. With no one around, no crazy dares to blame it on. That kiss changed us forever. We can never go back now.

My fingers travel to my lips as if I can somehow feel his still there. How can he be with Sabrina right now after that kiss?

A flicker of light pulls my attention to the winding dirt road up to Connor Ranch. Headlights shine through the trees, driving right up to the ranch house. Who could be driving up here this late?

I lean closer to the window, waiting for whoever it is to come into view.

Wade's truck.

I spring up from the bench and pad down the stairs, careful not to alert Katie. By the time I get to the front door, Wade's truck is parked in the driveway. He kills the ignition, stepping out into the night.

I open the door before he gets the chance to knock, standing on the porch in my bare feet. I probably should have put something else on before I came down, but it's too late now.

Wade waves, walking towards the porch in the same jeans and button-down shirt he was wearing earlier at Cisco's. "Hey Haze, sorry I probably should have texted you," he says, making his way up the steps. He smiles, standing in front of me, towering over me in his boots. "I just, I don't know, wanted to see you."

"It's late, Wade," I say curtly.

His smile falters a bit. "I know. I'm sorry. I probably should have texted. I just— Are you okay?"

My gaze falls to the wooden boards of the porch. I take a step back. "Yeah, I'm fine. Katie's here, we just got back from town, and I'm a little tired."

"Katie's visiting? Oh, I didn't realize. You two were out tonight?" He asks.

I look up, locking eyes with him. "Why were you out with Sabrina?"

His eyes widen. "Hazel, it's not what you think. Seriously."

"What else could it possibly be, Wade?"

"We aren't together again, she just wanted to catch up, remember?" He explains.

I sigh, sitting down on the wooden rocking chair. "It's fine, you don't need to explain anything to me anyway. I just don't want her to take advantage of you again. I hated seeing you like that."

He squats down in front of me, and even though I've seen him almost every day for the past nineteen years, he looks different somehow. His gaze pins me in place. I want to hide away from him. I never want to look away again.

"I appreciate the concern, but I'm not going back to her. Ever."

"Ever?" My voice comes out breathier than I want.

He nods, taking my hand in his. "I came here because I wanted to show you something." He takes the journal out from under his arm. How did I not see it there before? He flips it open to the first song, setting it open in my lap. "I've spent all summer trying to make sense of this damn journal, and I can't figure it out. Songs appear in it when I've had it with me all day long, Haze. I don't know who's writing it. But it's not random. It's every moment I've wanted to say something and didn't."

My fingers run over the fading ink. "What do you mean? That doesn't make any sense."

His eyes light up. "I started thinking about *when* each song appeared, and it started to come together. I'm not sure about the first few, and I don't know how it's even possible, but it's way too accurate to be a coincidence."

"What is, Wade?"

"I think it's about us."

A million different emotions run through me at once. "What do you mean?" I whisper.

"Haze I– I mean, reading this helped me realize something. And, I think you feel the same way. At least I hope you do. Otherwise, I'm screwed," he lets out a dry chuckle. "I guess what I'm saying is that somehow these songs feel like they're describing my thoughts this summer–"

"Wade, what are you saying–" I start.

"I think I'm in love with you."

The world stops spinning.

Chapter 31

Going, Going, Gone

My ears ring. Wade searches my face, waiting for any sort of response, but my brain is short-circuiting.

"Hazel?" He says, rubbing circles on my hand. "You don't have to say anything right now, I just– I needed you to know."

Suddenly, the night is too loud. The crickets sound like sirens in my ears, the wind whistling through the trees sends a shiver down my spine.

Nothing will ever be the same again. I'm going to lose him in the worst possible way.

The journal sits on my lap like an anchor, weighing me down. All summer long, while I've been deciding how to tell him I'm leaving. While I'm fighting something I don't even understand, creeping up to the surface and demanding to be let out into the air.

This whole time. He felt the same. He's *in love with me.* He was supposed to be safe. And his mouth is moving. Shit, he's talking to me.

"–and I know I'm just springing this on you and that's probably not fair, but I just can't go another minute without telling you." He glances down at our hands.

"I'm moving to Arizona," I blurt, way too loud.

"What?" His eyes snap up to mine, dark blue like gathering storm clouds.

"Probably," I add.

He takes a breath, rubbing his face through his hands. "Hazel, what the hell are you talking about? You're *probably* moving to *Arizona*? Is this some kind of code or something?"

"No," I say slowly. "I mean, I was offered a position at the Arizona History Museum. In Tucson. It's a really great job, exactly what I studied for, and they want me to come down for a trial period next week."

A humorless laugh falls from his lips. "Hold up. I'm trying to wrap my mind around this," He says carefully. "You applied for and got a job in Arizona? How long ago was this?"

"A few weeks ago," I mutter.

"When were you going to tell me?" he asks so quietly I almost don't hear it. "When did you even do all of this?"

"I tried to tell you all summer, I just... couldn't. I don't know why." Tears prick the corners of my eyes.

"You don't know why." He repeats. Wade's lips turn stiff, a hard mask slipping over his face. He straightens, standing and taking a step back. "You should go. It's exactly what you wanted. Just forget I said anything." He walks backwards, down the porch steps.

"Wade, please, I think we should just talk about it for a minute," I plead, standing up on shaky legs.

He smiles at me, but it doesn't reach his eyes. It cracks my heart right in half. "It's okay, Haze. You were always meant for more than this. I understand. We can go back to being friends."

His words knock the wind right out of me. I stop walking, unable to respond as the rumble of the truck engine fills the air, then fades into the canyon.

Once I can't hear it anymore, I turn and stumble back to the porch. The journal sits on the rocking chair, pages turning in the breeze. I pick it up carefully, as if it's made of glass, and stare down at the lyrics.

A song I haven't seen before in the journal stares up at me, taunting me. "Going, Going, Gone" by Luke Combs.

I snap the journal shut, dropping it at my feet as the tears start to fall.

I've spent the last two days holed up in my room, poring over spreadsheets, schedules, dude ranch cabin upgrades, and researching the most I possibly can about the Arizona History Museum. I'm so prepared that I'm worried I might know too much about it.

What if I arrive and accidentally call someone I've never met by their name because I recognize them from the staff directory? Yikes.

I don't think I'll ever feel ready to step away from the dude ranch completely. For now, I'm trying to keep myself sane by over-organizing and making systems.

Is it also taking my mind off of everything that happened with Wade?

Yep, sure is.

We haven't spoken in two days. I'm not sure we've ever gone two days without talking at all. There may have been periods of time we didn't see each other in that long, but we definitely still texted or talked on the phone. It's weird, and I feel hollow. He's been half of my life since we met. I suppose it's good for us to take some space, but instead of feeling clarity, I'm just sad.

At night, when there aren't any more tasks to keep my brain busy, I sit in that sadness. My mom always says that you can't go around a feeling; you just have to go through it and let yourself feel it fully. So that's what I'm trying to do. I'm not sure when I'll get to the moving-on part, but I hope it's soon.

A part of me was hoping he'd change his mind. Give me a call and tell me that he misses me. That we can be friends again. But a deeper part of me knows that might not be possible for us, and hopes for a different sort of call from Wade.

I leave for Tucson in three days, and hopefully by the end of my week-long trip, I'll have something figured out. Whether I want to take the job or not, my life has already changed pretty drastically. I just have to find what makes me happiest. I thought for a minute there that it might be Wade who makes me the happiest, but I can't be the only one who feels that way.

I hold my cowboy boots in my hand, trying to decide if I should bring them to Arizona with me or not. Likely, I won't use them, but they bring a sort of comfort from home with me. They might be my emotional support cowboy boots, and I'm okay with that. Much easier to bring on airplanes than a pet.

I toss them in my suitcase and zip it up. My theory with packing is that if I pack a few days before a trip, I won't forget anything important. I can throw in some last-minute necessities before I head out the door, like my charger and toiletries.

Once again, I find myself standing in silence in my room, having completed another task in record time. All I have to do now is wait for Katie to show up. We are heading into the mountains tonight, at her request. She let me know in no uncertain terms that she was getting me out of the house for a couple of hours tonight. As much as I'd like to stay in another night and curl up with a good book, I know it's good for me, and I don't know how many times I'll be able to do this before I potentially move away from Juniper Ridge.

My gaze snags on the brown leather notebook peeking out from underneath my pillow. If anything, I want to feel at least okay for my trip. I pick the notebook up, studying the wrinkles in the cover. It almost looks a little droopy.

Like a wilted flower. Sad.

Same, journal.

Turning the pages carefully one by one, I go through every song that has appeared since I found the journal empty. All happy songs, all detailing falling in love. Until the latest one.

My fingers trace the new, dark black ink of the lyrics as I see the love story in my head. It's eerily familiar to my life at the moment. A sad story about someone leaving.

I look out of my bedroom window as my mind races, trying to make sense of this. I just can't get a grasp on this journal. Song lyrics seem to appear out of nowhere, and all of a sudden, they're sounding a lot like my life.

With the exception of "Butterflies," I remember thinking that none of these songs matched up well with how I was feeling at the time. But every time I was stressed or scared about something going on between us, the songs were happy and upbeat. They talk about crushes, a rush of feelings, jealousy, and falling in love.

Wade seemed so sure it was about us. But how? I trust that he's not writing in it, I know he'd tell me. No one else knows that much about him and me.

I set the journal back down on my nightstand with a sigh. I've got a lot to focus on right now.

The new job. Possibly moving away. Wade.

The last thing I need is songs popping up in this thing left and right. If I need to get rid of it for this to stop bothering me, that's what I'll do.

Katie shows up at my bedroom door a couple of hours before sunset in hiking clothes and demands that I hurry up and get changed so we can go on a hike somewhere in the canyon. She's only here another couple of days before she heads back up to Wyoming.

She's panicking about missing out on so many summer hikes this year because of her busy schedule in Jackson Hole as we hop into the Bronco.

"I think I'm just in denial that it's almost winter. Don't get me wrong, I'm *very* excited for ski season, but I feel like we didn't summer it up enough, you know? Two gals in our twenties, living in mountain vacation towns, and we spent the entire summer working. So lame. And especially you, you're single," she rambles.

I laugh, pulling the Bronco out of the gravel drive and onto the dirt road that leads to the canyon highway. "Kate, you forget, that sounds fun to you, just not me. I'd much rather work and bum around the ranch than spend any time with cocky, rich, vacation boys. That sounds like my personal hell," I shudder.

"That's only because you're a horse nerd. So you'll have to find yourself a horse nerd boy. Or someone that is equally as overachieving as you and doesn't mind your workaholic ways," she replies.

I sigh. *Or a horse riding-fishing-boating nerd combo who lives on a dock and knows pretty much everything about me.* "You're probably right."

"Of course I am. I just want us to have as much fun as we possibly can, while we still have the energy for it," she says.

We pull into the parking lot of our favorite hike in the canyon, and I'm already excited to be outdoors at the sound of my tires on the gravel. We hop out and start the trek up the mountain through the trees.

About halfway up, we get to a field of tall cheatgrass, golden for the fall already and blowing in the wind so majestically it looks like a commercial of some sort. I'll never stop being amazed by the landscape of the mountains.

We stop for a break, and I take a swig of water from my water bottle. "This is so what I needed, thanks for forcing me out here." I turn around, looking at the beautiful mountains around us and the sun low in the sky.

"I needed it too. It's been a week," she breathes out a sigh. "So still no word from Wade?"

My heart jolts at the change in subject, but I push through the hurt. "Nope. Nothing for two days. Not that I'm counting."

She nods, "You don't think you should reach out, I don't know, break the ice?"

"I'm not the one who put the ice there in the first place. He pretty much dismissed me the other day. He looked so hurt that I didn't tell him about the job. You should have been there, Katie. He looked mad. I want him to reach out when he's ready, because he *wants* to. If I do it, he'll just talk to me to be polite."

"Maybe he's waiting for an excuse to talk to you," she offers.

"I'm not forcing him into this, okay? He said he wanted to go back to being friends. I heard him."

"Oh, Hazel," Katie says, pulling me into a quick hug. "I'm so sorry. I wish I could fix it for you."

"I wish I could fix it for myself," I say quietly. This is not the time to cry. "He told me he loves me. And then sort of went back on it? I don't know, it's a lot."

Katie pulls back, gripping my shoulders, forcing me to look her in the eyes. "Do you want my opinion on this?"

"Yes," I sigh.

She nods. "I think he's nervous, babe. It sounds to me like that little love confession was the actual truth from his heart. I wasn't there, so I can't be sure, but I know Wade, and it seems like maybe he's just scared of losing you. Hell, I don't want to lose you either. It's a long way south, Arizona. You're both a little codependent in your friendship. I don't blame him for shutting down." She rubs her thumbs on my shoulders, grounding me. I nod, wiping away a tear from my cheek. "I know you don't want to hear it, but that man loves you. He'd do anything for you. I think this is his weird, non-communicative way of letting you go. It's Wade. He just wants you to be happy."

"Yeah, you're probably right," I whisper. My voice is shaky. She always knows exactly what to say. "I just– I don't know how to handle all of that. It's always been the same between us. For years. I don't know what to do with this. It's a lot of change."

She nods, stepping back. Her auburn hair glows a little more vibrant in the sunset, the green mountain meadows making her stand out in stark contrast. "You don't have to solve it all right now, you know. You can take some time."

"But I want to," I laugh, wiping away another tear.

"I know," Katie chuckles, looping her arm through mine. "C'mon, let's head back to the car. We've had enough nature for one evening."

By the time we finish the loop up the mountain, back down, and to the parking lot, it's almost dark out, and we are both starving. We roll the windows down and blast music the whole drive back to Juniper Ridge, only turning the volume down from ear damage level when we get to the first stoplight of the town.

"Want to hit up Heidi's for a burger? I could eat a burger so fast right now," Katie says.

"That sounds unhealthy, but yes, I'm down. I could use a burger too," I laugh.

"Burger night!" She yells, pointing one hand in the air in celebration, and for the first time in two days, I feel like myself again.

Chapter 32

Wondering Why

I've read the same paragraph in my romance novel over and over again. I've lost count seven times. Nothing is sticking. I thought maybe trying to sit on my window seat in my room and read a book would help take my mind off all of the drastic changes currently happening in my life. But my thoughts are getting in the way far too much.

I keep replaying my last conversation with Wade in my mind. The pull between us has definitely intensified this summer, but I never would have guessed he felt that way about me. It scares me more than I thought it would.

He's my best friend. My favorite person to be around. My partner in crime. I'm terrified to ruin that.

And, how does the journal fit into all of this? There's no way it could possibly be about us. But he is right, it certainly seems that way when I put all of the songs together. It has to be a coincidence. Songs don't just appear in notebooks out of thin air.

I've tried so hard to focus on the job and the trip I'm taking this week, but it feels like everything in my life blew up all at once. Now that Katie has gone back to Wyoming and there's this horrible rift between Wade and me, I feel like a boat, untethered and drifting away.

I take out my phone and stare at our text thread. His photo smiles back at me from the top of my phone under his contact name, *Wadey Baby*, that I set as a joke five years ago when he visibly cringed to Katie calling him 'Wadey' one day.

The photo is of him sitting on a rock in the mountains, hair wet from swimming in the river, sun shining somewhere in front of him, in the middle of a laugh. I wish I could remember what he was laughing at. Probably some stupid joke I told.

My fingers hover over the screen.

The best I can come up with is "Hi." Truly riveting.

Less than a minute later, my phone buzzes with a new notification. I almost drop it trying to open it as fast as I can.

Wade: Hey

Hazel: What's up?

Wade: Reading a book. You?

Hazel: Same.

Hazel: I saw your mom today.

Wade: Oh yeah?

Hazel: She said to say hi. So, hi.

Wade: I'll make sure to let her know you follow directions well.

Wade: Miss you.

I fidget with my phone in my hands until I get the nerve to press call. It rings once before Wade's voice fills the silence.

"Haze? Are you okay?" Wade answers. His voice cracks just a little bit. I wonder if he was falling asleep. Probably sitting on his couch, alone in the little apartment above the shop. Moonlight shining across the water, reflecting through the windows. He likes all the lights off at night except for the TV. *It's cozier,* he always says.

"Yes," I rush out. "Yeah, I'm fine. I just–" I pause. My chest flutters. "Do you remember the summer we were eight and eleven? Or was it nine and twelve? I'm not sure. But we spent the whole summer on horseback. To the point my dad had to get on us for overworking the horses."

A pause. "I remember," he says softly.

"And there was that rainy day in the middle of July, we had no idea a storm was coming until it was too late. We were already way up on the trail. Those big fluffy clouds turned dark and scared my horse." I fiddle with the ruffles on the end of my comforter. "That was one of the scariest moments I'd ever experienced, when I got lost out there in the rain."

He sighs. "It was scary for me too."

"But I found that tree, stayed out of the downpour, and you found me. I knew you'd find me, and you did," I say.

"I'd never let you stay lost, Haze," he whispers.

I nod, even though he can't see me. The silence engulfs us for a minute. I wonder what he's thinking. Does he miss those days? When we were carefree kids with no responsibilities looming over us? No complicated feelings cracking through?

"Are you going to bring your wordsearch book on the plane?" Wade asks, his tone picking up just a bit.

Damn if my heart doesn't flutter a little bit at that. He knows me too well. "Yes," I laugh softly. "I've got it packed in my carry-on."

"Shame," he sighs. "I didn't have time to cheat a little bit for you."

I laugh. "I think that's probably a good thing, Wade." When I was a kid, I loved word searches. My parents got me one for my birthday one year, but they didn't realize it was for adults and... extremely complicated. So, Wade helped me out by putting a little dot next to one of the letters in each word.

But that made it way *too* easy. I accused Wade of cheating. Ever since then, whenever he can get his hands on a word search of mine, he places little dots in the wrong spots just to throw me off.

"Send me photo proof that you can do a word search without my help, and maybe I'll believe you," he teases.

I roll my eyes. "Your *help* isn't needed this time, thank you."

My eyes start to droop. I lean for the lamp, switching it off. An hour of reminiscing later, we hang up, and I finally start to drift off to sleep. I'm half in dreamland when I imagine hearing truck tires come up the driveway. My heart leads me into a dream that it's Wade's truck.

He came back for me.

I answer the door, and he's kissing me just like he did in the barn, full of passion, years of wanting wrapped up in a single gesture.

But I wake up at three in the morning with dried tears on my cheeks, and my heart sinks when I realize it was just a dream.

White lines on the road whoosh by as I drive down the canyon road away from Juniper Ridge. The airport is at least two hours away, so I'm off at four in the morning to catch my flight. Despite the hour, I turn the music up loud enough to hear over my loud engine as soon as I get out of town.

My parents woke up with me to see me off, even though I'll only be gone a week. Seeing them wave goodbye as I drove away from the ranch was the final crack in my heart. I'm crying through "Cowboy Take Me Away."

Ever since I called Wade the other night, we've texted back and forth a bit. Last night, he sent me a photo of Drew wearing his lake monster sandals at the rental shop.

All I can picture when I close my eyes is Wade, staring down at me that night like I was the center of his universe. I've never been looked at like that, and I'm not sure if I ever will again.

Now here I am, driving further and further away from Juniper Ridge. Driving to my dream job. The one I worked so hard for, for so long.

I'm so unbelievably lucky to even get this opportunity in the first place. It might be far, but it's closer than I'd ever thought I'd get to Connor Ranch. At a prestigious museum, no less.

My chest hurts. It feels like something inside of me is reaching out for him, aching for his proximity.

I grab the old journal from the passenger seat and hold it in my lap. I've been tossing and turning every night, not getting much sleep, worrying about this thing on top of everything else going on. I can't change everything with Wade, but I can get rid of this journal once and for all.

No more nagging feeling in my gut, no more songs appearing out of nowhere, no more trying to piece together what is going on with it and why.

I'll miss this piece of my childhood. The journal I found with Wade that same day that we met. But it's time for it to go. I just can't do it anymore.

Before I can change my mind, I grab the journal and toss it out the window into the tall mountain grass on the side of the highway.

Everything is going to be fine. You didn't need it anyway. It's just another distraction. Wade will come around.

Maybe I'll start to believe it.

Hopefully.

This is hands down the best taco I've ever had in my life. And I love tacos. Taco Tuesday is my favorite day of the week. I have custom taco holders with little horses engraved on them. I'm a big fan.

The restaurant is a little worn down and dusty. It seems like more of a local joint than a tourist trap. There's a mix of desert-themed decor and paintings of cats with little mustaches and sombreros. It's cute. I can definitely see why people around here like it.

So far, Tucson has been... hot. Extremely hot. But I don't mind it as much as I thought I would. My flight was a nightmare from hell. No less than four crying babies, which I could have handled with some noise-cancelling headphones, but I forgot to charge them. The real kicker was the combination of the snoring old man next to me and the tall teenager behind me, kicking my seat every five minutes.

But since I arrived in Arizona, it's been relatively chill. My hotel is a cute little pink building with wrought-iron fencing. There's even a little bookstore next to it, which I checked out when I had a free moment last night. I spent yesterday wandering the town until I got too hot and found an indoor ice cream shop with really great air conditioning.

Now, the night before my first trial day at the museum, I've ventured out to a little taco stand a couple of blocks away from my hotel. Sitting on the still-hot-from-the-sun cafe table in the tiny circle of astroturf next to the food truck park.

I snap a photo of my birria taco and send it to Wade. He said he wants to hear about what I'm doing, so I'm going to try. Ten minutes later, my phone buzzes loudly on the metal table.

Wade: You would find tacos five minutes into your trip. Don't lie, is that the reason you're there?

Hazel: Obviously. They're better than they look, by the way.

Wade: Eat an extra taco for me.

Hazel: I plan to.

It stings a little that he's not here with me to experience this. It feels like he should be. Maybe I *am* a little too attached. I just know we'd have a blast exploring the town, buying ridiculous outfits for the sake of a theme, and eating tacos to our hearts' content.

I'm not one to do many things alone. I'm almost always accompanied by Wade, Katie, a dude rancher, or my parents everywhere I go. The only place I ever spend a good amount of time alone is the horse barn. Going out to eat by myself isn't something I'd usually do, but it's nicer than I thought it would be.

Plus, if I do move to Tucson, I'll have to get used to this. Sure, I'll probably make friends at work, but it'll take a while to make real friends I can have fun with.

I take my last taco to go, strolling around the boutique town. It's so pretty at night. Twinkle lights hanging from the buildings, solar lights illuminating the tall saguaros. With the harsh sunlight gone, I can appreciate the southwestern architecture and old town charm.

Across the street, a couple emerges from a restaurant, arms around each other like they went in for a hug and never fully came apart. In front of me, an older woman walks a small dog, smiling up at the stars.

I thought I'd feel out of place here. It's so different from Juniper Ridge, in every possible way. But, maybe that's a good thing. Maybe that's what I need. It's hard to imagine living anywhere else, but I've got to try. I didn't come all of this way not to live out my dreams.

I worked hard for this opportunity. I know a few people in my graduating class who'd kill to be here in my shoes. I can't let it go to waste.

When I get back to my hotel room, I beeline right for my laptop. I've got a big day tomorrow, so I may as well be as prepared as I can be.

I'm gonna rock this.

Group Chat

Hazel + Wade

Wade: How is Arizona?

Hazel: It's good! It's hot. But fun.

Wade: Sounds like someone I know...

Hazel: Lol

Hazel: How's Juniper Ridge?

Wade: Barely holding itself together without you.

Hazel: I'm sure no one has even noticed I'm gone.

Wade: I beg to differ.

Hazel: Besides you, of course.

Wade: I was talking about Sage. I heard she was crying all night long.

Hazel: Stop it! Sage likes you better anyway.

Wade: I'm your sidekick, remember?

Hazel: How could I forget?

Hazel: I miss you.

Wade: Miss you too, Haze.

Chapter 33

Tucson Too Late

My week in the desert consists of meetings, tours, lunch with new people I'm getting to know, and not much sleep. The Arizona History Museum is beautiful. It's full of amazing things I've never seen before. The people are so nice and accommodating, especially Betty, the soon-to-be retiree.

She reminds me a lot of Heidi. She's a total social butterfly, seeming to know everyone personally. Her white hair is cut to her shoulders and stick-straight. She's a waif of a woman, and older than I'd imagined. Apparently, she's been thinking of retiring for the past ten years, but never felt quite right about leaving the museum.

A lot of my time is spent listening to her tell stories about her life as an archivist, her two adult children who live out of state, and more than a few tales of the exhibits. Betty has devoted a huge chunk of her life to the well-being of this place, and it really shows through her work how much she cares about what she's doing here. She's making a big difference in the local community. Exactly what I've always wanted to do. And she does it all with a smile on her face and very high heels on her feet.

She's a national treasure.

Each night, I collapse in the 90's hotel bed, springs digging into my back. I'm able to send Wade and my parents a few photos from the week, mostly of my favorite exhibits, and some of the highlights from my trip. Example: the taco truck was amazing, the cafe at the museum, not so much.

I reserve a few selfies just for Wade, making faces at him through my phone camera, holding a street taco, posing with a t-rex skull, and other general silliness. He sends back selfies from the back office, organizing the filing cabinets that we didn't get to before I left, and paragraph-long texts about a couple of customers they have had this week at the rental shop. I tell him about all of the fossil history I'm learning about, and stories of the archaeological digs that they participate in every once in a while.

I fully immerse myself in everything at the museum. I try harder than I've tried at anything in my life before. I journal in the mornings when I wake up, earlier than I should, because I'm used to a ranch schedule, writing down all of my thoughts and feelings about my research and the things I'm learning.

I get into a good rhythm by the end of the week, and I can see myself fitting in well here. I even have lunch with the other archivists every day at all of their favorite local restaurants. Apparently, they had planned out a lunch schedule for the week so I'd get to try all of the great restaurants in Tucson and pick my favorites before moving down here. Though the taco place I went to on my first night is still at the top of the list.

I enjoy spending time with everyone, and while I haven't gotten to spend a ton of time with each of them, there's no one that I actively dislike, which feels like a win at a new job. They are all so welcoming and very interested in my life back in Idaho.

I tell them story after story about the ranch, the lake, and all of my friends at home. They get such a hoot out of my Katie anecdotes that we video call her at one point so she can say hello to her adoring fans.

The best part is, I'm good at this job. It doesn't bring me as much joy as the ranch, but I could definitely make a career here. I contribute in meetings, I learn a lot, I use my knowledge from both college and my own historical research for the ranch that I've done to bring new perspectives.

Quite honestly, I feel like I'm rocking it. I just can't shake the feeling of emptiness that follows me everywhere I go. It's somehow worse than I expected, knowing I can succeed, and even already am, and now I'll have to make this choice based on what *I want* and not by default because I can't do the job.

Tonight, they invite me out for drinks with the whole crew to celebrate my first week at the museum. Greg, one of the newer hires, and I pair up for a game of darts while the rest of the team hangs out in a booth at a dive bar downtown. This bar reminds me a lot of Cisco's, and my heart aches just a little bit. Neon lights are covering the walls, very few windows, and a bathroom with floors that are so sticky, I almost lose a flat.

The bartenders aren't very talkative, but seem to know all of the locals by name, along with their preferred drinks.

It's bigger than Cisco's, with a stage in the front for live music shows, and a whole row of pool tables towards the back that always seem to be pretty crowded. I can't tell if it's dimly lit because they were going for that vibe, or if they just haven't replaced a few burned-out lightbulbs. I love it here.

Greg orders us another round of beers before our turn at the heavily used dartboard.

"You're up, Haze. Let's see what you've got," he says.

I laugh. "Not much, to be honest. But I can give it the old college try."

"You don't play darts often?" He chuckles. "We'll just have to see about changing that once you move down here."

A nervous laugh escapes before I can stop it. "Nope, we have exactly one bar where I'm from, and there isn't much in it. It's really small and really old. But also really full of charm. It's one of my favorite places. Actually, this place reminds me a lot of Cisco's."

"Sounds like the perfect place," he grins. "What do you do for fun there, anyway? I wouldn't know what to do in such a small town, but you make it sound so nice."

"Well, I spend a lot of my time on the ranch," I say. Images of home run through my head. God, I miss it already. "There's a lot to be done all of the time, but I love ranch chores. They're soothing. Unlike household chores, which make me want to pull my hair out." He chuckles at that, throwing his second dart towards the board. A bullseye.

"I ride horses a lot, as you can probably guess," I continue. My third dart just misses the dartboard, clanging against the wall and falling with a small thud to the floor. Yeah, darts definitely isn't my thing. "And, my friend and I spend a lot of time on the lake. His family has an old boat that we take out a lot. The water is so clear it's gorgeous. Mountain lakes are something else. Although Bear Lake is pretty special, you won't find any other mountain lakes quite like it. It's magic," I breathe.

"Sounds like you really love it there."

I think about the water, the horses, the mountains. The bright summer sun, thick flakes of snow falling in December, through the glow of a street light, collecting on the road. "Yeah, I really do."

There may be another reason I love it there. A tall, quiet, sometimes awkward, blond-haired reason.

Greg wins the game, unsurprisingly. He mentions "when I move to Tucson" so many times in our conversation that I actually feel dizzy. We sit on a couple of barstools to finish our beers and chat a bit. Greg tells me about his sister and her trip to the southern Idaho national parks (about five hours from where I live, but everyone tends to assume everything in Idaho is close).

He's handsome in a classically good-looking sort of way, which is usually my type. Dark brown hair cut short, chiseled jaw, strong, tan arms. I even catch a peek of a tattoo spilling out from under the sleeve of his short-sleeved black polo, which I'm pretty sure is his personal uniform every day.

He has kind eyes and makes a lot of eye contact when I'm talking, giving me the impression that he's actually listening to what I have to say, rather than just being polite.

I should be interested. He doesn't work on what would be my team at the museum, so it's totally above board.

And yet, I feel nothing.

Why is it so hard to see anyone else in that way? Why can I only see Wade telling me he loves me on the porch under a blanket of stars?

"Hazel?" I hear Greg say, bringing me out of my brain fog.

"Yeah?" I ask.

"I said, would you maybe want to go to dinner sometime? Once you move here, of course," he asks. He's relaxed. Confident.

"Oh. Thanks for the offer, but I'm kind of in a complicated situation right now," I say. Technically not a lie.

"Cool, no problem. Just thought I'd shoot my shot while you're here," he smiles. I'm impressed with how unfazed he is. Must be nice to not overthink every single rejection that comes your way. There's no way I'd handle that as well as Greg does.

"Your politeness is very refreshing and appreciated," I smile back.

When I go to collapse on my rickety, trampoline bed in the hotel that night, the butterflies return to my stomach. It's been about a week without them, and they definitely were not missed.

I'll see Wade in two days, I think to myself, *I'll see Wade, and my parents, and the ranch. I'll be home.*

The thought is highly concerning. I should love Tucson. I should want to stay, right? If this is going to be my new home, I shouldn't be pining for Juniper Ridge.

I unlock my phone and hop onto social media for the first time this week. I haven't had time to so much as sort through my photos from my trip, much less keep up with anyone else's. I scroll through friends' posts, liking smiley, happy faces. Keeping up with the town goings-on, watching trick riding videos from a ranch in Wyoming that I follow. My own feed is filled with horses, Connor Ranch, and the occasional sunset photo from the back of the boat.

I find myself mindlessly scrolling through my own pictures, reliving so many amazing memories. Wade isn't featured prominently on my page, since I'm pretty sure that would nuke my dating prospects faster than I can swipe right, but every once in a while, I sneak him in.

Seven posts down, there is a photo of Wade from the back, sitting on the back deck of the boat, looking into the water. I stare at the little square image far too long for a normal person, until I've memorized every detail.

I recognize the shirt he's wearing in this photo. I got it for him for Christmas three years ago. Wade and I have our own mini-Christmas with Katie every year, the week before the actual holiday. It usually consists of small gifts (white elephant gifts if you're Katie), a classic Christmas movie ("Elf" if I'm choosing, "The Santa Clause" if Wade is choosing), and sometimes, if we are lucky and no one has booked it, sitting by the fire in one of Katie's unused vacation rentals.

Every year, I buy everyone matching footie pajamas and a big bucket of popcorn to share. We drink spiked eggnog and laugh our heads off until well after midnight. The particular year I got Wade that navy blue rash guard shirt for the boat was one of my favorites.

I was fresh off a breakup. I thought I'd be more sad about it, but to be honest, it was a good thing. We weren't that close to begin with, and it was time. The relationship had run its course, and neither of us was having any fun anymore. We'd only been dating about four months.

Even so, Katie and Wade pulled out all the stops to get me out of a post-breakup depression they were sure I would be in. I'd been gifted a care basket from both of them, chock full of my favorite things like chocolate-covered cinnamon bears, cozy western-themed books, and lavender colored socks with tiny horses embroidered all up the sides. We were watching my choice of movie, eating my favorite foods. I could not have made up better friends in my head if I'd tried.

But the best part of that Christmas was the competitive game of Monopoly we played at one in the morning, delirious from the lack of sleep and a little tipsy from the hard seltzers Wade had brought for us. I don't think I've ever laughed so hard in my life. I can't remember the words we said, the subjects we discussed, or the jokes going back and forth between the three of us.

I can remember the feeling of belonging vividly. I felt that night. Like I'd found my chosen family. I remember thinking, and maybe even saying out loud, how lucky I was to have moved to this tiny mountain town to meet two wonderful people who I'm convinced are my soulmates. That's what I want forever.

I turn my phone off and get ready for bed. As I pack up the majority of my things, my eyes snag on the cowboy boots I packed at the bottom of my suitcase. I didn't wear them at all this week, and I miss them. They're a part of me.

I'm a small-town, mountain girl with a horse obsession that never calmed as I became an adult. I'm a dude ranch manager. I'm always just a little bit dusty from trail rides. I'm a wintertime reader, watching the snow fall outside my window.

I'm an occasional fisherman on a turquoise lake that looks like it belongs in a tropical paradise. I'm Wade's best friend.

And, most of all, I'm a good old-fashioned cowgirl who wears emotional support cowboy boots, traipsing through a field of purple flowers on a mountain top.

I'm proud of that.

Chapter 34

Dry Spell

THE HOTEL ROOM DOOR shuts behind me on my last night in Arizona with a soft click. Peeling orange paint falls onto the floor from the door frame. I take a deep breath, my back resting against the cool metal door. It's been a long night.

It's been a long week, actually. A nonstop week of work, meeting new people, and learning new things. I've never been more ready to get back to the ranch.

I should be excited for new opportunities and new friends, but I just miss my old ones. All night, I took photos to send to Wade. I haven't yet, I'd rather show him myself when I get home.

I did send some to Katie, but I know she's busy with winter prep at the ranch, so I'm not surprised she hasn't replied yet.

Kicking off my boots and dropping my purse on my bed, I make my way back to the bathroom. I run a hand through my hair, unraveling my braid.

My nose has a red tinge to it after an afternoon in the hot Arizona sun. My eyes look dull. I'm exhausted.

I plop down on the hotel bed after washing my face and changing into my pajamas. The book I brought lies on the nightstand, the same one I've been trying to get through all summer, but my mind is racing too fast to pick it up.

Maybe I should send Wade the photos from the bar. I wonder what he's up to. If he's sitting around wondering about me like I'm wondering about him. Probably not. He's got enough going on back home, too.

But a part of me hopes that he is. That he misses me too. I rub a hand on my chest, blinking his face from my thoughts.

A loud buzzing sound comes from the nightstand. My phone lights up with a text from Wade. Our faces smile back at me on my phone wallpaper. Mid-laugh, hair wet from the lake, sitting with our shoulders together on his dad's boat in the soft glow of a summer sunset.

My chest tightens. I miss him.

Wade: How was your day?

I shake my head, smiling down at my phone. He should be mad at me for keeping the job a secret from him. He shouldn't want to know how it's going. But he still cares. He's still Wade.

My thumb hovers over the keyboard. I'm sick of texting. I need to hear his voice. I press the video call button, holding the phone up in front of me.

"Hey, is everything okay?" Wade's deep voice comes through the phone, and my entire body relaxes. He's the calm water on a cool morning, as smooth as glass. His hair is wet, falling into his face and dripping down his neck.

He's shirtless. Again.

"Hey, yeah, I'm fine," I say. "I just wanted to talk to you, and I don't feel like texting. I wanted to hear your voice. Is that okay?"

He smiles. "Of course, that's okay, you can call me anytime." A single droplet of water runs down his neck and onto his chest, disappearing below his waist. He steps back from the camera to close his room door behind him, the towel he has wrapped around his waist coming into view.

"Why are you never wearing a shirt? You can't answer the phone half-naked, Wade," I laugh.

He lies down on his pillow, his wet hair falling back. He reaches to the side, pulling his glasses from somewhere and putting them on."Shit, sorry," he looks down, frowning at his bare chest. "Let me grab a sweatshirt real quick."

My pulse speeds up, warming my skin. "Let's not do anything rash," I tease. "I didn't say you had to cover up."

His features relax, turning from concerned to amused. I feel my cheeks heat. Hopefully, he can't tell from the video. "Okay, fine, I won't then," he grins, flexing his bicep.

I laugh, "Wow, it really doesn't take very much to inflate your ego."

"Not when it's coming from you," he winks.

The longing in my chest turns to something more heated, deep in my belly. I adjust, pulling the covers over me, lying back onto the pillow.

"You never answered my question," he says.

Another drop of water falls down his collarbone onto the pillow. His sheets look soft. The thought of Wade picking out bedsheets makes me chuckle. I wonder if he chooses them by thread count. Probably.

My mind wanders, stuck in a daydream where I'm lying next to him, wrapped up in his warmth and the soft blankets. Running a hand along his chest, through the droplets of water. His arms wrap me into him, pulling me close. Swaying on the lake. Leaning over to brush my lips against his—

"Haze?" He repeats.

"What? What question?" I stammer.

"The one I texted you. How was your day?" He asks.

"Oh yeah, sorry," I clear my throat. "It was good. I just got back from dinner and drinks with the group. They're nice."

"They'd better be nice to you," he mumbles. "I'll come down there."

"I wish you were here now," I hear myself say. *Shit.* It's too late to take it back now.

He smiles softly, his glasses falling down his nose just slightly. "I do too."

I bite my bottom lip, fighting the images competing for top billing in my head. It'd be a huge problem if he were here with how I'm feeling tonight.

He sighs, eyelids fluttering closed. He runs a hand down his face, shaking his head. "What are you doing to me, Haze?"

I can't hide my sharp intake of breath. My cheeks heat, the feeling of a blush running down my neck. His gaze tracks it, raking down my neck. Even through the video call, I can see his pupils blown out, darkening his navy eyes.

He sighs again, deeper this time. "I've gotta go." He looks physically pained by the admission. "I'm taking my mom to dinner tonight and I can't—" He sits up, pushing his hair back from his face. "We'll finish this conversation when you get home."

I nod, disappointment filling my chest like ice water. "Okay. Thanks for talking to me."

I kick the covers off after plugging my phone back in, suddenly too hot in the stuffy hotel room. It's too quiet with the soft timbre of Wade's voice gone.

There's no way I'll get any sleep tonight. Not keyed up like this. I grab my phone off the nightstand again, pulling up the photo album called "Wade and I." Scrolling through our old memories usually helps me.

The first photo in the album is, of course, at the lake. Shirtless Wade again. Not helping.

I let out a frustrated groan, throwing my phone onto the bed. It's going to be a long night of tossing and turning in a hotel a thousand miles away from the person I'd give anything to be next to.

Chapter 35

I Fall To Pieces

The low hum of wind whipping past and airplane jets fills the silence as I sit in my window seat on the way back to Idaho. I thought I was lucky to have the row all to myself, but now it just feels lonely. All of my early packing wasn't as effective as I had hoped; I forgot my latest novel to read.

Not that I'd be reading it anyway, I've been too lost in thought to even pull out my headphones. I'm anxious about getting home. The longer I sit here staring at the circular farm fields outside the window, the more my nerves will start to get the best of me. I've got to distract myself somehow.

Kicking my backpack up to where I can reach, I lean over and fish around for something, *anything,* to do. My hands collide with random pens, my wallet, a granola bar, my laptop case, and a leather binding.

A leather binding?

I open my backpack up all the way, looking through the mess of things I brought and things I collected along the way.

My eyes lock onto familiar, worn leather. I pull the old journal out from my bag, hands shaking. The same journal with the song lyrics that mysteriously appear. The one I *threw out the window* on the way here. I'm frozen in place, wide eyes staring at the wrinkled leather cover.

How is this possible? Why can I not escape this thing? Did I dream of getting rid of it? No, I'm sure I didn't. It was only a few days ago. I remember where I was in the canyon when it flew out of the window, pages splayed in the cool wind.

I look around, but no one in the rows near me is looking over. Everyone is either asleep or watching a movie on the seatback tablets. I run my fingers over the soft leather tab tucked into a loop on the front. Every time I've opened this journal, Wade has been with me. Should I wait for him?

What if there's another song waiting inside?

I should be worrying about why this thing showed up in my bag when I threw it into the mountains. But, for some reason, I'm oddly calm. I'm kind of glad it's here. I was regretting letting it go. This thing has been with me for a while, even if it was lost to us for a few years. It feels like a part of me.

I flip through the pages of the journal, the songs playing in my head to form one big love story. I can practically see it as if it were a movie. Two people who have known each other for a long time start to fall for one another slowly, and then all at once. Until one of them leaves. That's where it stops.

Only, this time, my ears ring as I see another song has been added to the journal. There, on a page that was completely and totally blank last time I saw it, are the lyrics to Patsy Cline's "I Fall to Pieces."

The same song that Wade and I listened to together growing up.

The same one that helped him through his dad's death.

Then, right before my eyes, ink spills onto the page. The liquid black pours out like water from the seam of the pages, a stream of wispy tendrils. It dances around the page, happy and light. I watch, frozen in place.

The ink forms into a vine, leaves lining the edges of the thin stem, moving as if they were blowing in a breeze. Flowers bloom from the vine, small blossoms like bluebells or lavender, coated in black. The plant sways a bit, then stops moving completely, the shiny, wet ink drying into the page as if it were drawn there.

I snap the journal shut as fast as I can, blood rushing behind my ears. Opening it back up to check the page again, I almost expect the flower to be gone. A trick of the eye. But, there it is, in the bottom right corner of the page. The same style as the songs in the book, the same ink.

How is this possible? How is the journal even here in the first place? Did someone slip it into my backpack at the airport? I haven't even been around Wade at all since I threw it out of my car window, and I'm sure the journal wasn't with me in Arizona. I've been using this backpack all week, and I would have seen it.

I pull out my phone, sending a frantic text to Katie (thank goddess for airplane wifi packages) and stare down at the journal.

Wade's theory of the songs being about us doesn't seem so crazy all of a sudden. Although they don't really match up with my perspective of the summer. It's almost like they're being told from his point of view.

Is this how he's feeling right now? My heart cracks right in half.

My phone buzzes on the seat next to me, startling me. I stuff the journal into my bag, kicking it back under the seat, and reach for the glow of the screen.

I spend the next hour of the flight back home trying to decode what Katie means by her reply.

> **Katie:** Sometimes I think these mountains have a way of leaving little messages for people who are paying attention.

I throw my Bronco in park as quickly as I can, practically falling out of my door and onto the pavement. I made it home from the airport in record time, staring straight ahead the entire time. I think I probably zoned out for some of the drive.

I can't stop thinking about the journal. It all clicked into place. My growing feelings for Wade, songs showing up all summer, how easy it was to kiss him, the squeeze in my heart when he told me he loved me.

I've been falling in love with him all summer long, and I had no idea. But now that I put a name to the feeling, it's spilling out of my heart. I just can't go any longer without saying it. The dam has burst, and I can't put it back together.

I can't explain it, but that journal is something... more.

I sprint down the parking lot and across the boat ramp. The sun went down sometime while I drove through the canyon, bathing the valley in a soft blue glow. I almost run into a boat trailer as a truck slowly backs it down the ramp and into the water.

"Sorry," I shout behind me as red brake lights shine at my back.

I push past a small family walking on the dock, steadying myself so I don't fall into the lake. Halfway down the dock, I stop to take a breath, hands on my knees. My chest heaves. I probably should calm down a little bit before I just burst into Black Bear like a crazy person.

"Haze," a voice shouts from down the dock. A voice I'd know anywhere. One I hear in my sleep, in my dreams, on the wind in the mountains.

I look up, and there he is. My very best friend. My favorite person.

Standing in a ratty, old Black Bear Rentals t-shirt with some sort of stain on the front that's probably either jetski grease or huckleberry jam. Cargo shorts with way more pockets than anyone should reasonably have. A soft ball cap that doesn't even have any sort of logo on it.

I straighten myself, taking a deep breath. I break out into another run, closing the distance between us. I'm aware my face is likely very red, my hair is probably a tangled mess of waves, and I probably smell like the inside of an airplane, but I don't care anymore.

I don't care about anything but Wade.

I barrel into him, holding him so tightly he has no choice but to hug me back.

"Hey," I say into his shoulder.

"What are you doing here?" He whispers. I'm not sure if he's even aware of one of his hands absentmindedly running through my hair.

"I just got back. I wanted to see you," I confess. I try to catch my breath, but I'm not making it easy on myself, squeezing the air out of both of us. I pull back a little to look him in the eye. His cheeks are a little pink, probably from the sun. Freckles fan out over his nose, definitely from the sun. Blonde waves peek out from underneath his ball cap, contrasting against his tan skin. He looks concerned and a little freaked out.

"Are you okay?" He says.

"No. I mean, yes. I mean, Wade, I think I'm in love with you," I blurt out. "No, I am in love with you. Not just as a friend." I search his gaze for anything, but it's like he's a statue, frozen in place. "I know it's not fair of me to say that, especially after how I reacted when you told me you loved me. I've spent all week thinking about this, and I think I may have been in love with you for a while, but I didn't want to admit it to myself. I guess I was just too scared that things would change between us. That we'd ruin this amazing thing that we have. But that night you kissed me in the barn, I don't know. Something changed inside of me. I can't just be friends with you anymore.

"I don't *want* to live without seeing you every day. I don't want to never be able to touch you again. You make me feel so loved. So supported in every way. I know it's not fair of me to throw this all on you. I'm really not expecting anything back. I just feel like I need to be honest with you. I've been lying to both of us for so long, and I just can't do it anymore. I don't know exactly when that changed, but I just can't help it. God knows I've tried. If you don't want to be around me anymore, I'll find a way to deal with it. I'll understand. But I'd rather lose you completely than keep pretending I'm okay with the way things are.

"I love you, Wade. And that's not going to change."

Three heartbeats go by in silence. My stomach sinks as Wade stares at a far-off place behind me.

I'm too late.

I didn't say anything back when he told me he loved me, and he doesn't love me anymore. I've ruined everything. I should have just let things be. We were talking again, and we were friendly.

Walls close in around me as my heart rate speeds up. I know I said I'd understand, but maybe I can't.

Then, Wade pulls me in, and our lips collide. It happens so quickly, I barely even register it. As if someone clicked a button, all of the chaos and worry in my head goes completely silent. I'm floating, everything around us muffled like we're caught in a big bowl of jello.

Until Wade's hand finds my waist, pulling me flush against him, and time speeds up. I kiss him back, pulling a startled groan out of him. My hands trail along the hair poking out from the back of his baseball cap. I pull his neck in closer, desperate not to let this moment end.

That's what we have, him and I. Fleeting moments of soaring high, the tide coming in and sweeping us away. Until one of us wakes up and we're drowning.

"I love you too," he murmurs against my lips, both of us grinning.

The dock bounces beneath our feet on the waves as a boat drives by. We separate, and I'm already itching to close the distance between us again.

"Should we–" I start, nodding towards the rental shop.

"Yeah, c'mon," Wade grabs my hand, pulling me in the door. The same way he has since we were kids. But this time, it's so very different.

Chapter 36

Slow Hand

We barely make it inside the shop before Wade is pushing me up against the back of the door. The bell rings loudly over our heads, but it sounds muffled in my head. I'm swimming deep in Wade's touch. His hands trail up my side, stopping at my waist. He squeezes once, like he can't help it.

"Haze," he groans, pushing a thigh between my legs. The pressure is just right. "Better than I could've imagined."

I laugh against his lips, "You've been imagining this?"

"Yes. Only every day for the past ten years."

I can't hide my sharp intake of breath. Heat radiates through me, landing below my belly. He presses light kisses against my jaw, trailing down my neck. I grasp at his shirt, pulling him impossibly closer.

My hips roll of their own volition against his thigh, pulling a groan from deep in his chest. I knock his hat off his head, threading my fingers through the soft waves of his hair. An ache blooms within me, wanting to be closer. Wanting more.

His hips push into mine, searching for friction. I'm suddenly all too aware of him hard against me. I reach down, pulling at his belt. He captures my wrist, pinning it back against the wall.

"Not yet," he murmurs. A whine I've never heard myself make escapes my lips. "I've waited way too long for this, and if you do that, I'm not going to last."

"I don't want to wait," I protest.

He laughs against my lips. "So impatient." He trails his thumb along my lower lip. "Behave."

Wade slowly pushes the loose cardigan off my shoulders, sending goosebumps in its wake. I instinctively push up the hem of his t-shirt, greedy for more contact.

"Upstairs?" He pants.

I nod fervently as he pulls the cardigan all the way off, tossing it to the side.

"Shit," he says, his gaze roaming over my tank top. His hand absentmindedly reaches up, brushing his thumb against my nipple, poking through my shirt. A moan escapes my lips.

"I don't wear bras on travel days," I whisper, suddenly conscious.

"You've been walking around all day like this?" He practically growls. His thigh lifts, putting much-needed pressure back between my legs. "Without me?"

He pulls away, cold air rushing between us. Taking my hand, he pulls me towards the stairs, past the rows of fishing gear and lifejackets. The stairwell is dark as we make our way up to his door. He fiddles with the doorknob, chest heaving.

Wade opens the door, pulling me into his apartment by my belt loops. His lips find mine, a hungry, desperate pull. I barely notice him pushing my hips backwards, lifting me, and setting me on the table next to the front door.

"Are you sure about this? Is this what you want?" Wade pants.

I answer with a kiss. It should feel wrong, kissing him like this. I should feel embarrassed or something. But all I feel is Wade. "Yes," I breathe, running a hand over his bicep. "Is it what *you* want?"

His lips brush against mine, a whisper of a kiss. "I want you, Haze. I always want you. You have no idea how hard you've made this for me." He peppers kisses along my jaw. "That first night in Jackson, it took every ounce of control I had not to touch you."

My eyes flutter shut as his mouth makes its way down my neck. His tongue darts out, marking a hot stripe along my pulse. Breathing becomes difficult.

"I had to take care of myself in the shower after you left."

My eyes fly open. "Wade!" I gasp.

He chuckles. "Do you want me to apologize for how you make me feel? To hide it from you? Because I won't."

"Never," I whisper into his mouth.

Something clatters to the ground. His tongue explores my mouth as his hands find my chest again. I reach for his shirt again, and this time, he lets me pull it over his head.

He steps back, and I don't think I've ever seen him look more beautiful. Hair mussed, lips red and swollen, eyes dark.

This is how Wade looks when he's in love. It's brand new to me, this side of him. I love it.

"I need to see you," I say quietly.

"Me first." He reaches forward, running his hands slowly up my thighs. "You're so beautiful like this. You look like... mine."

"I love you," I whisper. He smirks, undoing the button on my jeans. I gasp as he slides them off my hips. He looks up at me from his knees, his gaze clouded with lust.

Slowly, he spreads my legs open, a sharp intake of breath through his nose. I should be squirmy with him looking at me like this, but I'm not.

It's Wade.

He rises, his mouth finding mine again. His hands brush my bare thighs, trailing higher and higher until he pushes inside me. He breaks away, bending down and capturing my nipple in his mouth through my shirt.

A groan escapes me, my head falling back against the cool wall behind me.

"So fucking gorgeous," Wade mutters. "I can't believe I get to have you like this."

His fingers continue to move inside of me, the pressure coiling up until it hits its breaking point.

Wade's name escapes my lips as I fall over the edge, and he swallows it with his mouth, kissing me as I come back down to earth.

"Holy shit," I gasp.

"Yeah," he says.

"We should have been doing this a long time ago."

He nods, lifting the hem of my shirt up and over my head. He lifts me off the table, carrying me carefully across the small apartment, into his bedroom, and onto his bed. I sink into the covers and watch as he undresses all the way.

He reaches into his nightstand drawer, pulling out a small foil packet. My pulse races. I've seen his room countless times. I've seen that exact nightstand every time I've been over, sleeping on the couch just feet away.

But I've never once thought about what's in it. Never thought about this side of Wade I've never seen before. I thought I knew everything about him, but this is all new.

Wade covers me, the bed dipping beneath me as he lines himself up. Last time we were in a bed together, it was all I could do *not* to think about this exact situation.

Now, it's all-consuming. We're desperate. Needy.

"Lift your hips," he growls into my ear. He slides a pillow under my lower back, causing a shiver to run through me.

He pushes into me, and it feels like coming home. His hands run through my hair, tracing the long strands fanned out above my head. I close my eyes, giving in to sensation.

"How is it this good?" I breathe.

"Because it's us. Look how good we fit," he says.

It is us. Wade and I, after all this time.

Wade is tracing my cheek with his thumb.

Wade's eyes staring deep into mine.

Wade's back flexing beneath my fingertips, moving in and out in a rhythm that makes me come undone.

His name is on my lips as my vision blurs. I open my eyes as our lips collide, a low groan rumbling from his chest.

"Haze," he whispers as he stills above me, pleasure taking over his features. A breathy giggle falls out of me.

"What?" he laughs.

"I just can't believe we haven't — I didn't know it could be like this," I confess.

"Ruined you for everyone else, have I?" He teases.

"There's not going to be anyone else." My eyes widen as what I just said hits me. I rush to cover it up with another joke, but he cuts me off as soon as I open my mouth.

"You're it for me too," he states, as if our fate has already been decided. He and I, for the rest of our lives.

I ruffle Wade's shower-damp hair as we slip back into his sheets. Moonlight spills in the window, casting his face in a blue glow. His navy eyes stare so longingly into mine, I swear he can see my very soul.

"Go on a date with me," he whispers, bringing a hand up to trace my cheek. I shiver under his touch, sliding closer so our chests are touching. "I want to take you out."

"We go out all the time," I breathe, planting barely there kisses along his collarbone. We've settled into this new side of us easier than I could have ever imagined. Like it was meant to be all along. It's a weight lifted off of me, not having to resist wanting him.

"Not like that." He hugs me into him, pressing a kiss onto the crown of my head. "A real date. Like you deserve. I want to wine and dine you."

I laugh into his hard chest. "Deal."

I let myself sink into him, let him pull me in closer, and bury his face into my hair. It feels indulgent, all of this taking. I never allowed myself to feel even a fraction of anything for him in fear of ruining what we have. But now, I can't imagine ever going back to that.

We have this *because* of our friendship. All of the late nights spent talking, days at the lake, all of the history between us. It's allowed us to know each other on a molecular level. I feel like tonight I've finally locked in the final piece of Wade Monroe. The one side of him I hadn't experienced.

I love the Wade squished up against me like he can't get close enough.

But I also love the Wade who races me on horseback through the mountains. The Wade who dances with me in the barn, at Cisco's, or on a floating dock anytime he hears music. The Wade who finishes the last few bites of my huckleberry shake because I can't possibly eat any more.

All of those sides come together to make up my favorite person in the whole world. And now, I can have all of them.

My eyelids grow heavy. I nuzzle into his arms, snaking around my waist, his chest hard against my back.

"Let's never sleep alone again," he whispers into my ear as I drift off.

Group Chat

Miles's Prison

Katie: So, how are the lovebirds? Excited for tonight?

Hazel: I'll call you!

Wade: How do you know about tonight?

Wade: Hazel, how does she know about tonight?

Katie: Did she not tell you? I'm coming on your date. As a chaperone.

Wade: You are NOT invited on my date with my girlfriend.

Katie: Oooooh, girlfriend, huh?

Wade Monroe left the chat.

Hazel Connor added Wade Monroe to the chat.

Miles: HOW DID YOU LEAVE?

Katie: No one tell him.

Miles: Please let me be.

Katie: I'd sooner divorce you.

Miles: We aren't married!

Hazel: Sorry, Miles.

Chapter 37

All Your'n

"THIS ISN'T SUPPOSED TO be this complicated," I huff, throwing another shirt onto the pile of discarded outfits. Wade and I are going on our first official date tonight, and Katie's face is about two inches away from her phone camera, picking an outfit with me.

Although it's more of a fashion show of all of my clothes in my closet than actually picking anything.

"It's not, babe," Katie says. "It just has to be absolutely perfect, or I'm not letting you out of the house."

"Oh, okay. So no pressure then," I roll my eyes. Out of the two of us, Katie is by far the more fashionable one. She loves clothes and can rock pretty much anything, whereas I'm more of a functional t-shirt and jeans kind of girl.

It feels different to be going on a date with Wade. He insisted that we go on a real date like a real couple, and apparently, that requires me to dress up. He was also very specific about picking me up at seven, and knocking on my *front* door, not my room door, after he lets himself in like usual. The formality of it all is making me a little nervous.

I kind of love it.

"Hey, where is that dress you have? You know, the one with the slit?" Katie says from the beanbag chair she's lounging in, her auburn hair splayed out on the back in a fan around her head. The soft glow of the fireplace illuminates half of her face.

"You're going to have to be more specific than that," I say, "I have literally no idea what you're talking about."

"Oh, you know this one. It's floral and blue, I think. And it has a super high slit on the leg," she says, exasperated.

I rummage through my closet some more until I see something she might be talking about. It's a blue velvet dress with white flowers embroidered all over.

"This one?" I pull the dress out of my closet and hold it up to my body, stepping in front of the camera.

"Yes! Try that one on with the light tan cowboy boots," Katie claps with excitement.

"Isn't this one a little formal? And a bit revealing?" I ask as I pull the dress over my head. The velvet is so soft.

"I'm not hearing a problem in either of those questions," Katie says, studying the dress as I straighten it out. "It's perfect!" she declares, "Throw on your tan leather jacket. The one that matches the boots. Yep, that's it! You look gorgeous," she says as I pull the jacket on. I do a little turn for her, and she squeals.

I walk over to the full-length mirror and take a look. I really do love this dress. The jacket and boots dress it down just enough to wear anywhere, even though it's probably the nicest piece of clothing I own.

My boots are plain enough not to clash with the dress. They aren't the kind I'd wear on a horse in a million years, but the heel is fun for nights out. My dark hair falls down my back in my usual waves.

"I think you're right, Kate," I beam, "It's perfect. I don't know how you do it."

"I'm a genius, I know," she closes her eyes with sass and flips her hair over her shoulder.

I do a little twirl in the mirror again, then plop down onto my bed, holding the phone in front of my face. "I'm ten percent less nervous now."

"You don't need to be nervous, you silly goose," Katie waves me off. "It's just Wade. He already loves you. This is the fun part."

"I think that makes it worse than a date with a random guy," I say, "If that doesn't work out, I'll just have lost one night and maybe the price of my dinner. But with Wade, the stakes are higher, you know? Also, we've never done this before. What if it's weird? Oh my god, what if he sees date-Hazel and doesn't like her? Then what do I do? He's never seen date-Hazel before!"

My heart picks up speed. I know I sound ridiculous, but right now, all I can think about is what could go wrong. "We just started dating, it can't be over already."

"Whoa, whoa, whoa," Katie says, sitting up. "Slow down. Date-Hazel is just regular Hazel with a bit more sparkle.

There's no possible way to hate her. She's the best. He's not going to decide he doesn't love you anymore after you go on a real date," I breathe a deep breath, focusing on her. "He's known you for, what, like twenty years? I don't think there's a single person on this planet who knows you better than Wade. That includes me."

"Yeah, I guess you're right," I whisper.

"Oh, I know I'm right. I've been watching you two for the better part of a decade," she assures me. "If there are any two people made for each other, it's y'all. He loves you, Hazel. Let him love you. All you have to do is sit back and enjoy the happiness."

"Thanks, Katie."

The doorbell rings downstairs, startling me.

"Shit," I jump up, hurriedly smoothing out my dress and hair, "Why is he always five minutes early? Who does that?"

"He clearly does not know how girls work," Katie says. "You look great. Knock him dead!"

I feel like I'm sixteen years old again, walking down the stairs for prom to meet my date at the bottom. The soft timbre of his voice floats up the stairwell as I make my way down, followed by my mom's laugh.

As soon as I come around the corner, his eyes lift to me as he takes me in. I can practically feel his eyes slide up my body, landing on my own. A smile spreads across his face, and all of my nerves melt away.

"Wow. You look... really pretty, Haze," he says. Heat creeps up my cheeks. I'm still not used to this from him, especially in front of people. My mom smiles, stepping aside.

"Thanks, you look pretty too," I joke. He blushes, and I decide that I'm going to compliment him a thousand more times just to see his cheeks turn pink. It's adorable.

We head out to his truck, and like usual, he opens my door for me as I climb in. Unlike usual, he kisses me after I climb in before he shuts the door.

"So I was thinking we could get out of Juniper Ridge for the night. I have somewhere else in mind," he says once we pull out onto the highway heading the opposite way of town.

"Oh yeah?" I smile. "Where would that be?"

"I guess you'll just have to stick around to find out." He looks over at me with a grin, and his eyes practically twinkle.

If you had told me a few months ago that I'd be headed out on a date with my best friend, I would have laughed. I never would have ever expected this to happen. Partially because I hadn't allowed myself to think about the possibility. Every time I found something about him that I loved, I thought about how lucky I was to have him as a friend. Or, how happy he'd make someone someday.

Now, when he does something especially nice for me, or smiles big when he laughs, or brings me a coffee, I don't have to deflect my feelings. It's the best feeling ever to love him without limit.

We drive until just before the canyon empties into another, bigger city. Wade pulls onto a dirt road and heads up a couple of minutes until we get to a big white barn. He backs up to the barn, a little ways away from it still, and kills the ignition.

"Is this where you say you were just kidding about wanting to be with me, murder me with an axe, and leave my body for the wolves?" I ask.

"Not tonight," he says, reaching for something behind his seat. "I have a surprise up my sleeve. But it's in the tailgate." He steps out of the truck, walking around the front end to get my door.

"It's a surprise in the tailgate in the middle of the mountains at night, and you expect me to believe it's not a murder axe?"

"I promise it's not," he says, reaching for my hand. "Where would the fun be in that?"

"I'm sure an axe murderer would think it's a whole heap of fun," I mutter as I step out of the truck. It's chilly outside, the first hint of fall in the mountains. Crickets chirp, wind whistling softly through the aspen trees.

He leads me to the back of the truck, opening the tailgate and letting it down. It's so dark out here that I can barely see.

I can just make out several blankets, fluffy pillows, and a bin towards the tailgate. He grabs a remote from inside the bin and clicks it, aiming at the barn behind us. Twinkly yellow lights light up the night, lining the roof of the white barn.

"Oh my god," I breathe. "This is like a movie. Whose barn is this?"

"I know some people," he shrugs, taking more things out of the bin. First, a big white box with a lens on the front. He jumps into the tailgate and places it on the top of his truck. After straightening it perfectly, he clicks it on.

Light pours out the front, illuminating the barn. It's a projector. The opening scene of "Casablanca" plays as he pulls a giant popcorn bucket, two sub sandwiches wrapped in Heidi's branded paper, and a tray with two soda cups out of the bin.

"Is that a magic bin?" I say.

"Yes, it is." He smiles as he sets the bin on the ground.

"I can't believe you did all this, Wade. This is amazing. I've never had anyone do anything like this for me."

"Well, you deserve it," he says, helping me up onto the tailgate. "Next time, we'll just go out to dinner somewhere. But I wanted our first real date to be extra special."

"This is easily the best date ever," I grin. I mean it too. No one has ever come close to doing something so special for me.

We lay against the back of the truck bed, on top of a bed of pillows. Wade gathers a few blankets to put over us and grabs our food.

"I love this movie," I say in between bites. "I mean, obviously, everyone loves this movie, but there's just something about a sad, pining Humphrey Bogart in a Moroccan cafe."

He laughs. "Casablanca never gets old."

"Casablanca lives forever," I nod.

After we finish the sandwiches and about half of the popcorn bucket, Wade puts his arm around me, and I snuggle in a little closer. I look up at the stars above us, and the twinkle lights around the barn, and it hits me how magical this is.

My best friend in the whole world loves me.

He planned this entire move-in-the-mountains date for me. He got us food from his mom's restaurant and popcorn from the only movie theater in Juniper Ridge.

A breeze blows by, sending a chill up my arms.

"Are you cold?" Wade says, his thumb tracing along my goosebumps. "Here, let's scoot the blankets up."

We slide down a little bit until we are under the blankets all the way. His arm slides under my waist, pulling me closer to him. The warmth from his body heats me right away. We stay like that for a while, pretending to watch Ingrid Bergman in Paris. His other hand lands on my thigh, pulling my leg on top of his. The velvet of my dress falls away as the slit opens up.

He turns towards me, his gaze firmly set on my lips. "I love this dress," he murmurs.

"Oh, really?" I whisper. "What is it about this particular dress that you love?"

"The color is nice," he shrugs.

"Yeah, I'm sure that's it."

"Among other things," he adds, moving his hand up my thigh another inch. His touch sends goosebumps down my arms, and this time they're not from the cold.

I lean in, pulling him closer by his belt loops. His soft lips capture mine, moving slowly as I sigh into his mouth. He runs his hand up and down my thigh, but never any further, even when I try to nudge him. I make a frustrated noise after my third attempt to nudge him forward, and he actually laughs against my lips.

"Seriously?" I grumble.

"Hey, this is our first date. Cool it," he laughs, eyes glinting in the string lights. He pokes me in the side softly, making me giggle.

He kisses my nose, turning us back to the movie. I nuzzle my head back into his shoulder.

I imagine Wade coming out here during the day and stringing up these lights, figuring out how to work the projector, asking his mom for picnic food, and packing it into a bin.

I can't help but smile.

Wade looks down at me, raising an eyebrow. "What?"

"Nothing," I grin. "I was just thinking about you setting this up. Must have taken some time."

"Don't think about it too hard, you'll ruin the magic," he whispers, pulling me closer.

"Okay," I promise. But my smile never quite fades. Eventually, Casablanca comes to a bittersweet end on a rainy tarmac, and the projector switches off, bathing us in darkness again.

Wade helps me jump down from the tailgate, taking my hand. He spins me into his arms and kisses me one more time. I get butterflies for the millionth time.

"I love you, Haze," he whispers against my mouth.

We spend the whole drive back to Juniper Ridge talking and giggling. The drive goes so quickly, I'm surprised when he turns onto the road to Connor Ranch. We pull up at exactly ten o'clock.

He walks me up to the door and grabs both of my hands at my sides, pulling me into another kiss. If it weren't so cold outside now, I could probably drag this out for a while. But I start to shiver, and he pulls away.

"Goodnight, Haze," he whispers so softly I can barely hear him, "I'll call you tomorrow."

"Goodnight, Wade," I whisper back, leaning back against the wooden boards of the house.

His gaze turns heated in a way that I can feel all the way down to my toes. "I'm trying very hard to be a gentleman right now, but you're making it difficult with that goddamn dress."

I don't have time to respond before he closes the distance between us, capturing my lips in a rough kiss. I melt into his arms, running my hands through his hair. I'm about to jump into his arms when he pulls away, hair mussed and out of breath.

Wade's forehead rests on mine as he whispers, "If I don't leave right now, this is going to get really inappropriate for a first date."

I suppress a shudder. "Sounds fun, how inappropriate?"

I feel butterflies in my stomach as he leans into my ear, brushing his lips against it.

"I really, really wish we were at my place right now." He trails kisses down the column of my throat, stopping at my pulse. I feel the pull of his tongue on my skin, sending a current down my spine. I grab onto his shirt, pulling him closer.

"This dress would look much nicer on my floor." He steps back, cold air filling in between us. My heart sinks at the loss of contact with him. I'm consumed by him. Even a couple of feet away from Wade is too far.

“Maybe on our next date,” he winks, backing off the porch. He jogs over to his truck, and the next thing I know, his headlights are slinking off into the distance.

I’m left standing against the wall, my chest heaving as my senses come back.

don’t think I’ve ever been this happy before. It feels good. I can’t believe he took me on a real date. One that was thought out, and so perfect for me. I’m so into him it’s unreal.

I text Katie the second I’m in my room. Ten seconds later, my phone is vibrating with an incoming call.

“Hello?” I answer. All I hear on the other end is a loud, high-pitched squeal.

“Okay, tell me all about it. Spare no details. I mean, maybe spare some details,” she says excitedly. I tell her all about the date, her only interruptions being some giggles and a *stop it right now.*

“Seriously, Hazel. What did I tell you?” she says once I’ve finished.

“You were right,” I admit. “I felt like I was in a rom-com the entire time. I still can’t believe that happened.” I brush out my hair and start my nighttime routine.

“You cannot let that man go. Ever.”

“I don’t plan to.”

Chapter 38

He Loves Me All The Way

"Well, Hazel Mae, what did you want to tell us, honey?" My dad says from the soft saddle leather recliner in the living room of the main house. I texted both of my parents this morning, letting them know I have some news to share with them.

We are a family, but Connor Ranch is also a business. All ranch-related decisions are run through all of us until we all agree. And this time, I'm nervous. I'm betting they're expecting me to tell them that I'm moving to Arizona any day now. I still feel like I'll be disappointing them.

I can't remember a time in my life when they weren't talking about me moving away from Juniper Ridge one day to pursue my dreams.

My mom sits on the couch across from me, smiling at me and clutching her clipboard. She's been overworked lately, especially with me being gone on the trial run. Our extra ranch hands have gone home for the season, so now it's just us taking care of everything, getting the ranch ready for the long winter ahead.

"I wanted to let you guys know that I've made my decision about the job in Arizona." I take a deep breath. Might as well get right into it. "I'm not going to take it. The trip went well, as I've told you. I did well at the job, I liked everyone, and it seemed exactly like I figured it would be. But I realized while I was down there that I don't want to leave the ranch. My work here is my passion. I'd like to start historical tours to add to the dude ranch activities. I'm planning on doing lots of research and planning this winter, and could have the addition to the business ready by summer. It's something I've been thinking about for a while now, but I didn't think it was realistic until I did my research and found other ranches with similar programs. I'm confident it'll be a great addition for our guests."

I pause. Both of my parents are completely unreadable. They always are when they've locked into business mode. I take another steadying breath and push on.

"I love this place. I always have. I love taking people on rides, I love teaching them about our history here and showing them all of my favorite spots in the area, and I love Juniper Ridge. It's my home, and I want to keep it that way. However, if you don't think that historical tours would be a good addition to the dude ranch, I understand." I force myself to stop talking. I'm proud of myself. My point has been made, and now I'll just have to see what they think.

Dad is the first one to break the silence. He clears his throat, arms still crossed across his chest, "You're sure about this?" His tone is gruff, but not harsh. I can't get any sort of read on what he thinks, and it's killing me.

"Yes," I nod. "I'm sure."

"Oh, sweetie, we're so happy for you," Mom gushes. She stands up and runs over to me, engulfing me in a hug. She squeezes me so tight that the air rushes out of my lungs. I stumble to catch my balance when she releases me.

"I think historical tours are a great idea, Hazel. I trust that you'll build something great for the ranch," my dad says with an approving nod.

"Really?" I ask. "You aren't disappointed that I didn't take the museum job?"

"Why would we ever be disappointed? We are so excited you want to stay and add onto the ranch," Mom says. She steps back towards Dad, clasping her hands together in excitement.

"I just thought that you guys wanted me to move away and do something big with my life. You've always encouraged me to do that. I didn't think you wanted me sticking around at the ranch," I say.

"We encouraged you to dream big because we never wanted you to feel stuck here. The ranch is our dream, but we didn't want you to feel like it had to be your dream too. We didn't mean you have to leave, of course, we want you to stay for our own selfish reasons. You're a huge help around here, the guests love you, and we get to see you all the time. What could be disappointing about that?" my dad says.

A wave of relief crashes over me. The weight I've been holding for years now falls off my shoulders. Now that they've approved my new idea of historical tours, I can spend the next few months working towards that goal. I've never been this excited for the future in my whole life.

Plans rush through my head, fighting for top billing on my to-do list. I can't wait to get started. I can't wait to call Wade and Katie and let them know the good news. It's going to be a lot of work to get up and running, especially since we are already low on help, but I know I can do it. I feel it in my bones.

"Oh, and one more bit of news," I start. "Wade and I are kind of together now. As a couple. Like, not as friends." I clasp my hands in front of me, swaying on the heels of my feet.

"Hah!" My mom yells, pointing a finger at my dad. "You owe me twenty bucks, Elliot!"

"Excuse me?" I cross my arms, eyeing my mother. My dad grumbles in her direction. "Did you have a bet with Dad about Wade and me?"

"Oh, honey, it has been just a matter of time between the two of you since you were kids. I'm surprised it took this long," Mom laughs.

"I'm going to pretend not to be offended by the fact that you two are betting on my life," I admonish. If I'm being honest with myself, it is kind of funny. Now that I look back, Wade and I were always inevitable.

"Does this have anything to do with the fact that you're staying in Juniper Ridge?" My dad asks, cocking an eyebrow at me.

"Honestly, no. I would have stayed either way. I made that decision before I knew if we were going to be together or not. It's just a bonus. A really great bonus that I'm super excited about," I smile.

"Good," he says, standing from the chair.

"I'm so happy for you, Hazel Mae. I've seen how you look at that boy, and I've seen how passionate you are about this place. I'm so glad you've decided to say yes to what you love." My mom looks at me with pride, and I can't help but think about how lucky I am. She's right.

I love this place, I love my parents, and I love Wade. All this time, I've had everything I love right here in front of me.

All I had to do was say yes.

I close the door to my room, throwing my jacket onto the chair in the corner. I've got plans with my *boyfriend* tonight, and less than half an hour to get ready. As usual, my hair is a windblown mess under my cowgirl hat, and dust is caked onto my face.

I walk over to my desk to hang my hat on the hook above it, but stop short when I see the journal lying open. I laugh to myself. So much time this summer I spent wondering what Wade was feeling about me, and here it was the whole time. Right in front of me.

It's not on the same page it was on when I left. In fact, it's a whole new song. I flip backwards, but every other page remains the same. Turning back to the new song, I read through the lyrics.

Written on that last page is "Forever and Ever, Amen" by Randy Travis. Another classic country song that James Monroe used to overplay in his office. He always used to make a big deal out of dedicating this song to Heidi every time she came to visit. He'd look at her with adoration and pull her over to dance with him behind his desk. Maybe that's why Wade is always dancing with me.

This song means so much more to me now that I see it in writing in the journal that holds our love story. Happy tears leak out of my eyes as I imagine Wade at home playing this song and thinking about me. I don't know what I did to deserve such a perfectly imperfect person, but I'll always be grateful to be loved by Waylon Monroe.

I lay the journal carefully onto my desk again, closing the leather flap. I don't know how to describe it, but it just feels complete now. Sure, it's the beginning of a new chapter for Wade and me, but this one from our childhood is done. We're different now.

As I step towards my door, a flicker of light catches my eye. I spin towards my desk just in time to see another bright sparkle, then the journal is gone. The smooth wood of my desk is empty, like nothing was ever there.

A humorless laugh escapes me. It's gone. The journal is gone, just like that. I should probably be more surprised than I am, but it just feels right. As if it did its job, and now it's gone.

Maybe Katie is right. Maybe there is a little bit of magic hiding in these mountains if you look closely.

About A Year Later)

Epilogue

Wade

THE CHAMPAGNE CORK FLIES out of its bottle with a loud *pop*, clearing the dock completely and falling lightly onto the surface of the turquoise lake.

"Shit, sorry," Haze laughs, a grin on her face, her eyes sparkling in the sunlight.

"I've got it." I squat down onto the dock, my shirt brushing on the dock as I reach out as far as I can.

"So close," Hazel giggles from behind me.

My shoe brushes against a dock cleat. The perfect leverage to reach out just a little bit further. My fingers pinch the cork, grabbing onto it as I lean back onto the grey wood. I collapse onto my back, handing the cork up to Hazel.

She stands above me, still laughing, her long brown hair cascading around her face. Her lavender tank top blows in the breeze around her hips like petals on a flower.

She's so pretty.

Hazel holds out her hand to pull me to my feet. I brush off the back of my shirt, taking the cheapest bottle of champagne we could find from her to pour into coffee mugs. The only cup adjacent thing I hadn't packed away.

We're celebrating today. Today is our last day at Black Bear Rentals.

Black Bear Rentals itself will still exist. The buyer wanted to continue it the way it is, including keeping all of the long-term employees. They'll add to it, I'm sure, but for the most part, it'll still be a vacation rental shop on the lake.

This past winter, Hazel and I spent a lot of time talking about our futures. I just never felt like mine included the rental shop. Cleaning out all of my dad's old things last year was cathartic. It also showed me that this place is just a building. I'm proud of what Wyatt and I did with it, just like I'm proud of my dad buying it all those years ago. But it's time to move on.

He's with me no matter where I am, and keeping the shop around to feel closer to him when it's not bringing me happiness just isn't right. He wouldn't want me to do that.

So, Hazel and I really cleaned it out in the spring, moving my limited belongings into an apartment just outside of town. Closer to the mountains. It's a little weird not living on the water, but I love being a little bit closer to Haze.

It'll also be more convenient with my new job. Hazel has done an amazing job with her new historical tours at the dude ranch, and I'll be there for the busy season, adding a fishing guide business to the thriving ranch. In the winter, I'll take locals and the occasional skier out on the lake. In the spring and fall, I'll guide the river through the canyon for fly fishing.

It'll be something different every day. Hazel says my dad would be proud.

"Wade!" A familiar voice cuts through the quiet marina. "You couldn't wait for the party to arrive before popping the champagne?"

"I couldn't hold him off any longer," Hazel says, looking just past me.

I turn around to see Katie and Miles walking down the dock, hand in hand. Behind them, Codie waves to us, tote bag full of snacks in hand.

"What are you doing here?" I can't help but smile. This has Hazel written all over it.

Katie pulls me in for a hug, then stands next to Hazel, an arm around her shoulder. "Your girlfriend wanted to surprise you," she winks.

"Is that true?" I ask Hazel. I don't think I've ever smiled as much in my life as I have in the last year.

Hazel nods. "I wanted you to have a real celebration. I know you wanted to keep it low-key, but people care about you, Wade. They want to celebrate you."

"Don't start without me!" Another voice yells. The four of us turn to the parking lot just as Parker rips his shirt over his head, throwing it on the ground. He runs down the dock towards us.

"Is he going to stop?" Hazel says.

Codie shrugs. "Probably not."

Parker lets out what sounds like a battle cry, sprinting past us and off the edge of the dock. Water falls all around us from his splash.

"Parker's here," Miles deadpans.

Parker surfaces from the water, shaking his hair out of his eyes. "How come none of you are swimming?"

"Because there's no swimming in the marina, dumbass," Miles says.

"Oh," Parker's smile falters for half of a second before it's back. "They'll have to catch me then." He winks, swimming back over to the dock. He lifts his arms, resting them on the edge.

"I appreciate you all driving down here, but I don't really have anything planned," I say.

"We don't need plans, Wadey, we just wanted to say congrats on selling the shop and hang out for a bit. We're all proud of you," Katie says.

Miles shakes my hand. "Excited for you, man. We're telling everyone that stays at the cabin about the setup you two have down here at the ranch."

"Thanks, Miles," Hazel smiles. She hands Parker one of the towels we brought to sit on as he climbs back onto the deck, dripping wet.

We set up a makeshift picnic on the dock, a mess of every color of towel from the shop, cheap champagne, and a couple of cases of beer that Miles brought. The sun peeks behind the mountain, casting the lake in shades of pink and blue. At some point, Hazel switches on the string lights over our heads.

"This is so pretty," Codie says. "I'd love to live on the water someday."

"Have you always lived in Jackson Hole?" I ask.

She nods. "Yep. My parents are there. I love it. But it'd be fun to have a change someday."

Twilight turns into night as we chat about our summers, Connor Ranch and its new additions, and Miles's latest Fourth of July firework mishap at Lone Pine.

I'm distracted by Hazel, as usual. The warmth in her smile, how animated she gets when she talks about the historical tours, the way she leans into my shoulder even when she's not thinking about it. Letting me know she's always there.

"I'll miss this place," she says, opening a bag of popcorn.

"Me too," I nod. "But, I'm excited for everything else we have planned. Plus, we can still come down here every once in a while."

"If Parker doesn't get us kicked out for swimming in the marina," Codie adds.

"Live a little, Tourmaline," he quips back.

Katie dissolves into a fit of giggles.

"Is that an inside joke?" I ask.

"No, that's her—" Hazel is cut off by the sound of an engine pulling into the parking lot. "Hey, who's that? No one comes out here this late."

A yellow Volkswagen Beetle pulls into a parking spot near the doc. Parker stands up, grinning ear to ear.

"Is that who I think it is?" Katie gasps, clapping her hands together.

"Who?" Hazel asks again.

We stand, following Parker as he makes his way to the parking lot. He stops about halfway there, turning back towards us with a mischievous grin.

"Everyone," he says, arms outstretched. The car door opens behind him, but it's too dark to see anyone. "I'd like you to meet my fiancée."

Acknowledgements

Fun fact: Lilac Creek was the first book I wrote all the way through. Well, kind of. The storyline was different, but the characters were the same. It was set at Bear Lake. I wrote that story years ago and came back to it a couple of times before sitting down and rewriting it from scratch after I wrote Ember Meadow. Ember Meadow wouldn't exist without Lilac Creek. Katie was originally written as Hazel's best friend, and I never intended to write her a whole book.

Writing is funny that way. I'll always be so grateful for Hazel and Wade and everything they inspired. I'm so elated to share their story with you.

Huge gigantic thank you to my sister, Sami, who has read Lilac Creek more than any person should ever have to. I literally could not do this whole thing without you, for real. Time to celebrate!

Thank you to Tyann, who was one of the first readers of this book and helped it become what it is. You're the coolest.

Thank you to the cover designer of my dreams, Brooke. You continue to knock everything out of the park and make these books so pretty! Your talent is unmatched.

Thanks to Kellianne, the coolest editor in the world, for being a true wordsmith and a bright sparkle in my life. I appreciate you more than I could ever put into words, for book things and life things. Mahalo.

To Daylen for always enduring the drafting cave and bringing me sweet treats, coming to far-away book signings, sending emails and finding really cool opportunities. I appreciate everything you've done for this little book.

Thanks, Mom and Rob, for always showing up at my local signings and supporting my dream.

Thanks, Dad, for marketing my book to everyone you know and reading all of my new material.

Thank you to the best book club ever for showing up to signings, buying multiple copies of Ember Meadow, and shouting your support from the rooftops. I do not deserve y'all! Also, let it be known I did skip one book this year. Sorry.

Thank you to my Ranch Hand Crew for showing up and supporting Ember Meadow and Lilac Creek as if they were your own! I seriously cannot believe how lucky I am to know all of you, and that you spend time reading my words and loving my characters. You are so cool!

Thank you to everyone who was an ARC reader for this book. It's because of you and your dedication that I get to live this insane dream!

And, of course, thanks to you! I appreciate you buying my book, reading this story, and giving Hazel and Wade some room in your heart. It means the world to me.

Abigail Morgan writes stories with her boots in the dirt and her head in the clouds. Usually the kind drifting over the Rocky Mountains at sunset. Her romance novels mix the wild west with cozy charm and always carry a dash of mountain magic. She is the author of The Elements Series: *Ember Meadow* and *Lilac Creek*.

authorabigailmorgan

authorabigailmorgan

Made in the USA
Coppell, TX
19 July 2026

84600697R00208